Against My Will

Frederick Fell Publishers, Inc.
2131 Hollywood Blvd., Suite 305
Hollywood, FL 33020
www.Fellpub.com
email: Fellpub@aol.com

For more information about special discounts for bulk purchases. Please contact Fredrick Fell Special Sales at Business@fellpublishers.com.

Designed By : Social Agency / www.socialagencyinc.com
Cover Photo By : www.Philbrick.com

Manufactured in the United States of America

---

10 9 8 7 6 5 4 3 2 1
Library of Congress Cataloging-in-Publication Data

Berkley, Benjamin.
  Against my will / by Benjamin Berkley.
    p. cm.
  ISBN 978-0-88391-279-9 (alk. paper)
  I. Title.
  PS3602.E7568A73 2012
  813'.6--dc23

                    2012018514

Against My Will

Will

by Benjamin Berkley

"Woman must not depend upon the protection of man, but must be taught to protect herself."
- Susan B. Anthony

To my beautiful wife Phyllis, my biggest fan, who always believes in me.

And to the brave souls of the Mauthausen Concentration Camp.

Prologue

It used to be commonly believed that a husband had a right to have sexual relations with his wife. A topic that was ignored for many years, spousal rape is now recognized as illegal in every state in America, and this type of rape was officially declared a human rights violation in 1993. Unfortunately, however, many states still make a distinction between stranger-rape and rape that occurs within the context of marriage, with the former carrying harsher penalties than the latter.

Further, it is estimated that up to 15% of married women in America have been victims of spousal rape. Many women who fall victim to this type of violence blame themselves for staying in an abusive relationship while many women do not have the means to leave. Others see sexual submission as something that they must do because of their religious convictions.

If you are a victim of spousal rape, help is available. Call the National Domestic Violence Hotline at 1-800-799-SAFE. They will direct you to places in your area where you can seek help.

Tumbalalaika

PART

ONE

Chapter One

My bridal party lined up like airplanes waiting to be cleared for take-off while I remained parked in my small dressing room hangar. All alone, except for my reflection in the floor length mirror, my thoughts drifted back to only ten months ago.

I had just taken the New York State Bar Exam. Since I just reached my goal of experiencing financial independence for the first time, marriage was definitely not on my radar screen. But my father said it wasn't right that a 29-year-old Jewish girl was not already married. At the time, maybe he was right. I had a closet full of bridesmaid dresses, enough diplomas to fill an entire wall, and a desk calendar that was counting down to my 30th birthday.

Focusing on the mirror now, I admired my mother's dress. It was slimming, which was definitely a good thing for me as I have always been apprehensive about my weight. It covered my arms, and elaborate lacework and crystals trimmed the heart-shaped bodice and train. As I stared at my image, a tear formed in my eye. I was only three years old when my mother died and my memories of her are limited to a grainy black and white photo of my parents under the *Chuppah* that sat on the rectangular mahogany server in our dining room.

The raucous voices of Jacob's groomsmen distracted me as they departed from the hallway en route to the sanctuary, replaced by the sounds of rustling dresses and my bridesmaids laughing about something that I am sure was silly. But I wanted to be part of the silliness. Then the laughter disappeared with their on-time departure. Next came the groom and his parents. All that was left was a deafening silence as I waited.

I wanted to rub my eye but my makeup was set. I considered scratching my ear but knew it might leave a red mark. I thought about running away. But I had nowhere to go. And my remaining time was flowing faster than the last grains of sand in an hour glass.

Rose's First Diary Entry

A young nurse with a very kind face told that me that I have been in this hospital bed for more than two weeks. But I have lost all sense of time and place. I am tired, I am weak and it hurts so badly when I try to eat. But I am hungry and I must get strong.

I am told to rest. But as soon as I close my eyes, I hear voices and can't discriminate if I am dreaming or awake. A defiant storm rages outside but not as violent as the storm within my aching body. I lift my body up and stare out of the small inch of glass that is not obscured by the pelting rain on the window. There is thunder and lightning but I cannot distinguish between reality and nightmare. And I take no comfort from the howling storm through which I now relive the previous nights and days of torment, pain, and humiliation. My spirit was bruised, as well as my body, and sorrow was an unwelcomed friend.

Someone touches my wrist and I twitch with fright. Has my end finally come? But the touch is quickly followed by a soothing voice which assures me that I am all right and doing fine.

Ironically, I suddenly have the gift of time while only recently my life was passing faster than the sands in an hour glass.

I will sleep now and maybe write more tomorrow as I am told that I may soon forget. But I never will.

Chapter Two

Feeling a little lightheaded, I stepped away from the mirror and walked towards the window. Outside, a very tiny sparrow had found a resting place on a branch. I marveled how he balanced himself with one claw tucked up inside. We exchanged glances before he flew away and I was envious of his freedom.

Looking up at the sky that was slowly changing from shades of reds and oranges into darkness, my mind began swirling with thoughts, good and bad. I had slept so poorly last night anticipating today. I remembered looking at my alarm clock on the night table. I squinted my eyes to see the numbers. It said seven but I did not know if it was seven in the morning or at night. I mused that perhaps I missed my own wedding. But rather than panic, I pulled up the sheets, which felt so crisp and cool, and fell back asleep.

Upon awakening, I had a terrible headache, which I never get. I had thought that a long, hot shower would ease the pain. But instead it left me more tired. And I am not one to take pills to mask the pain.

There were so many things I still needed to do and I had prepared a list. But oddly, I did not feel pressured. Instead, I leisurely ate my Honey Nut Cheerios and a banana and entertained myself watching *I Love Lucy*. It was the one where Lucy was working on an assembly line packing candy, and the candies started coming out faster than she could pack them into their boxes. I had seen this episode dozens of time before but it still made me laugh. And I so needed to laugh.

My stomach growled as I looked at the plate of once piping hot hors d'oeuvres that were brought into the dressing room earlier. But I was too nervous to eat and elected to finish the poured glass of champagne with which only moments ago my girlfriends toasted me. As I brought the rim to my lips, I fixated on the thousands of tiny bubbles releasing their energy in such a small area.

I returned to the mirror and stared again looking at the reflection. The person I saw there was dressed in a white gown that would be the envy of every young woman. Yet from the depths of the mirror reflected a face stricken with fear.

I pulled the thin veil down over my olive skin and suddenly a transformation from girl to woman occurred right before my eyes. Before me stood a stranger. This was not the face I had known for almost thirty years but a frightened young woman looking like a china doll in a glass case.

I touched my own face under my veil as I wanted to make sure it was me. My brown eyes looked sleep deprived and were barely visible because my pupils were so wide.

Outside the room, the music played and my heart began to thump. Not a steady thump, like a heart beating, but an uncontrollable pound. It was so loud in my ears.

I took one more glance at the girl in the mirror. But the girl was gone and had been replaced by the stranger's face. I knew once I turned, I was not only leaving that young girl's face behind, but the life she once led. I knew as I walked out the door, I was going to take on the life of the stranger in the mirror. And the same thoughts crossed through my mind that had crossed many times in recent days. Thoughts of fleeing, images of wandering lost. But the sounds outside the room became louder and clearer. And I began to sing softly the song my Nana sang to me when I was frightened:

Tumbala, Tumbala, Tumbalalaika
Tumbala, Tumbala, Tumbalalaika
Tumbalalaika, shpil balalaika
Tumbalalaika freylekh zol zayn

Rose's Second Diary Entry

It was dark when I opened my eyes and I tried to focus on the clock on the wall opposite my bed. Was it seven in the morning or was it night? Or does it even matter?

My body is frigid and I cannot get warm. There are many blankets on the bed but they don't stop the cold that is running through my bones.

The same kind nurse from earlier fed me a few spoonful's of water. But the spoon felt so cold against my parched lips that I shivered as I tried to swallow.

She told me that it would be good if I could sit up. She said it might help bring down my fever. I was too weak to resist as she placed me in a chair by the window and wrapped me tight in blankets.

Through the window, I imagined my vegetable garden back home. My father had cleared a small area in our yard near our neighbor's pine tree that provided just the right amount of shade. And each spring we would plant seeds which in a few short weeks became vegetables. My favorites were the tomatoes whose plants grew taller than me and strong enough to hold dozens of fruit. Poppa always reminded me that a tomato was a fruit.

And how much fun it was getting down on my knees digging for potatoes and onions. I remembered how I would fill the basket and then run into our kitchen and dump them all over the kitchen counter. Mama would pick out the largest to use for making soup.

Sadly I also recalled the end of each season. We had picked the last of our crop and the once green leaves that carried life had now turned brown and wilted and died. Along with the fallen pine needles, all that was left was a stark contrast to only a few months earlier. I helped my Poppa till the area and we talked about when we would plant again next year.

I am not ready to become a wilted plant and die. I pray to see my garden again.

Chapter Three

I finished Nana's song and blotted a tear from my eye with a tissue, trying not to disturb my makeup.

"That song is pretty. What is it?" my wedding planner Diane asked as she entered the dressing room.

"Oh," I said, startled. "I am embarrassed. You weren't supposed to hear me."

"What was that?"

"It's a song my grandmother sang to me when I was a little girl," I said, setting my glass of champagne on the small table by the window.

"Well, it is beautiful. And Danielle, you look amazingly beautiful."

I shrugged and said thank you as Diane handed me my bouquet of small chocolate, orange and cream colored roses that were held together by a narrow band of crystals designed to match the crystals on my dress. The bouquet resembled the flowers in the photo that my mom carried on her wedding day.

"Where's my dad?" I asked quietly as we approached the doors that opened into the sanctuary.

"He went to the restroom."

"I sure would like to."

"Oh, well, I don't think we have time."

"I am only kidding."

Diane smiled. "Now, after your daughter reaches the end of the runner, she will sit down and your music will start. At that moment, I will open the doors."

As I listened to her instructions, my heart beat faster and my face felt flushed.

"Hi sweetie. Thought I forgot?" Dad joked as he took his position to my right.

"And I want you to count slowly to three before you start to walk,"

Diane continued.

"You understand that?" my father said smiling broadly as he lightly brushed back the side of his hair with the tips of his fingers. My father had never given in to the fact that he was bald. Instead he grew this enormous strand of hair that started on one side and wrapped around the top of his head and down the other side.

"Don't be so nervous, Dad."

"Me? Nervous?" he said, touching and straightening his bow tie, which was another nervous habit of his.

"And remember to walk slowly. You only do this once," Diane added as she moved behind me to straighten my train.

Waiting for our cue, I pondered Diane's choice of words. I had spent my entire young life following instructions; always obeying, and wanting to please, especially my father. So why should today be any different?

"Do I have time for a cigarette?"

I looked at my father in amazement. "Dad!"

Diane smiled warmly at him. "No, no. It's ok. We still have a few minutes. The patio door is just to the right. You can smoke outside."

Diane and I laughed as my father's black patent leather shoes made this odd clicking sound as he walked across the black and white tile floor to the door.

"Can I take a peek?" I asked as I stood on my toes and looked through the small rectangles of opaque glass in the doors that would soon swing wide open.

I did not want a large wedding but my father said that he had been saving up his whole life for this day. And that he only had one daughter. And that he wanted to share this *Simcha* with everyone!

"The *Chuppah* looks amazing."

The four posts were wrapped in hundreds of roses, and adding support for the canopy were the *Talits* of our grandfathers who were there in spirit.

"The room will become even more beautiful once you step inside," Diane murmured.

"You must use that line on every bride."

"No, I really don't."

"Then you are truly very kind," I said as we watched my father puffing away outside the glass patio door. "He told me he was going to quit."

"It's a horrible addiction. My father also smokes and he has tried to stop many times."

"Well, maybe I should have started smoking. I hear you lose weight. And then this dress wouldn't be so tight."

"The dress fits you perfectly."

"Is that in your wedding planner contract to make sure you say the right things?"

Diane politely laughed.

"It's ok. Anyway, I never asked you. Are you married?"

Diane laughed again. "No, I have been with this guy for a while. My parents are thrilled. And he is ok. But I haven't found Mr. Right yet--only Mr. Right Now. But it looks like you have."

"Yes. That's what my father said."

Diane appeared puzzled by my answer. "I'll go get your dad."

As she stepped away, I craned my neck and stood on my toes to look through the small glass windows and watched my niece drop white rose petals from her basket that softly landed on the white laced runner which ran from the back of the sanctuary and stopped just before the steps leading up to the *Bema*. Standing at the end of the runner and focused on the back of the sanctuary was Jacob, who was standing so stiffly he reminded me of a photo I saw of the palace guards in front of Buckingham Palace. But they weren't wearing *yarmulkes* on their heads.

"I am sure that nicotine must feel real good on your lungs, Dad," I said sarcastically as my father resumed his position. He rolled his eyes in response.

Diane smiled and adjusted my tiara. "We're almost there."

My palm was sticky with sweat from holding the flower bouquet and my hands started to shake.

"Are you ok?" Dad asked.

I really had to pee though I knew my window had long ago closed to get out of and back into my dress. I was also thirsty and I wanted something to drink. But I was too nervous to ask and afraid if I did, I would spill all over myself.

Always wanting to please, I answered, "I am fine."

"It's time," Diane announced excitedly as my niece dropped the last petal and the sound of the four string quartet playing Pachelbel's "Canon in D" filtered through the space between the doors. I repeated Diane's words *"it's time"* to myself, musing that it is the same words a condemned person hears before taking his first steps to the gas chamber. But unlike the condemned, I did not know my fate.

As I was about to take that first step, I felt paralyzed and unable to move.

"Dad, I don't know."

My father ignored my plea and extended his arm so I would not try to run away.

"You're so beautiful. My precious little angel."

For as long as I can remember, that was my dad's favorite phrase when he addressed me affectionately.

I looked into my father's eyes that were now flowing with tears.

"Your mother would be so proud of her little girl. And her wedding dress looks so amazing on you. I am sure she would have wanted you to wear it."

Another tear started to form in the corner of my eye as I blinked to blot it and stop its track down my cheek.

"You cleaned up pretty good yourself, Dad," I said, softly brushing my hand across the satin lapel of my dad's black tuxedo as Diane started the countdown.

"One, two."

As Diane whispered *"three,"* the oversized double doors swung open and I smiled like a pageant queen atop a parade float as we began the procession slowly down the aisle, walking past each row of our family and friends who had risen to their feet to welcome the bride.

"Slower, Dad," I whispered to my father who was getting ahead of me, causing my veil to bounce in front of my face. He quickly got in sync and my fourteen-foot long train now flowed gracefully behind me. As I took each step, I inhaled the music inside the synagogue which was sweet and calming even though I felt a crescendo of mistake as we moved forward.

Five more steps and I wobbled slightly, stepping forward on my right foot. Is the strap on my heel too tight? Will I fall out of my shoes? Will everyone laugh? I remembered all of the items of the list that I was supposed to do today. I wished I was sitting in front of my television watching Lucy with my cereal bowl in my lap.

Four more steps and there was my law school friend Marcia mouthing *"beautiful."* I bet her $1,000 that she would be married before me. She should have taken the bet. Well, too late now.

Three more steps and the fragrance of the roses was intoxicating. It was as if the synagogue had been turned into a floral shop and was overtaken by the pungent smells.

Two more steps and the flash from the photographer's pierced my eyes. I blinked in rapid succession, momentarily losing my sense of where I was.

One more step and I looked up at the stained glass windows lit up by the setting sun as they met the ceiling of the sanctuary. And standing at the base of the bema was the man I was to marry. Suddenly, the music became so loud I did not even recognize the song and my eyes focused on Jacob. His back was toward me.

And then it happened. The words of my Nana rang in my ears louder than the music. *"If he keeps his back to you as you make your way to him, he will not love you. Instead, he will think of you as a prize and will never show you warmth. But if he turns to face you as you walk down the aisle, he will love you and cherish you for the rest of your life."*

Jacob turned to face forward but his eyes continued to wander. He looked all over the room. But not at me. And with each step I took, my thoughts drifted slowly back to that first day almost a year ago.

The bar exam was three long, exhausting days. Add in the stifling heat and humidity, and by the end of each day I was both mentally and physically drained. Today was even hotter and last night's rain only brought more humidity to Queens, which had been narcotized by the heat.

But this morning, with no test to take, I slept in until 10. I then spent the rest of the morning catching up on all of the things I had to put on hold for the past two months while I was studying, including making an appointment to get my teeth cleaned, changing my cellular calling plan, and going online to schedule a time to take my written test for my driver's license.

After lunch, I went to Barnes and Noble, which was only a two stop ride on the #7 subway, and enjoyed a relaxing afternoon browsing the bookshelves before purchasing Ina Gartner's latest cookbook. On the subway ride home, I hung onto to the overhead rail with one hand as I flipped through the pages of all these wonderful recipes I couldn't wait to make.

As I exited the Roosevelt Boulevard subway station, I thought about stopping at Schwartz's Bakery. My dad loved their apple turnovers, which he so enjoyed after dinner with a cup of tea. If I got there before five, they would still be fresh and right out of the oven. But when he had called me this morning, he'd said he had a surprise. Perhaps he wanted to take me out to some fancy dinner in celebration of my surviving the bar. But knowing my dad, we were probably going to Benjie's, his favorite deli. And that would be fine with me as it gave my dad a chance to *kibbitz* with the cashier whom he always seemed to have a thing for although he never asked her out.

So instead of stopping, and feeling in desperate need of a shower from the humidity, I walked briskly the four blocks to 35th Street where I had lived my entire life.

34th and 35th Street were sycamore lined and consisted of row after row of five story brick and stone buildings built in the 1940s that shared a garden (really a narrow patch of grass in the middle). When they were first built, my dad said they were the "talk of the town" and were called garden apartments which was the closest thing in Jackson Heights, Queens where you could have your own backyard. But unless you lived here, the buildings all looked so similar except for the street number that it made it almost impossible at night to tell them apart. Our building was full of families and single moms, a noisy beehive of babies, kids, bikes, strollers, scooters and walkers.

"Hey Sammy," I said to the red-haired, snub nosed, freckle faced boy playing stoop ball against the steps of our building. "Who's your friend?"

Sammy was in the fifth grade. His parents worked long hours and I often helped him with his homework.

"This is Raj."

Raj was much shorter, a little huskier, dark haired, and had a very thin face with deep dark circles under his eyes.

"Hello Raj. Are you new here?"

"Raj don't speak much English. His parents just moved into the building," Sammy explained.

"He *doesn't* speak much English," I corrected him. "Well nice to meet you," I said, extending my hand.

"Hi," the short boy answered.

"Danielle, do you want to see my baseball card collection later? I got the whole Yankee team!"

"I *have* the whole Yankee team," I corrected him again as I started to walk up the four brick steps. "Maybe later. But Raj, watch out for Sammy. He always wins," I joked as I pushed in the massive, wooden door that led into the darkly lit lobby.

The lobby had been recently renovated. But built long before there was central air conditioning, without windows, and a weeklong heat wave that had driven temperatures higher each day, the fumes from the fresh paint were choking as I waited for the one elevator. After a minute of gazing at the elevator dial that appeared to be stuck on the fifth floor, I put my hand over my nose and ran up the three flights of stairs.

"Dad, I'm home," I shouted as I turned the key and opened the metal door. As I stepped inside, I smelled cigarette smoke.

"You told me you quit," I yelled as I shuffled through the mail on the small wooden table in the hallway.

"I'm in the den," he barked back in his heavy New York accent.

Aside from the new flat screen television that my dad bought last year after our old television died of natural causes, our apartment looked the same as when I was a little girl--oatmeal colored carpeting that was so worn that the vacuum cleaner's wheels no longer left track marks; dark, mahogany furniture that lost its luster back in the '80s; bare walls except for a Yankee calendar that hung on the wall with a thumb tack in the kitchen next to the phone, and ceilings that were white at one time but have now taken on an ugly shade of yellow as a gift from my dad's decades of cigarette smoke.

"Ok," I said as I pressed the blinking amber light on the phone. "I will be right there. I am just checking the messages. Your accountant called. Something about the store. He can't read your handwriting. And Uncle Eugene wants to know if we can come to their house for dinner on Sunday."

"Don't worry about that now. Come in here."

"All right, all right. I am just getting something to drink," I shouted back as I walked into the kitchen and opened the refrigerator. "So what's the surprise?"

"Just get your drink."

Holding a can of Diet Coke, I complained as I walked and talked.

"It is so hot in here. That air conditioner is not cooling off. You need to call-- Oh, I am sorry. I didn't know we had company," I said, stopping in surprise at the entrance to our living room.

My dad was sitting on his favorite brown leather recliner, which faced the new flat screen. Seated on the couch next to him was Mrs. Nadel, an old family friend who professed to be a matchmaker, though she had difficulty matching her shirt with her shoes. Next to her was someone I had never seen before. As I went to kiss my dad and Mrs. Nadel, the stranger got up from his seat.

"Danielle, I want you to meet Jacob."

The stranger appeared to be in his mid-thirties. He had a trimmed beard and wore a tweed suit and horn-rimmed glasses. At that moment, I realized my dad's idea of a surprise and immediately became annoyed.

"It's 90 degrees out and you're drinking coffee? Not anymore. And you told me you quit," I said as I pulled the cigarette from my dad's lip and extinguished it in his cup of coffee. As I did, I noticed that there were beads of sweat on my father's forehead.

"My daughter wants to be a prosecutor. Guilty," he said, mocking me with his hands held in front of him like someone who was just about to be handcuffed.

I could smell the coffee from his breath. "It's not funny Dad," I said, pushing his hands down.

"I have been rude. I am sorry. Hello," I said to the stranger, accepting his handshake.

"Hello, nice to meet you," the stranger uttered in a husky voice as he lowered his head revealing his thinning black, curly hair.

I smiled and took a seat on the other couch that faced Jacob.

"How are you, Mrs. Nadel?"

"I have been fine but I am sorry," she said looking at her watch, "but I have to go. I did not realize how late it is. Besides, my work is done here."

"I walk in and you have to go?"

"Mrs. Nadel. You're invited to stay for dinner," my dad announced with open arms.

"Thank you, thank you. Don't get up. But my granddaughter is in a piano recital and my daughter is picking me up."

As Mrs. Nadel rose from her seat, she pointed to me and said to my father, "Soon you'll have grandchildren from this little one and you'll know the *nachas* they bring."

"Dirty diapers?" I said wryly.

"My daughter is such a kidder. You should be on stage. A young Joan Rivers."

As Mrs. Nadel walked passed me, she stopped and placed her hand over my cheek. "You'll see. He's a nice boy. I can find my way out."

Her hand smelled of fish and I wrinkled my nose. The sound of the closing door quieted the conversation in the room as I again took my seat.

"So, are you a business associate of my father's?" I asked the stranger, already knowing the answer.

Both my father and Jacob laughed.

"No? You're not?" I responded, not surprised. "What's so funny?"

"Jacob's parents live on Long Island. And he recently moved to Queens. So Mrs. Nadel one day came into my store and told me about him.

She thought you would like to meet."

"Good old Mrs. Nadel," I said with a smirk. "Always working."

"Tell my daughter where you live."

"Dad."

"No, I want him to tell you."

"Well, I bought one of those converted lofts near the bridge," Jacob said. "You know. They're revitalizing the whole area. Anyway, it needs a lot of work. But when it is done, it will be nice."

"You hear that, Daniella. He owns real estate." My dad called me Daniella when he wanted to make a point.

"Wow. Another Donald Trump," I whispered to myself.

"What'd you say?"

"So I hear, Dad," I nodded.

"And I am an investment banker. I work for Morgan Stanley," Jacob continued.

"Oh, that is very nice. Well, then, I assume you two have business to discuss so I will excuse myself," I said.

"Danielle, Jacob will be joining us for dinner," Dad said.

"OK, but--"

"And I stopped on the way home and bought dinner."

"You did what?" Except for buying his cigarettes, I did all of the grocery shopping as my father rarely ventured into the market.

"Well I guess I will just set the table." I stood up.

"Danielle, please sit down. I invited Jacob to meet you."

"Oh," I replied in a sarcastic tone.

"Your father has told me some very nice things about you," Jacob asked as if I were interviewing for a job and he was reading my résumé.

"I have trained him well."

"I understand that you are in law school," he remarked.

"No, actually I graduated in May and just took the bar. Yesterday was the last day," I replied.

"Congratulations. That is amazing."

"What, that yesterday was the last day?"

"No. I know the commitment you have to make. And I respect that.

I thought about going to law school after college but I wanted to start making money."

"Law school's not for everyone." I quickly realized what I said sounded pompous. "But I am sure what you do is very interesting."

"So when do you get your results? I hear it takes several months."

"Yeah. They stretch it out. Not until around Thanksgiving time."

"Well, I am sure you did fine. Just to get through law school, you have to be very bright," he said.

"Thanks. Anyway, I really should set the table. If I leave it up to my dad, he may put out cereal bowls," I joked.

"Danielle, you sit. Get to know each other. I'll take care of the table." My father winked at me, which I returned with a stare and a roll of my eyes as he walked out of the room.

"So, I'm sure you want to know all about me," Jacob said.

I pressed my lips and glanced at the stained colored ceiling as Jacob began reciting his résumé as if he was reading from a prepared text.

"I graduated NYU and was fortunate to get a job on Wall Street for an investment banking firm that was based in England. I had a chance to transfer to their London office which would have been exciting. But after a year, and saving some money, I enrolled in Columbia. Two years later, I earned my Master's degree in finance and took a job with Morgan in their Cincinnati office. Then a managerial position opened up and I moved back to New York. And here I am," he said, stretching out his arms which revealed his protruding belly as his suit jacket opened.

Jacob looked for a reaction but I sat with my hands crossed against my chest as he continued.

"I have two sisters. Lindsay, the youngest, goes to Adelphi. She is in a Master's program to become a speech and hearing audiologist. And Sherri is a teacher. She got married last year. I am the oldest. So tell me about yourself."

"Well I thought I did. I am waiting for my results. There is not much else to say." Just to make conversation, I added, "So, aside from the job, why did you move back to New York?

"I missed my family. And Cincinnati is not the most exciting place to live."

"I have heard that. Well, that is great, and you seem nice but this is a little awkward."

Jacob hesitated. "I don't know what you mean."

"Look, I don't know what my father told you but I am not on J-Date or any other dating service. And I am not looking to meet anyone right now. All I want is to pass the bar exam, hopefully get hired on by the DA where I am clerking now, and find my own place to live. So I have plenty of time."

"I had an elderly aunt who said, 'Arukot Chikit, Le'Olam Lo Tid'eeh Ma Hechmatzt,'" Jacob quoted.

"I know. She who waits will never know what she missed. But my time for waiting has not yet begun," I retorted.

"You're missing the point and…"

As Jacob was about to further prophesize, my father shouted from the dining room.

"Come, come. Talking makes you hungry." Dad entered the room waving his hands to follow him like he was directing traffic around a car accident. "We're sitting in the dining room tonight."

"The dining room, Dad?" I reacted with surprise. Except for the Jewish holidays, my father and I have our dinners in the kitchen. And as I took inventory of the table he had set, I was so embarrassed and wished that we were eating at Benjie's.

"Dad!"

"What?"

My father had unfolded the turkey, corned beef and pastrami but left it in its butcher paper wrappings, placing all the deli on a chipped white platter that I could not remember when we last used. And circling the meats were the plastic containers of coleslaw, macaroni and potato salad, a jar of mustard with a butter knife sticking out of it, another jar of Kosher pickles, and a dessert-sized plate of unevenly stacked Jewish rye bread.

"Ok. So I am no Martha Stewart."

"Dad, this is so embarrassing. Who sets a table like this? Everything is still wrapped and where are the napkins?"

"Jacob," my father said, turning to the stranger as he handed him a paper plate. "It's food right? As long as it is good, who cares how it looks? And when you have your own home, Danielle, you do things your way. Ok, you sit there," he said pointing to me, "and Jacob you sit next to my Daniella."

Jacob smiled and nodded with approval as I rolled my eyes again and took my seat.

"Good. Everyone's seated." My dad held up the dessert plate and recited the blessing over bread.

"Baruch, ata, adonai, eloheinu, melech, hoalam, hamotizi lechem menhaoretz.... Ah Men."

As I sat quietly, my father and Jacob attacked the deli and entertained themselves talking about the Yankees and the stock market. Finally, my father realized that I had become a spectator to this conversation. "You're quiet tonight, Danielle."

"No I am not. I'm just enjoying the ambiance," I said in a now too familiar sarcastic tone.

"Don't be rude." He turned to Jacob and said, "My daughter is usually non-stop talking. I sometimes can't even get a word in."

"First I am a comedian, now I am a mute. Make up your mind Dad."

"Whatever."

"Whatever" was my dad's most often used expression when he wanted to change the subject.

"Let her eat," said the stranger as he guided more than a bite full of his sandwich into his mouth, revealing his mustard stained fingers and chewed and bitten fingernails.

I wanted to barf but politely sat and finished my half sandwich as the two men resumed their conversation. After they solved all the problems of the world including how our country can avoid going into the next great depression, my father pulled away from the table as if he was the chairman of a board of directors.

"Jacob, come in the living room with me. We'll watch the end of the Yankees game while Danielle puts away the dishes. Danielle, if you could make me a cup of tea. Jacob. Do you want? And if you could bring us in some of those Danishes from Schwartz's."

I was sorry I had not stopped at the bakery to buy something fresh apple turnovers.

"I'll be right there, Mr. Landau."

"Ok, talk, but don't be long. Andy Petitte's pitching."

My father walked down the hallway and I was again left to make conversation with Jacob.

"I'm going to go ahead and make some tea. Do you want some?" I asked.

"No, I am fine. But can I help you?" he replied.

"No, it's only tea, not a casserole, but thank you."

I filled the mug with water and put it in the microwave as Jacob talked to me from the dining room. "You have many beautiful photos here. Is this your brother and his family?"

"Probably. They live in Chappaqua."

"You mean where the Clintons live."

"Yeah, but they don't have Clinton money. My brother hasn't written any best-selling books and his wife is not the secretary of state," I joked.

"And they have two kids?" he asked.

"No, I think they only have a daughter, Chelsea. I am kidding. Yes they do," I replied.

"I can see the resemblance. And this picture must be your mom and dad."

"Yes," I said as I entered the room and set the tray with the mug and a tea bag on the dining room table. "My mom died when I was only three. I don't have many memories. She was very pretty and died too young. She had breast cancer. And if doctors knew what they know today, who knows, she might still be here." I looked at the grainy black and white photo before putting it back on the mahogany server.

"You look just like your mom."

"Really?"

"Sure, I see it. Your eyes, your smile. She was very beautiful."

"And a lot thinner, but thank you. That was very sweet. I will be right back. I am just going to bring my father his tea."

My father was sitting in his brown leather reclining chair watching his Yankees.

"Here is your tea." I made a crashing sound with the tray as I set it on the coffee table. "And the Danishes were stale. I would have stopped at Schwartz's but…"

"Whatever," he said as he waved me off with his hand. His hand gesture was his favorite nonverbal way of dismissing me.

"And we need to talk when your surprise leaves."

"Ok, whatever," he said again with the wave and without turning his face away from the screen.

"Whatever," I replied as I walked back to the dining room expecting to find Jacob.

"Hello, where are you?"

"I am out here." Jacob had stepped outside onto the balcony to smoke.

"I hate smoking," I said.

"Your dad smokes," he said as he stepped back inside.

"I know, and I hate it." I reached to grab the cigarette from his mouth. But before I could, he walked into the kitchen and extinguished it in the sink.

"Thank you."

"You are welcome."

"Anyway, I am just so tired. It's been a long week and I haven't had much sleep. So I am going to say goodnight. But the game is still on. So if you want to stay and watch it with my dad, go ahead."

"Well that's fine but it is more fun in person. So I will see you Tuesday night."

"Tuesday? What's happening on Tuesday?" I asked with a puzzled look.

"We have a date."

"A date?" I shook my head in disbelief. "Look, I don't want to be rude and you seem like a nice person. But like I told you, I am not looking to meet anyone right now."

"Well you are being rude to your father."

"What?"

"Before you got home, your dad handed me two tickets for Tuesday night's game. The seats are right behind third base and I am sure he paid a lot of money for them. The Yankees are playing the Red Sox. So I'll meet you at six in front of the advanced ticket window."

"Goodnight Mr. Landau," Jacob shouted as he opened the door to leave. "Thank you for dinner."

"So I will see you Tuesday night," Jacob said assuredly. Not waiting for the door to close, I marched directly into the den.

Chapter Four

From the time I was a little girl, my dad and I have been attached at the hip. He was my dad and trying to be a substitute for a mom I really never knew, so we did everything together. He also raised me intelligently though he taught me more through common sense rather than books. And whenever he could, he would quote from the Talmud, or as he liked to refer to it The Good Book. He was also the center of my life from the very beginning and my first memories are of his easy smile, gentle nature, and loving embrace.

My dad was a source of comfort and support to me and I was encouraged to follow my dreams and to indulge my creativity. But I was not spoiled. I learned the value of hard work, of honesty, of friendship. I learned responsibility and how to make difficult choices for the good of others over myself. A widowed father trying to raise two children, he treated my brother and me with respect, love, and kindness. I also learned what a healthy home looked like, and of the peace and acceptance in a home where all family members are truly happy.

But from the time I was a teenager, my dad and I have battled. It was usually over the petty things. Like he would think my skirt was too short or I was wearing too much makeup. But I always had the upmost respect for him and would never hurt my father. I also did not want him to be alone and, until recently, put off finding my own place to live.

Baseball was his passion. Not just baseball, but New York Yankees baseball. From the day the season started to the last out, he lived, slept, and breathed the Yankees. Being a widower for more than 27 years, it became the reason he gave for not remarrying though he has had some chances. But as he often said, with work, raising a family, and being the biggest Yankee fan, *"who has time for marriage?"* However, though he will not admit it, his other passion was seeing that I get married.

"Dad." I was standing next to him though he appeared unaware that I had even entered the room.

"Dad." My voice grew louder.

"What?" my father acknowledged while not moving his head away from the television.

"Dad, please talk to me."

"You going to tell me again about the crack in the wall," he said not looking at me. "I know about it. I have called the building maintenance number three times. No one calls me back. So if it bothers you that much, hang a picture over it."

"Dad, I did not come in here to talk about a crack in the wall."

"Then what," my father responded by throwing his hands up in despair.

"Dad!"

"Jeter's on first and there's no outs."

"Dad." I stepped in front of the television blocking his view. "We need to talk now!" I wrested the remote from his hand.

"All right. They're losing six to nothing in the bottom of the seventh. They're in God's hands now. Ok, sit down. Talk to me."

I sat down on the couch, crossing my arms across my chest and took a deep breath.

"What the hell was that all about?"

"Don't talk like that to your father."

"Ok. Dad. Sorry. But please explain how Mrs. Nadel, a *Shadkham*, so happened to be in the neighborhood."

My dad acted surprised at my question.

"Dad, I am not stupid."

"Ok, Ok, I wanted her to be here for the introduction."

"What introduction? This is the 21st century!"

"He's a good man," my father answered. "He has a big job. People look up to him. He will be a good provider."

"Dad, I am going to be a lawyer. I intend to be able to provide for myself. Besides, I have my career to think about first."

"Ok, ok but the calendar knows the truth."

"What does that mean?

"What does it mean? You are 29 and it is time to meet someone and get married and have a family. So Mrs. Nadel comes into my shop. She tells me about this nice boy. I mean a man. And I say why not. He should meet my Daniella. So what's the big deal? You want to convict your father of the crime of wanting his daughter to meet someone and get married, and have children, and have a house, and make her father happy so I can go to my grave knowing my daughter will be ok. So convict me," he said, again offering his hands to be cuffed.

"Ok Dad, you're not dying and enough with the handcuffs but I just think that…"

Before I could finish my thought, my dad jumped from his chair but quickly collapsed back into his seat.

"What's the matter?"

"Look at that. Jeter stole second. He can still run."

"Dad, look over here. We're still talking."

"What were you saying?" he said, grabbing the remote out of my hand.

"I know how old I am."

"And you are not getting any younger. And I don't want you spending your life alone. Like Aunt Esther."

"You are now comparing me to Aunt Esther?"

"Yeah, your aunt made lots of money. And she had a beautiful apartment in the Upper East Side and traveled. But she had no one to enjoy it with. Is that what you want?"

"Well at least I'll have a nice place to live."

"I'd rather live in a prison. Not funny. But you know what happened to Aunt Esther with all her money?"

"What Dad?"

"She went *meshuga*. She started talking to herself every night because she had no one else to talk to. They finally locked her up with all the other nut cases."

"I don't believe you."

"Whatever."

"And I will also know when I meet the right person. Besides, it is not like I don't go out. I have had plenty of boyfriends."

"Boyfriends yes, husbands no."

"But you have never approved of any of my boyfriends."

"Like who?"

"How about Richard?"

"A Momma's boy."

"Joey."

"He was in the Mafia."

"But he bought me nice gifts. Scott."

"Not Jewish."

"Hyman."

"Too Jewish."

"Todd."

Dad holds up a limp wrist.

"Ok, so he didn't like sports."

"Sweetheart. He didn't like girls."

"Maybe I don't want a husband."

"Then you will be like your Aunt Esther and die all alone."

"Well, regardless, the man I marry is not going to be someone that Mrs. Nadel finds."

"Whatever sweetheart. But the good book says--"

"The good book! What good book? Do you now think you are Tevye from *Fiddler on the Roof* quoting the good book and you are going to find a groom for your daughter?

And do you really think that after I meet this man, and have dinner with him, and by the way he has no manners as he was shoving that pastrami into his mouth and there was mustard all over his fingers, that I am going to say thank you Dad for bringing to me the man of my dreams? Where do you think we live, Anatefka?"

"Huh?"

"Well I am not Tevye's daughter Tseidel."

"You should have gotten that role in high school. That Chapman girl. You had a better voice then her."

"No, Dad, she had a better voice. And why are we talking about what happened in high school? Stay focused," I said as I put my hands on his head and pried the TV remote from his hands again.

"Daniella, you are so dramatic. Just like your mother was. Besides, sometimes you have to listen to the words from the mouth of someone with experience. You think your mother and I knew each other that well? But our parents approved and that was what was important."

"Don't talk about my mother that way."

"That was a good way. That is the way she made me know how she felt. And I know how you feel. But I want you to give him a chance. Who knows? Maybe he is the one and your old poppa will soon have little *kinda* jumping up and down on my knees and we will be rolling and playing on the floor just like I use to do with you and your brother when you were little."

"Ok, Dad, I will see him again. But if it doesn't work out, that's the end. Deal?"

"Deal. Now can I finish watching the game?"

I kissed my father on the forehead and gave him back his remote. But while my father's mind returned to Yankee Stadium, that night I pondered being Mrs. Danielle Liebowitz. And all of a sudden, my life felt like it was passing faster than the remaining sand in an hour glass.

Rose's Third Diary Entry

The kind nurse said I slept well for the first time in a week of nightmares. Before last night, she said I would sit up in my bed and stare at the wall, though no one was there, and scream. This would happen several times during the night before I fell into a restful sleep. Perhaps fear is slowly becoming a thing of the past. But the past is still with me every waking moment.

Lunch was a bowl of soup filled with carrots, onions, celery and large strips of chicken. Seeing it brought memories of my mother preparing a big pot in the kitchen for Friday night dinner. Even before I tasted it, I was filling up on the rich aroma that filled the room.

As I brought a filled spoon to my mouth, it smelled so good. I managed a few bites before my stomach hurt. The doctor said it would take time to reintroduce food to my body as it had been so long since I had proper nourishment. I had also lost a tremendous amount of weight and if I forced myself to eat, I would be rewarded with a wrenching gut and nausea.

I felt a little stronger this afternoon, and my nurse announced that it would do me good if I left the room. Without asking, she placed me in a chair and wheeled me through the corridors of the hospital which seemed endless and all alike; the unmistakable scent of disinfected linoleum floors clung to the gleaming white walls and ceilings.

I pleaded that I felt more comfortable in my room, so she returned me. But upon leaving the chair, I was determined to take my first steps and walked to the window. My nurse pushed open the glass and I felt the invigorating air sweep inside my lungs and circulate around me. Outside were baby sparrows searching for food. As I placed some crumbs of bread from my lunch plate on the windowsill, I thought how ironic it was how in the camp we risked our lives for even one crumb.

This evening, a young aide came by my bed side. She asked if I needed anything. I said I would like to brush my hair and pointed to my brush by my bed side. She smiled and quickly returned holding a mirror. From the depths of the mirror, a frail, wan face with a determined chin and sensitive lips, now as pale as a winter rose, reflected back at me. I began to tremble as I examined my ashen cheeks and the dark purple abrasions encircling my swollen eyes which had once been pools of blue water. My hair, once finely spun gold, was now tousled carelessly above my bandaged head. I had seen a corpse and it was me. As bitter tears poured down my weathered face, the look in her eyes stared, haunted, into mine. I looked into the stark face that seemed so empty. I had seen the devil and I never wanted to share what I saw with anyone.

I am now tired and need to sleep.

Chapter Five

Nothing is more disgusting then riding the New York subway system on a hot humid summer day as the smell of perspiration combined with body odor permeates the rail car. With the temperature hovering in the 90s and the humidity index even higher, today was one of those dreaded days. But, like the good girl that I am, and wanting to please my father, I rode the subway to meet his Prince Charming.

As I exited the rail car, a handwritten sign read that the elevators were out of order. Of course, of all days, they picked today to break down. Walking up the two flights of stairs, droplets of sweat accumulated on my eyebrows and my upper lip. I helplessly licked the top of my lip, hoping to extinguish the sweat mustache that formed without many people noticing. But my tongue came up short and returned to my mouth with the waxy flavor of my lipstick. I now knew why the color was called burning burgundy. Feeling as if my face was melting in the overbearing humidity, I tried to slyly wipe my nose on my sleeveless shoulder but again failed, leaving a salty smear of makeup clearly visible on my arm. I felt paranoid that my face looked just as smeared.

The air was thick as I joined the growing crowd of fans moving toward the stadium entrance. As I walked, I noticed that my watch, which usually flopped around my wrist, felt tight. I felt swollen from wrist to toe.

It was still a few minutes before six as I walked up to the box office where we had agreed to meet, hoping that Jacob would be a no show. But, to my chagrin, deep in a sea of Yankee fans adorned in blue and white, he spotted me. He was wearing a crisp white shirt and tie and his fingers appeared mustard free.

"Were you waiting long?"

"No, I just got here," I said with a wry smile, feeling a trickle of perspiration running down my back.

"Good. Your dad arranged for the tickets to be at Will Call. I'll get on line."

"Ok."

I used the time while Jacob waited to check my face and reapply my lipstick.

A few minutes later, I was following Jacob through the stadium gate and into the ball park. But, with the crowd pouring in, I had difficulty keeping pace with him as he walked several steps ahead of me and increased his pace before I finally lost him in the crowd. And now, with no ticket in hand, beads of sweat pouring from my forehead and upset with myself that I had agreed to go, I stopped to catch my breath before reversing my direction to leave.

"Danielle," a voice called from behind me.

"Danielle." The voice sounded closer.

"Danielle." The voice was now in my face.

"Yes," I answered upset and out of breath.

"I thought you were behind me?"

"Well, if you even bothered to look, you would know that I was not. Anyway, this was a mistake. So I am going to go. Enjoy the game." I started to walk away.

"Wait. Are you hungry?"

I did not answer.

"Let's get something to eat."

Having sprinted for what seemed like a mile and dripping from perspiration, what I really wanted was a shower.

"Please, let's get something to eat."

I am always hungry and I thought I should at least get something to eat for all of my effort so I accepted his offer.

"Ok," I answered reluctantly.

"Great. Let's get some hot dogs." Hot dogs was not my first choice but I followed him to the concession stand a few steps, feeling confident that I would not lose him again.

"Three Hebrew Nationals," he shouted to the lady behind the counter. "A bag of peanuts and two Cokes."

"Excuse me," I said, poking my head so that the food server could hear me. "Could you make mine a Diet Coke? Thank you."

"Diet?" he questioned.

"Yeah, something wrong with that?"

"No, I just did not figure you to be a diet type of girl."

"What does that mean?"

"Well, you know. You don't look like you diet."

"Excuse me. That is the rudest."

"I did not mean it like that. I take it back."

"You can't. You already said it."

"Well, what I meant to say is that you're just going to gain more weight once you have babies."

"Are you for real? I am out of here."

I had always been very sensitive about my weight as it had been a struggle.

"I am sorry. Truly sorry. That was tactless. Again, poor choice of words."

"You make it sound like I am going to have a litter. Anyway, I am not having babies that quickly," I said as I took my hot dog and Diet Coke and walked over to the table of condiments.

"Whatever," I answered as I pumped out a fine line of ketchup onto my dog while Jacob drowned his hot dog in mustard.

"You sure like mustard," I said.

"One of God's greatest creations," Jacob proudly responded.

Jacob was right about one thing. My dad must have paid a lot of money to get these seats as they were four rows behind the Yankee dugout.

"I don't think I have ever had seats these good," I commented.

"Well, it's a special occasion," he smiled.

"And what is that?"

"Let's watch the game and I will tell you later."

With that cryptic message dancing in my mind, I ate my hot dog, shared the peanuts and sipped on my Diet Coke as the Yankees were cruising to a crushing defeat of their arch rivals.

By the seventh inning stretch, as we stood to our feet and sang "Take Me Out to the Ballgame," all I could think about was taking me out of the ball park and heading home for a shower. But as I was about to say my good night, Jacob startled me with his announcement.

"Well, you seem to check out. So I think we should make a commitment."

Commitment! At first, I thought he had used the wrong word.

"Could you repeat what you said?"

"You know. Commitment."

I did hear right. "Commitment for what?" I asked, settling back into my seat.

"Well, I am not going to see anyone else and I don't want you to. And we'll continue seeing each other for a few months and see where it goes."

"Are you fucking out of your mind?"

Jacob looked startled that I used the F word, as did the guy sitting next to him.

"I came here tonight because of my dad. I respect him and I know he spent a lot of money. But I am not into arranged marriages or anything that you are suggesting! You are really messed up. You need help."

I got up from my seat and walked toward the exit as Jacob followed me and yelled my name to stop me. But I ignored his pleas and walked faster and faster, finally arriving at the sign that pointed to the subway when I felt a sweaty hand on my shoulder.

"Danielle."

I pulled his hand away.

"Please, this was a mistake. I am tired, I am hot and I want to go home."

"Can we talk?"

"You had seven innings. And all you did was inhale your food, burp, and check your Blackberry. I don't even think you knew I was sitting next to you."

As I yelled, a very cute college age girl wearing a Yankee jacket and matching baseball cap heard what I said and flashed me a thumbs up in approval.

"I am sorry," he said, feebly looking at the pavement.

"Ok, well if that is all you can come up with, it was nice meeting you but I am going to go now."

"Wait. I really want to get to know you."

"Hello, did you not hear me? I am going home."

"I heard you," he said but this time looking squarely into my face. "But I would like, if possible, another chance. Can we start over?" Jacob asked followed by one of those uncomfortable pauses. "Hello, my name is Jacob." Jacob offered his hand his hand which I loosely grabbed. "What is your name?"

"I don't like games."

"Please. And what is your name."

"It is Danielle," I responded robotically as the stadium crowd inside roared. "Perhaps you should go back to watch the end of the game."

"No, I'd rather be here," Jacob said as a passing fan shouted that A-Rod had just hit his second home run of the night.

I stood quietly.

"Well, Danielle, do you like gelato? Because I know the best place in all of New York. And if you would so honor me, I would like to take you there."

Against my better judgment, but not wanting to upset my father, I agreed, but thirty minutes and eight subway stops later, there I was having the most amazing butter pecan and chocolate mint gelato I had ever had. And the conversation tasted a lot better than an hour ago.

"I did have a nice time. Thank you. But I should go."

I was drained from the heat and was still looking forward to that shower.

"So, no go on that commitment?

"I don't think so but…"

"Well, do I at least get a second chance?"

Jacob got his second and many more chances, which pleased my father. And with the Yankees in the playoffs, my father had a new best friend to watch the games with while I tried to figure out if there was a relationship worth pursuing. Regardless, Jacob was no longer a stranger in our home but a welcomed guest. And my father could not have been happier.

Rose's Fourth Diary Entry

My eyes were bigger than my stomach and I ate too much over the last few days. Just as the doctors had warned, I had a horrible stomach ache accompanied by bouts of diarrhea that left me dehydrated. Now, five days later, I am finally feeling oriented as to night and day and have the strength to write my story.

Reports had been circulating that Jews of Poland were being taken from their homes to internment camps or worse. With the little money that my Poppa had saved up, he arranged for my older sister to go with this couple he knew. The husband was an industrialist and had owned several milling factories near town. Poppa had done several favors for him and he promised my father that his daughter would be safe. But for two days after Hannah left, my mother cried and cried, worried for her safety. I remember how my father would hold her hand trying to reassure her that Hannah would be all right.

The third night after Hannah left, it snowed and the temperature dropped to bitter cold. Sometime in the early morning, we were awakened by several loud knocks on the door. The pounding at first went unanswered but quickly grew louder and the sound echoed to the marrow of my bones. I heard my father open the door and there was yelling. I ran to into my mother's arms. Three men in dark brown uniforms walked into our home and we were told to gather all of our things; we had to leave now. Within minutes, we were walking in the snow covered street under a somber, moonless sky. As we passed each home, our neighbors joined us. It started to snow again as I looked up the angry sky.

We continued to walk but no one knew where we were going or what our destiny would be. It was freezing cold and we stood for hours in this terrible weather in an open field waiting for everyone to assemble while the Germans went from house to house to make sure no Jew remained. They also warned the non-Jews in the town that if they hid any Jews, they would be killed.

After a few more hours, a long caravan of open bed trucks arrived and the Germans started to beat us on our backs with their rifle butts to hurry us into the vehicles. Everyone scrambled to stay with their family members and no one knew what would be done with us. After we all entered the trucks, they began to move but we had no idea in which direction.

After what seemed like hours, the trucks stopped suddenly as other trucks joined. Traveling together, we proceeded again as more snow and darkness fell and the night grew blacker and blacker. It was freezing cold but we did not utter a word.

Finally, in the middle of the night or perhaps it was morning, we arrived at a place no one recognized. The Germans began to shout and shoot their rifles in the air so we would get out of the trucks. There was an empty school with big rooms and we were herded in there with shouts and beatings. Later they threw some stale bread at us which was to be our nutrition.

We slept on the floor and those that had brought blankets from home could cover up with them; the others just froze. The next day, under guard of German soldiers whose rifles were always pointed at us, we were allowed to wash our faces in the nearby lake. But the water was freezing and my mother was upset that we even made the trek. Walking back, we passed a large fire over which the Germans were cooking soup, drinking, and appeared to be telling jokes. But as our cold and hungry faces passed them, there was no offer to share their meal.

That night, two male friends of mine from my village escaped through an open window. But we were told that they were caught after a few hours, and since we didn't see them again, we were sure that the Germans had shot them. Before they escaped, they had offered for me to come with them. But despite my strong desire to join, I couldn't leave my family.

On the third day, we were lined up and ordered to remove any jewelry that we had and place it on a long table. The once empty table now grew full with rings, necklaces, bracelets, brooches and watches. An old woman fumbled with her wedding band. I also watched as a little girl, no more than five or six, was told to remove her tiny gold earrings. When she started to cry, the soldier yanked the rings through her ears, tearing and bloodying her tiny ear lobes. Her mother screamed and the solder hit her in the face and dragged her by her hair outside. A murmur of fear filled the room, quickly followed by the sound of a gunshot. Then there was silence.

Afterwards, the soldiers made us go on another long walk at the end of which we saw trains. We were thrown into the railcars and everyone tried to hold onto their family. The Germans squeezed so many people into the cars as if we were animals, with no place to sit or stand.

In one corner there was a tin can and above it was a tiny window. The can was the train's toilet. The next day the train door opened briefly and the Germans haphazardly placed a bucket of tepid cabbage soup that was leaking from its sides inside, with no spoons. The doors then quickly closed and locked and the cattle cars continued on their journey.

After a few more days the doors opened again to let in some air and the Germans watched like hawks so that no one would get away. A guard had also discovered that a woman had given birth on the train and he took her and the baby away. Moments later we heard gun shots.

At each subsequent stop, as impossible as it was, more people were stuffed into the trains. By this point there were many dead bodies in the train as it was so difficult to sustain life in these squalid conditions.

At one stop, I peered through the tiny window and I saw a family. The mother was pretty; her hair was pulled back and held by a fancy clip. There was also a young girl, probably my age. She was wearing a heavy coat and gloves and her shoes were shiny. We gazed at each other from the platform. As the train's wheels started to clang and groan, I never stopped looking at the young girl until she completely disappeared. And I hoped, my God, there is still civilization; the world has not come to an end. But hope can be paralyzing.

Chapter Six

The Yankees did not make it past the first round of the post season. For my father, that also marked the end of his baseball season as he couldn't care who went on to the World Series; his mind was already on spring training.

But for Jacob and me, after a picnic and boat ride in Central Park, a birthday dinner and concert tickets at Madison Square Garden, and a stroll under the moon at Jones Beach, we had entered our own post season and I agreed to Jacob's "commitment." Of course, it was an easy choice for me to make as there was no "someone else" that I could call up to play. But if "someone else" came along, I would not turn down a late season trade from another team.

Jacob and my father were also both pleased with my decision to stay with the current lineup. However, except for a kiss good night, Jacob did not make any overtures to becoming intimate, which I found a little strange. But I rationalized that perhaps he was very old fashioned that way and wanted to move slowly. I was fine with this as I did not have much sexual experience and felt a little shy about sharing that kind of intimacy. I equated sex with love and wanted to share it with someone special.

Work also took on a new dimension as my boss in the DA's office allowed me to interview witnesses and prep the cases that were going to trial. And though the bar results were still a few weeks away, except for actually going into court and trying cases, I was for the most part acting like a real attorney.

By the beginning of November, and after flirting with the calendar for several weeks, fall had finally arrived with a vengeance, sending the daytime temperatures into the low 50s. With the sudden change in seasons, tank tops and tees were exchanged for sweaters and coats, which I preferred wearing anyway as they better covered up my body.

November also meant that we would soon be celebrating my favorite holiday. Enjoying Thanksgiving dinner at my Nana's house was just a given in my life. As a little girl, I fondly remember how much fun I had helping Nana stuff the turkey, make the cranberry mold, and glaze the sweet potatoes. Of course, no traditional Thanksgiving dinner was complete without homemade pumpkin and pecan pie. And the validation for all of Nana's hard work came when she presented her perfectly roasted golden brown turkey to our beautifully set table and my father would make a toast, choosing the loveliest and kindest of words to profess his appreciation.

But this year would be very different. My brother invited Nana to spend the long weekend with his family. My dad and I were also invited to my brother's for dinner but Jacob's parents extended an invitation and he really wanted us to go. And though I had been to Jacob's parents' home for a Labor Day barbeque and his sister's birthday party, Thanksgiving dinner would be the first time that both of our families would sit down at the table together.

Earlier in the week I called Jacob's mother to ask what I could bring. She insisted that we *"just come and enjoy"* though she finally accepted my offer to bake my favorite pumpkin and apple spice muffins. But with my euphoria on learning only a few days
earlier that I had passed the bar examination, I wished I had not volunteered as I was having difficulty focusing on anything.

I only wished that Jacob would have shared my excitement. Instead, he lectured me on his very strong opinions on how difficult it was for working mothers to balance raising a family and furthering their career. Not wanting to engage in a subject that I thought was too premature for our relationship, I elected to not respond. This only angered Jacob as he expressed how important it was for his wife to be "home with the kids," just like his mother was. Realizing that I could not remain mute, I voiced my counter points to his position.

After I rested my case, it was clearly evident that we had had our first major fight and I was sensing that Thanksgiving at Jacob's parents might not happen. But the next day, Jacob again surprised me. He texted an apology which he sent seconds before he knocked on my apartment door holding an arrangement of flowers with a card that invited me to a "make up, I am sorry, may I take you out for dinner" dinner. With no other plans for the evening, and turning to see my father wearing a Yankees cap and a big smile, I said yes.

Following dinner at my favorite Italian restaurant, Jacob invited me to his apartment for dessert, where we finally consummated that part of our relationship. As for the sex, there was more humping than kissing. But my mind was on the chocolate cake he had bought for dessert that was waiting on the kitchen table and which became the highlight of my evening.

———————————————

Jacob's parents lived in Long Beach on the southern tip of Long Island. As parking on the streets of Queens was so limited, my dad did not own a car. Rather than us renting one for the day, Jacob offered to drive. I told my father to sit in the front so that he would have more leg room.

As we drove, my father and Jacob talked about the stock market and the Yankees, only occasionally turning over their shoulders to ask why I was so quiet. I would return their questions with a smile and simply say, "I'm fine," which more than satisfied their inquiry.

When we were a few minutes from his parents' home, Jacob called his mother, and she was waiting at the front door waving when we arrived.

"Hello, come in," his mother said, hugging me.

"This is my dad."

"So nice to meet you. Thank you for coming," Jacob's dad said, extending his hand.

"Your daughter is lovely," praised Jacob's mother.

"Like her mother. Thank you," Dad grinned.

There was a momentary pause.

"I brought you something, I hope you like them." I handed the basket of muffins to Jacob's mother.

"You didn't have to."

"But I wanted to."

"Thank you. Let's put them in the kitchen."

As we followed her into the home, the smells of all of the foods cooking wafted together in a wonderful, home cooked aroma. And in the kitchen, set out on the counter was a parade of desserts including pecan, pumpkin and chocolate pies.

"Any traffic?" Jacob's dad asked as he took our coats which only a week ago were still hanging in our closets.

"No, not bad," Jacob responded as he headed to the kitchen. "Anyone thirsty?"

"Well let's go sit down. My oldest daughter and my sister should be here shortly," Jacob's father said as he guided us out of the hall.

We followed Jacob's parents into the den where his mother had set a beautiful tray on the bar countertop of cheeses, grapes, and crackers neatly arranged and sitting on paper leaves that represented all of the fall colors. There were also small dipping dishes of humus and eggplant dip.

"I have a feeling you are a scotch man," Jacob's dad said to my father as he picked up a glass from the bar.

"Well, since I am not driving, why not."

A few minutes later, Jacob's sister and aunt arrived and Jacob's father ushered everyone into the dining room. Jacob's mother loved to decorate for the holidays and her festive table looked like a picture out of Gourmet magazine. Along with a holiday tablecloth with matching napkins, holiday china plates, and amber colored glasses, the serving plates carried the Thanksgiving theme. Even the cranberry tray had small turkeys adorning the border. And each chair was perfectly positioned so as to allow everyone just enough room to get in and out with ease.

"These are so cute," I said, admiring the chocolate covered turkey wrapped in amber colored cellophane that was placed on top of each plate as a hostess favor.

With everyone comfortably seated, Jacob's father raised his glass for what I thought would be a toast.

"As is our family tradition on Thanksgiving, we begin our meal with a festive joke:

"Three men, an Italian, a Frenchman, and a Jew, were condemned to be executed. Their captors told them that they had the right to have a final meal before the execution.

"They asked the Frenchman what he wanted.
'Give me some good French wine and French bread,' he requested. So

they gave it to him, he ate it, and then they executed him. Next it was the Italian's turn.

'Give me a big plate of pasta,' said the Italian.

So they brought it to him, he ate it, and then they executed him.

Now it was the Jew's turn. 'I want a big bowl of strawberries, said the Jew.

'Strawberries?! They aren't even in season!' his captors exclaimed.

'So, I'll wait...'"

Amidst the laughter and applause, Jacob's father asked everyone to start eating, and we gladly obeyed. The food tasted as good as it looked and everyone overate, prompting Jacob's mother to suggest that we take a break before we have dessert.

"Great idea," replied Jacob's aunt.

His mother then said, "So Danielle, that is such wonderful news about passing the bar. You must be so excited."

"Thank you. I am."

"So what are you going to do?"

"Well, I just learned that there is an opening in the DA's office where I have been working. But I am also going to put together my résumé and see what happens. At least that's the plan."

"She'll get a job. Who wouldn't want my beautiful Daniella?"

"Thanks Dad. My biggest supporter."

"Why not? I should be. She makes me very proud."

Jacob's father nodded his head. "Spoken like a true father."

As if he was following a script and that was his cue, Jacob rose to his feet and tapped the wine glass with a spoon.

"I have an announcement."

I turned to Jacob with a puzzled look and shrugged my shoulders as his mother looked to me to see if I knew what Jacob was about to say. As he spoke, I was absolutely clueless where he was going.

"As you know, Danielle and I have been seeing each other for a few months. And the times we have shared together have been wonderful."

I was now feeling embarrassed and felt my face turn red.

"So, it being Thanksgiving, and having everyone who means so much to me being here together, I thought this would be a great time to ask a question."

I bowed my head and wished that I could hide under the table, fearing the words that were about to come out of Jacob's mouth. But as he cleared his throat, I panned the room from left to right and saw a sea of smiles.

"Danielle, you are the most amazing person I have ever met. And I want to spend the rest of my life with you."

At that moment I wished I was a turtle and could bury my head inside my shell. Instead, I pasted a blithe smile on my face.

"Will you be my wife?"

Wife? I thought of another four letter word as my mind was flushed with emotions and my heart was racing.

"I don't know what to say." I said, gazing at the ring that he was holding in my face.

"For once my daughter is speechless. Of course she says yes," my father yelled as he jolted from his seat and raised his glass of wine. "And let me be the first to toast the future bride and groom. *La Chaim*!"

A nanosecond after Jacob placed the ring on my finger, I was buried under my father and Jacob's family hugging and kissing me.

"Look at you," my father said. "It reminds me when Mariano Rivera got the last out in the World Series and all the players charged the mound."

As I came up for air, I looked at the ring which hung loosely on my finger.

"Let me see," Jacob's mom requested as she reached for my ring finger. "Oh, Grandma was a much larger woman and she had big fingers. We'll get it resized. I know someone in the city I can trust."

As everyone took turns holding my hand in theirs, Jacob was waiting for approval like a puppy wagging his tail after he had peed on the paper rather than on the carpet. But all I could muster up was a smile that looked like the kind your teacher gave as she handed you your report card.

"It's a little warm in here. Is it just me?" I asked.

Jacob's father opened the sliding door. I thought about running away. But I was too embarrassed to say no, or for that matter to say anything at all, so I just walked to the door to breathe in some fresh air. But the conversation quickly turned to wedding dates, where to register, and color schemes. Everyone was talking around me, yet I could not process what anyone was saying except for Jacob's oldest sister, Sherri, who was noticeably reserved. Politely I said, "I think now the bride and groom need some time to go over everything."

"That is a good idea," remarked Sherri and she nudged me into the kitchen.

"I am very happy for you but I am sure you would have preferred a more private proposal."

"I am a little shaken."

"But are you surprised?"

"I don't know. I guess not. From our first date, your brother has always talked about marriage."

"Well, I am very happy for you. And I welcome you in our family. I always wanted a little sister."

I pointed to my hips. "I don't know about little."

"Oh, come on. You are beautiful. But I want you to know. Maybe I shouldn't say this since you just got engaged, but my brother can be a real jerk."

I nodded my head.

"No seriously, he is very headstrong."

"Yeah."

"You know Jacob had a serious girlfriend before you."

"I know. Kristin."

"Close. Tristan. They were together for almost a year. She was wonderful. We all loved her. She was in med school. And we thought they were going to get married. "

"But she wasn't Jewish."

"Right. But that is not why they broke up."

"No?"

"I don't know. After they stopped seeing each other, I wanted to talk to her. We were very close. But I left her many messages and she never took my call or called back. I finally gave up but I always thought there was more to it. Anyway, my brother can be very demanding."

"Yes, he is."

"Just be careful."

"What do you mean?"

"Look, I probably already said too much."

"Who wants dessert?" Jacob's mother asked as she walked into the kitchen and picked up the pies that were on the counter."

In the car ride home, Jacob and my dad resumed their earlier conversation while I nodded off in the back seat. And though whenever we were together I wanted to ask him about Tristan, I never did. Instead, we spent the next several months planning a wedding rather than discussing a marriage.

Rose's Fifth Diary Entry

It was December 10, 1944. The only reason why I remember that date is because there was a little girl in the same rail car that said it was her birthday today. However, for most Eastern European Jews, the time for celebrating had stopped long before.

As the train came to a screeching stop, we heard the voices of German soldiers shouting from outside and I kept my arm tightly around my mother's waist. Within seconds, the cattle cars doors opened revealing barking dogs and uniformed men touting rifles. "*Raus! Raus! Schnell! Schnell! Raus! Raus!*" the men shouted. "Get Out! Get Out! Quickly! Hurry Up! Hurry up leave your luggage behind!"

We were in the back of the car. But I immediately felt the freezing cold air that consumed the train car. As we stumbled forward, I cautiously stepped over the stiffened body of an older lady who had died during the trip. A few more steps and I squinted from the bright sunlight and almost lost my balance, having been in total darkness and without food or water for days squeezed into the rail car with no place to sit or stand.

We approached the opened rail car door and confronted the frightening face of a German shepherd that lunged towards me with his mouth wide open exposing these huge teeth. Surprisingly, the guard pulled back on his collar and then smirked and laughed in my face, saying something in German that I did not understand.

More guards and dogs then boarded the car, and with the barrels of their guns, the guards pushed us onto the platform. Those who did not walk fast enough off the train were thrown to the ground. At this point, many of the women were crying as they lay in the snow too weak to get up on their feet. Those poor souls who did not get up fast enough were shot in the head. But maybe they were the lucky ones.

Once on the platform, everyone wanted to move about and search for their family members. But I had lost my shoes when I was hurdled into the train and my feet were turning blue from the icy pavement.

While standing for what seemed like eternity, I wondered what was on the other side of the barbed wired fence. I could see a church. There were roofs and chimneys. And in the houses there were beds and sheets and blankets. The people had clean clothes and nobody was screaming or being screamed at. Nobody was treated like cattle. They were there, on the other side of the fence, in a clean little village where children played and had food to eat. And I was here.

Finally, a gray car pulled up and the soldiers jumped to attention as a burly man in his forties exited. The uniformed men saluted him as he passed them and moved towards us. He announced that we were in Mauthausen, Austria and that we were lucky because this was a work camp. If we did our work, we would be treated fairly.

As he talked I looked down at my feet and noticed I could no longer feel my toes. So I stepped onto my mother's shoes and somehow she managed to hold and balance herself with the weight of my body on her feet.

Suddenly, the commandant gave some order and the guards began separating us. On one side they pulled out the sick and elderly. On the other side were the younger and healthier looking men, women, and children. Then we were further separated; women from the men, boys with their fathers and girls with their mothers. All the while, uniformed men were barking orders like their dogs to move faster.

As families were divided, there were screams and cries. The sick and older men and women were then ordered to march away from the train station and within minutes they were out of view.

For the rest of us, the massive wood and steel gates behind where we were standing opened and we were ordered to march into the camp. Again we were pushed and shoved as the guards used the barrels of their guns to move us forward. As we did, a young mother in front of me tripped and fell to the group releasing her baby from her arms. A guard immediately shot them both. I stepped over their bodies and painfully walked past.

Once behind the gates, we heard repeated gun fire and I saw a cloud of smoke in the direction of where the sick and older men and women had been taken. The sound of gun fire was followed by a woman next to me reciting *Kaddish*, the prayer for the dead.

Chapter Seven

As my father and I approached the end of the lace runner, I looked again at Jacob. But instead of him looking back at me, his eyes continued to wander around the sanctuary. Annoyed, I focused on my brother David. He was sitting in the front row with my sister-in-law Denise, my nephew Michael and my niece Rebecca, who was making curly cues with Denise's long hair. Sitting to the right of my brother was my Nana Rose, looking so aristocratic in her dark blue dress and her treasured pearl necklace that floated like a halo around her neck. My grandfather gave it to her for their 50th wedding anniversary.

She blew me a kiss as our eyes met. *"I love you."*

"I love you too, Nana," I whispered, as I had now taken my final step and awaited my fate.

My dad lifted my veil and he kissed my forehead. "I love you so much."

"I love you too. I only wish Mom could be here."

"She is here sweetheart. Now go get married."

"Ok," I said with a laugh and tears in my eye as he took my hand and placed it around Jacob's extended elbow and the two of us walked up the three steps taking our position under the Chuppah.

In Jewish tradition, the bride walks around her husband seven times to symbolize the contract between a husband and wife. As I completed the first of the seven turns, I again looked at Jacob. Surprisingly, he had cleaned up pretty good; his beard was trimmed, his hair was styled, the shirt was crisp, the suit was pressed, and outwardly he broadcast a message of confidence and self-assurance. However, it was his inner being that I feared.

Completing my second turn, I turned to my Nana and remembered the day I first told her about Jacob.

I tried to visit Nana at least twice a week and always on Friday when I would first stop at Schwartz's on Queens Boulevard to buy her a fresh *Challah* for Shabbat.

Each week, going to the bakery reminded me of the movie *Groundhog Day* as the same scene repeated itself. The air was heavy with bread baking. A worker in a stained white apron scurried from the back of the store to the shelves against the wall carrying loaves of Challah that were steamy, soft, and shiny with a light glaze.

For me, the real treat was what was behind the waist high glass counters. They were filled with vanilla crescents, lemon squares, linzer törts, hazelnut spirals, chocolate-dipped sablés, and rugelach. I was in heaven and sweets were my passion as each week I wouldn't leave without sitting down in one of the three small booths in front of the glass counter. And each week, the same older woman, no taller than five feet, with a bouffant hairdo, her skin a milky white except for the smear of rouge on her cheeks, shuffled toward me. As she did, I watched her apron almost snag her legs so that she might tumble forward. But she never did.

She asked me with a generous smile and a wink if I wanted a cup of coffee. I said yes and felt guilty for having sat down to be waited on by this elderly woman. But she did not seem to mind and brought back my extra light coffee with my choice of pastries. And sometimes, to my surprise, a piece of freshly baked rugelach and another friendly wink.

Nana's building looked identical to ours. Aside from it being around the corner, the only difference was the color of the front door. Having our grandparents living so close made it very special for my brother and me. When my mother died, my father found himself with two small kids to raise and a business to run, so my Nana became my surrogate mother as she cooked our meals, cleaned our clothes, and stayed with us each night until my father would come home from work.

"Who?" Nana's voice asked from the intercom speaker in the lobby at about three million decibels.

"It's me, Nana," I shouted at the top of my lungs.

"Vaht?" she blasted back.

After three or so tries, during which I alternated shouts of, "It's meeeee!" and "C'mooonnn Nana," she buzzed me in.

I took the elevator to the fifth floor and walked past three apartments that all had the same aroma of chicken soup seeping through the walls until I reached the end of the hallway, rang the bell, and waited for Nana to look through the peephole.

"Who's there?" she asked even though we'd just spoken on the intercom. My Nana was never a very trusting soul and justifiably so considering that she was a Holocaust survivor who lost her entire family to the Nazis. But when I felt weak, she gave me the words to be strong and I often wondered where her strength came from. Regardless, I enjoyed kidding her that, after all, the big bad wolf could have killed me on the way up, donned my clothes and then figured out which was the correct apartment door to approach.

"It's Danielle."

"Coming, coming, coming," My Nana replied as the sound of the whistling tea pot on her stove quieted and was replaced by her shuffling feet as she approached the door.

"All these knobs," she said as she slowly turned the three locks.

Nana was less than five feet tall but someone I always looked up to.

"Look at you, so beautiful, my *Shana Madela*," Nana said as she reached for my face and gave me a kiss. "So sweet you are."

"Oh Nana, you always say that."

"What. I can't tell my granddaughter how beautiful she is? Come, come," she said as I followed her into the kitchen.

"Here is your Challah from Schwartz's."

"Smells good. Put it in the kitchen in the bread box."

"Breadbox," I thought to myself. "Where? I don't see a breadbox," I said searching the kitchen. And then I realized. "You don't mean the microwave?"

"Yes, that's now the breadbox."

"Nana, my brother just bought you a microwave so that it would be easier to heat up things."

"Well it works just as good keeping my bread fresh. Anyway, I can't figure out how to use it. And who needs all that radiation. I read this article in the New York Times that those microwaves are not safe. You'll see."

"Nana, you read too much."

My Nana has always said that you cannot begin your day without reading the paper.

"And the article also said the same thing about those cell phones. You hold them long enough against your head and you going to get a brain tumor."

"Nana, everyone has them."

"And everyone will soon have brain tumors."

"Nana. What are we going to do with you," I said hugging her. "You want me to show you how to use the microwave?"

"No, it works great as a breadbox," she said as she walked away.

I put the challah on the counter and opened her refrigerator to make sure she had plenty of food.

"Do you need anything?" I asked taking inventory of what was in the refrigerator.

"I have food. Don't worry. Come. Let's play cards."

Satisfied that everything looked in order, I walked into the living room where Nana was seated in her favorite over-stuffed chair that sat angled in the corner of the room and faced the window. The cards for our weekly gin rummy game were already dealt and the New York Times was in her lap. For 85 years, she has remained extremely alert and up on current affairs.

"You have so many things in here," I said as I passed the ceiling-scraping curio cabinet. It was filled with her prized collection of assorted cups and saucers that she received as gifts from all her friends who would bring her back a cup and saucer from wherever they traveled.

"What do you want sweetheart? Everything I have is yours."

"Nana. You're being ridiculous. You love looking at everything. And what I am going to do with it?"

"I rather you have it now. Anyway, it is better to give while your hands are warm."

Sitting in the center of her dining room table was her Shabbat candlestick holders. They were wobbly and brass but Nana kept them well polished. I paused to admire them and remembered every Friday night, to commemorate the start of the Sabbath, Nana would cover her head with a shawl. With my brother and me standing beside her, she lit the white candles and waved her hands over the flames and covered her eyes and prayed.

"Someday they'll be yours," Nana said with her sweet smile as she caught me looking at the candleholders.

"Stop talking that way Nana," I snapped back.

"Ah, my *kindelah*, even at 85, I do not feel old. But I know my time is soon."

"Don't talk like that."

"You're right. I am not ready to go."

"Then you won't go."

"But I look in the mirror and I see someone I do not recognize. Who is this old face? I do not feel on the inside the way I look on the outside."

The rest of her furniture was circa 1950 though it has held up amazingly well. Family pictures covered the faded wallpaper with some hanging so close together that the frames overlapped. Nana also collected needlepoint doilies which she draped over the four foot stools that were in front of the matching couch and which elbowed each other for breathing space in the small room. In the living room was also a very small mahogany table with more family pictures on it.

"Look at this," Nana said, pointing to the article in the NY Times about poverty in Appalachia. "It is shameful that a country as rich as the United States allows poverty to exist. It is sad."

"It is Nana."

As I watched her read the article, I thought about what an amazing person she was and how this world would be so lost had she not survived the Nazis. She had a great will to live; someone who found meaning in life despite the pain of her life. But it was not only this strength of will but also this great, hard-edged determination to survive. When I was seven, I remembered falling off my bike and my lip was cut and bleeding. Nana bandaged me up. But a week later, she pushed me back on my bike and taught me not to fear.

As we played cards, I inhaled the sweet smell of hydrangeas; her favorite flower reposed in a sparkling glass vase on the dining room table.

"Those flowers smell so wonderful, Nana."

"That's what I worry about. Who will water my plants when I am no longer here?"

"Stop it Nana or I am going to hit you."

"All right."

"And it's your turn to pick a card."

"Ouch!"

"What's the matter?"

"Something hurts."

"What hurts Nana? What's going on?"

"My *tuchas*. It's my *tuchas*."

"Something hurts there?"

"Feels like a stab, like someone is jabbing me in the *tuchas*!"

My Nana rarely ever complained about anything.

"Let me check."

"Ahhhhhh, that hurts!"

"Nana, you are sitting on the telephone handset. That is why it hurts," I said as I picked it up and put the phone back on its cradle.

"No wonder why nobody calls me."

"You're very funny. So, you had a good time with David?"

Nana had been visiting my brother and his family for the past few days.

"He worked, and that sister-in-law of yours. She has this *punim* and never smiles. She doesn't even offer you a cup of water. You could die.

She's no *baleboostah*. But she's busy with the children. Such beautiful *kinda*. And they wanted to take me here and there. They think I am a young girl. But I don't have the *koyach* like I used to."

"They just want to do things with you."

"I have aches and pains but I don't tell anyone. I make the best of it. But you remember the show the 'Golden Years'? *Fe*. They should call it the tarnished years!"

I smiled.

"I just hope God loses my address for many years. I have too many things I still want to do."

We finished our card game. And just like every other week, we walked into her bedroom which she always kept clean and tidy. Inside her room were her bed, nightstand, dresser, and her beautiful cedar hope chest that was covered with a lace shawl. Next to the window was a plain slat back rocking chair under a standing lamp where she loved to sit and look at the window which faced the park. On Nana's dresser was her silver hairbrush sitting on a glass tray. The back of the brush was made of mother of pearl and the handle was silver plated with the initials I.O.

"For years Nana I have asked you. But you never tell me. What do the initials stand for?" I asked, pointing to the initials on the brush.

"The brush was a gift."

"I know Nana. You've told me that. But from whom? Was it a boyfriend? Who was it?"

"That is all I can tell you now. But someday you will know."

From the time I was a little girl, Nana would rock in her chair and we would talk while taking turns brushing each other's hair. But in recent years, I mostly did the brushing. It also allowed Nana and I time to talk about everything and anything. And the world outside was forgotten.

"So. What is new with my Danielle?" she asked as I took the comb out of the side of her head, releasing her long, thick, wavy white hair.

"You have the most amazing hair Nana. I hope I have hair like you."

My Nana laughed. "You have a long time before you will have hair like mine. So, *vooz*?" (What's new?)

"Nana, remember how we would talk about the man someday I

would marry."

"Yes, and we said he would be tall and handsome with eyes that would be brighter than Times Square. He would have a kind, sweet smile and soft hands, like butter so that he could hold you tenderly. Your husband would be hard worker with his mind, not his body."

"Well I have some news," I said as I continued to brush. "You know the man I have been seeing?"

"Yes, I think. And he has a name?"

"Jacob, Nana. His name is Jacob."

I cherished my visits with Nana and selfishly did not want to share them with some guy that I was seeing. Besides, I was not really serious with any of my past boyfriends. And my relationships always provided interesting stories to tell Nana. But with Jacob's proposal, it was different. To put on my dad's thinking cap for a moment, I am now the manager of the Yankees. And I have to decide whether to let the batter swing and take my chances that he gets a hit or sit him down and call someone else up to bat.

"It's a nice name."

"And where did you meet this man with the nice name?"

"Remember a few months ago. I came home and he was in our apartment."

"A stranger was standing in your apartment. Did he rob you?" Nana asked.

"No Nana. Mrs. Nadel knew him and told my father," I reassured her.

"That Mrs. Nadel should mind her own business. You don't need her help to meet someone."

"I know, but my father thought I did."

"So now he's Tevye!"

I laughed. "That's what I said. Anyway, he stayed for dinner and we talked and…"

"And, vooz?"

"And two nights later we went to the ball park."

"He's a ball player?"

"No. Nana," I laughed.

"Then what does this man do?"

"He works for Morgan Stanley. He apparently has a good job. And, he has asked me to marry him."

Nana put her hand over my hand that I was brushing her hair with and said, "So, what did you say?"

"It was so sudden."

"Go on, "she said releasing my hand so that I could continue brushing.

"You know we went to his parents' house for Thanksgiving."

"Yeah."

"And right after dinner, he stands up, he says he has something to say, and next minute I know, there's a ring on my finger."

"And where's the ring? Is it a good stone?"

"It was his grandmother's and it is being sized."

"Ok, so I'll see it soon. But did he get down on his knees?"

"No."

"Did he ask your father first?"

"He did. Dad told me he came over a few weeks before and they talked."

"Well that was the right thing to do. Your grandfather would have asked my father before we were married, if he…"

"I know Nana. I wish I had met my great-grandparents."

"They were wonderful people." Nana momentarily turned her head away from me. I felt that if I were not in the room, she would start to cry. "Well, I have only one question. Do you love him?"

I did not answer.

"Danielle, do you love this man? You can't marry him unless you love him."

"I don't know Nana."

"Vooz."

"He's not the best looking guy. He has the worst manners. But I am almost 30. And he has a good job so maybe…."

"Danielle. When you first saw him, did your heart go pitter patter?"

"What?"

"Hand me that photo." Nana pointed to the picture frame sitting on her nightstand.

"Look at that man. Your grandfather was such a good looking man. Tall, big shoulders, and strong. That is where your brother gets his looks."

Nana then took my hand and puts it over my chest.

"When I first met your grandfather, before he could even say hello, my heart did this little dance. A flutter," she said as she demonstrated with my hand over her blouse. "And that was a sign. I knew, when I met my husband, let him rest in peace, that he was the one. "

"I don't know Nana."

"Well, is he a good kisser?"

"Nana!"

"Vooz. You don't buy a cow to put milk on your table unless you already know that the cow can make milk. And you can tell a lot about a man from the way he kisses. If he is gentle, and takes his time, this is good. If he rushes you to get to the finish line, you need to slow down."

"I don't want to hear any more about this," I said as I continued to brush her hair.

"So, did you give him an answer?"

"No, not yet but…"

"You have to milk the cow before you buy it."

"Nana!" I screamed, startled that she would use such a phrase.

"What do you think, that I was born yesterday? You think in my day we just walked up to the Chuppah and…"

"I don't want to hear any more about this."

"So when are you going to give him an answer?" Nana pressed me.

"Tomorrow night. He's taking me out for dinner to Bacchus, the Italian restaurant."

"Oh, fancy shmancy. You order the veal. It is the best. Your grandfather loved their veal."

"So what should I tell him Nana?"

"Well, if you love him, you should marry him. But if you don't, there are plenty of other boats in the sea and they are building new boats every day."

"Ok Nana, where did you hear that?"

"On Oprah. She knows everything."

"Yes she does. But what if I don't love him? My father said I will learn to love him."

"What? You have to go to school to learn? You've been in school long enough!"

As Nana spoke, there were the voices of children coming from outside the window.

"Look, look," Nana pointed to the window. "Look at all the little children playing. See their smiles? They are so happy."

"They are."

"And someday you'll have little ones just like those."

"I hope so. Nana. What if I am wrong? What if Jacob is not the right one?"

"We don't talk about that now."

I resumed brushing Nana's hair. And as she rocked in her chair, she softly sang:

Tambala, Tambala, Tumbalalaika
Tumbala, Tumbala, Tumbalalaika
Tumbalalaika, shpil balalaika
Tumbalalaika freylekh zol zay

Rose's Sixth Diary Entry

The gates closed behind us. Holding on to my mother's hand, I watched my father being pushed along with a group of men into one room while my mother and I were marched into another and told to remove all of our clothes. As we stood naked, anyone who tried to shield their body parts was beaten with the butt of a soldier's gun.

After a humiliating examination to make sure we were not concealing anything, we were taken to a dimly lit room where we showered with freezing water. In the showers we were given soap where I heard someone say that the soap was made out of the fat of the bodies that were burnt and that combs were made from the bones and purses from the skin.

From the shower, we were ushered to still another room where the air was stuffy and foul. We were told that our old clothes may have carried infections and we had to quickly select new clothes from a pile of clothing that was on a table. I grabbed the first things I could find along with a pair of shoes, hoping that they were a left and a right, not giving any thought whether they were wood or leather; just that they would fit.

From there we were led into a huge room filled with German clerks. We were told to stand in line and push up our sleeves. We had a number tattooed on our arms with an electric pen. My Mama told me to be brave and not cry. I tried to hold back the tears as the hot needle of the pen burned into my arm a small triangle and the number 44117.

A soldier started shouting at us and pulled me from my mother's grasp as other officers pulled other girls of similar age. There were probably twenty of us; all blondes with fair skin. My eyes remained fixed on my mother who was only a few feet away but far enough to know that if I crossed that distance I would be killed. As I gazed at her face, her eyes were dulled and she looked white and sickly and filled with fear. In only days, the woman with the voluptuous figure had become gaunt and pale. It was as if my mother knew she was already dead. I tried in vain to mouth words but my mother appeared to look through me and not at me.

All of a sudden, a young woman not wearing a uniform and carrying a large sack in her hand walked into the room. She handed a paper to the soldier. As he read it, she seemed impatient and argued that he was taking too long. Moments later, she walked up and down the line of girls and stopped in front of me and my heart leaped.

She was probably in her mid-twenties, and had blonde straight hair which was pulled back into a severe bun and fastened at the nape of her neck. She was very pretty but I was afraid to look at her and kept looking down. But she put her hand on my face and I looked up and saw a very sweet smile greeting me. She took my hand, stroked the hair out of my eyes and shouted something to the soldier before walking away.

There were more shouts as my group was led in one direction and my mom began to move further away from me. "Please, please," I pleaded as I stretched out my hands, trying to grab my mother's hand. But all she could do was look at me with sadness in her eyes and a tiny brave smile as she nodded that I would be ok. That was the last time I saw my mother. And I never had a chance to say goodbye to my father.

Chapter Eight

I had been standing for over 30 minutes and my feet were really hurting. Why do women sacrifice comfort for style? I asked myself as I turned my right ankle in so that I could momentarily relieve the pressure from my other foot. And as the Rabbi continued with the blessings, all I could process was blah, blah, blah and thought of the movie "The Graduate" when Dustin Hoffman appeared high up in the church and professed his love for Katharine Ross. But that only happens in the movies.

The ceremony had now reached the point where we exchange rings. But from standing for so long, my fingers swelled and Jacob had to push the thin gold band on to my finger. As he did, I looked for Nana to jolt up from her seat and shake and shout her disapproval just like in "The Graduate." Instead, she returned my glance with her sweet smile. And now, like the grains of salt passing through an hour glass, my time had run out as I slid the band on Jacob's ring finger.

"Harai at mekudeshet li, b"taba- at zu, k'dat Moshe v "ysiroe,"
"Be sanctified to me with this ring, according to the laws of Moses and Israel"

The Rabbi continued, "By the powers vested in me by the State of New York, I now pronounce you husband and wife."

"Mazel Tov," the crowd erupted as Jacob stomped to pieces the symbolic glass wrapped in a white linen napkin. After lifting my veil for a very brief kiss, we walked hand in hand down the three steps quickly passing all of our well-wishers who were on their feet clapping with their approval.

Waiting to greet us at the back of the sanctuary was Diane.

"Mazel Tov. Congratulations. That was beautiful."

"Thank you," Jacob said smugly as if he had just won a spelling bee contest.

"Do you want a few minutes?"

"We're ok but now I really have to pee," I said.

Diane laughed as she walked me to the bridal room where I had first dressed while Jacob stood and shook hands with our guests on their way into the ballroom.

"Could you find my grandmother? I really would like to see her."

"Sure," Diane said as she opened the door to the bridal dressing room and I made a mad dash for the bathroom, wiggling out of my dress as I filled the bowl fearful that it would overflow.

"Danielle."

"I am in here Nana. I will be right out."

"It was a beautiful ceremony. And Rabbi Asa did such a wonderful job."

"He did Nana," I said as I came out of the bathroom rearranging my dress. "But I feel sick."

"Do you want me to get you something? Are they serving soup? I am sure they can get you some. It always makes you feel better."

"I am ok. I am just a little light headed. It's my nerves from standing so long. I'll be ok."

"Could you get my granddaughter a little soup?" Nana asked Diane.

"Thanks Nana. But I am sure it would not be as good as yours," I protested.

"I am sure I can," Diane said as she left the room.

"Vooz?" Nana turned back to me.

"Nothing."

"Oy. Such a beautiful girl should not have such a sad face on her wedding day."

The kitchen was only steps away from the bridal room and Diane quickly returned with a cup of steaming hot chicken soap.

"Thank you dear," Nana said.

"My pleasure. And I think I will leave the two of you alone for a little bit while I check the ball room." Diane left.

"Take some soup," Nana urged me.

"I will Nana," I said as I put a spoonful to my mouth. "Nana, do you remember when I did not feel well when I was young, and you told me that the soup was blessed."

"I do."

"And you would say, *Sweetheart. It is magical. The first drop of chicken soup was blessed by God and each drop made after that is also blessed.*"

"That's right. God blessed the first drop of soup and every drop after that was blessed."

"And you would say, 'Eat some soup, Danielle. It will make you feel better.' And I would say, 'But Nana, I am not hungry'."

"I remember. So many years ago but I remember it like yesterday. So what's wrong sweetheart?"

"Nana, I think I made a terrible mistake."

"Mistakes can be fixed."

"I don't know, Nana."

Nana and I talked for a few more minutes until Diane back came into the room.

"Are you ready for your grand entrance Mrs. Liebowitz?"

"Wow. You are the first person to call me by that name."

"Well, it takes a little getting used to. But a year from now, your face will light up when you hear your name."

"Like this?" I moved my lower lip as far right as I could so as to distort my smile.

"Kind of," she said, frowning.

"I love you Nana," I said, turning back to my grandmother.

"You'll be fine. But smile so everyone can see that beautiful *pu-num*," she replied.

I shrugged away my anxiety with a careless smile as Nana left the room.

"Ready?" Diane asked, not offering me any opportunity to respond as she walked me to the ballroom entrance where Jacob was waiting by the door.

"It's show time," Jacob announced. I wanted to wipe that shit eating grin off his face as he took my hand. And as we awaited the band leader's introduction, I fantasized about taking a long, hot bath to soak my aching feet.

"Ladies and gentlemen, put your hands together as we welcome for the first time, Mr. and Mrs. Jacob Liebowitz."

Diane pushed open the doors to more cheers and shouts as Jacob led me directly onto the dance floor where we had our first dance followed by the father-daughter dance. And as my dad waltzed me around, he again told me what he had said so many times before; that Jacob *"was a good man."*

"I know Dad."

"And I know you will give him a chance."

"I think I did. I just married him!"

My father shot me an inquisitive stare and looked anxious to respond but was quickly swept away on his feet by our family and friends who circled us as the band started to play the traditional *Hora*. And just when I thought the dance floor could not fit any more people, a chair was pushed under me and I was lifted into the air. Seconds later, Jacob was rocketed up in his chair holding the end of a white napkin and we were guided towards each other.

After I snagged the other end of the napkin, our lifters spun us around the center of the dance floor like wobbling tops that were about to lose their momentum. But each time I thought the ride was over, we were thrust even higher into the air as our chair lifters kept in sync with the rhythmic beat. And as I continued to be tossed and jostled in my seat, I lost sight of my father and felt unsure about the man who was to replace him as my protector.

The rest of the night was a blur as I drank too much champagne and ate too little food.

By midnight, only a handful of our friends and family remained. Holding my shoes in my hand, I told Jacob that I was going to change. But Jacob waved me off with his hand while he continued talking to his best man.

When I returned, we said our last goodbyes and drove to the hotel that Jacob's parents had arranged for us to spend our wedding night. And as Jacob inserted the room card key into the door, I asked in a flirtatious tone, "Well, are you going to carry me over the threshold?"

Jacob did not respond as he opened the door, switched on the light and walked inside, leaving me alone in the dimly lit hallway.

"Are you coming?" he questioned in a tone that would be more appropriate for a boss asking his employee rather than of a husband of his new wife. Accompanying the question was Jacob's now too familiar shit eating grin. I crossed my arms hoping my body language would send the right message. But instead Jacob continued examining the room as if he was a quality control inspector while I stood at the door. And for a fleeting moment I planned my escape. I could take the elevator down to the lobby. Have the desk call me a cab and this nightmare would be finally over. But, like the good girl that I am who always wants to please, I stepped inside.

The room was not just a room but a huge suite and seemed even bigger as Jacob opened the drapes.

"My folks must have spent big bucks on this room. And it probably has a great view during the day. But we'll be leaving early," my tour guide announced. He then proceeded to toss off his shoes and unbutton his shirt as I walked passed him and sat down on the edge of the bed.

"Are you ok?"

Looking around the room, I wished I was in my in my own bed holding my pillow.

"Yeah, I am still feeling lightheaded. I think it was too much champagne. And my feet hurt."

I was hoping my words would convey to Jacob that I wanted to put off consummating our marriage for another day.

"Are you scared?"

I thought the question was strange and I now wanted the moment to be over
before it even started.

"Should I be?"

"No," he replied, though I was not satisfied by his answer. And though my aunt had bought me this beautiful silk nightgown to wear on my wedding night, after Jacob's remark, I had no burning desire to disappear into the bathroom and come out throwing myself on my new husband.

"I am your husband now. And I will protect you."

Jacob's announcement sounded like an actor auditioning for a part in a play. But with that unconvincing performance, he would never get the role.

"And you never have to ever feel afraid."

Hearing him say just those words made me feel more frightened.

"Tonight we are one."

Jacob's line was so corny that I panned the room for whoever was feeding him these lines. As I did, Jacob sat down next to me and lowered my head onto the pillow. I closed my eyes, expecting him to kiss me. Instead, his hands reached for the top of my pants. After twisting the top button open, he pulled my pants and panties off and I felt his finger probing inside me.

"Open your eyes."

My head was spinning from the champagne and I wanted to sleep.

"Sweetheart. Open your eyes."

Sweetheart? I wondered. Jacob rarely ever used words of affection.

As I raised my eyelids, Jacob stood by the bed and removed his shirt exposing his very hairy chest. His pants and boxers followed and I closed my eyes again. And with my blouse still buttoned up, he climbed on top of me and attempted to thrust inside me as he spread my legs with his hand.

"Ow," I yelled, arching my back.

But my announcement of pain was met with deaf ears as Jacob thrust again and I yelled louder.

"I am not ready."

"Shh," he said as he put his hand over my mouth signaling for me to be quiet as he thrust harder and even deeper. And I wanted to cry but did not. Instead, I grabbed the piping on the side of the mattress. He thrust again, and again, and again. And each time he withdrew was followed by an even harder and deeper thrust and I felt the same jerking, uneven sensation I felt like only a few hours ago when we were lifted up in the chairs.

"Jacob, it really hurts."

But again my pleas were ignored as he began an uneven in and out and in and out motion. I felt his sweat pouring from his chest and through my top. Seconds later, his body stiffened as he gave out a horrendous, ugly moaning sound before crashing his chest on mine. And for the moment while he lay on top of me, I could feel the pounding of his heart lessen.

Finally, he withdrew and rolled onto his side while I remained still. We exchanged no words as Jacob fell into slumber while I continued to feel pain from the ordeal. Scared, I hummed to myself

Tumbala, Tumbala, Tumbalalaika
Tumbala, Tumbala, Tumbalalaika
Tumbalalaika, shpil balalaika
Tumbalalaika freylekh zol zayn

and prayed that tomorrow I would learn to love this man.

Rose's Seventh Diary Entry

"Raus, Raus, Schnell, Schnell," the soldier shouted with the butt of his gun jabbing in my back. And as I hobbled through the wooden gates that only a short time had opened to accept its newest group of displaced Jews, I passed row after row of tall evergreen trees that dripped in necklaces of ice. With one shoe too large and the other way too small, I stumbled through the crunching snow as the wind was howling and shaking off snowflakes that slammed to the ground.

A few hundred kilometers from the gate stood a stone and brick house which I had not seen when we entered the gates as it was on the other side from where the train had stopped.

Waiting behind the glass front door of the house was the woman with the kind face that had pulled me out of the line.

"You're cold. I poured you a bath. It's all right," she greeted me.

The woman had soft blonde hair, was very fair skinned and spoke softly. And I had the feeling that those wayward hairs dangling over her eyes would be whisked back into place as soon as she passed the nearest mirror.

She pointed to a room down the hallway and as I walked through the house, a rich smell of food wafted toward my nose.

"Don't be scared. You are the lucky one." She stroked the hair out of my eyes and I started to cry as I repeated to myself *"you are the lucky one."*

I followed her to the bathroom where she helped me out of my clothes and into the tub. I will never forget that wonderful bath. There was real soap, the water was hot and the tub was clean. Soon my weary body was covered with sweet smelling sudsy lather and I did not want to leave the tub.

"My name is Irene," my savior said, handing me a warm cup of very strong black tea which I sipped very slowly, treasuring each steaming drop and wondering why I had been singled out. Why was I so lucky?

Irene had placed some clothes on the sink counter and she waited for me in her room which was next door. Her room appeared to have been converted from an office as there were gray file cabinets that lined one wall along with what appeared to be a few text books that barely filled a very large book shelf. Other than her bed, the rest of the room contained a small table, lamp, and radio, and a very large chair.

Irene explained that she was the commandant's housekeeper and supervised all of the cooking and cleaning of the home for the commandant who loved to entertain. I would be working with her. She also said that the work was very hard and the hours long. But so long as I did my work, I would survive. I was also not to talk to the commandant, not ask questions, and only speak if I was spoken to. I was not to make conversations with any visitors and just do my work. If I had any questions, I should ask her.

Sensing I was hungry, she took me into the kitchen and fed me some leftover chicken and potatoes. There was even a basket of black bread that she warmed up in the oven. I ate with a gusto having not had a meal in days. She continued to explain my job duties. But as she spoke, I wanted to ask her about my parents. Would they be ok? And why were the other girls pulled out of line? What happened to them? But I was frightened of what her answers might be.

Finally, she opened a door and led me down six steps from the kitchen into the basement. Irene pointed to a metal framed bed that was very low to the ground. She said that this where I would sleep and she handed me a blanket and told me to go to sleep as tomorrow would be a long day. It was dark and cold, and every time I closed my eyes, my mind could not escape the last images of my family. I eventually cried myself to sleep.

Chapter Nine

Though I had known Jacob for almost a year before I said, "I do," getting married was still the most impulsive thing I had ever done in my entire life. But my father had repeatedly told me that "*Jacob was a good man.*" Perhaps my father really was Tevye. And, being older and wiser, he saw qualities in my husband that were not transparent to me. So I pledged to myself to be patient.

"Good morning, Mrs. Liebowitz," a male's voice announced accompanied by a tapping on my shoulder. "Rise and shine."

I must have been in that stage between sleep and consciousness and I did not immediately respond. The last thing I did remember was staring at the ceiling and humming "*Tumbala, Tumbala, Tumbalalaika.*"

"Mrs. Liebowitz, this is your husband. Time to wake up." The tapping now moved to the top of my head. And I thought I was dreaming as I slowly lifted my head from my pillow.

"What time is it?"

"Time to go. I want to be on the road by 10."

Through my half closed eyes, I searched the room looking for something familiar.

"Mrs. Liebowitz."

I lifted up the blanket and saw that one leg of my pants was free but the other was down around my ankle and I tightly crossed my legs as I felt the pain all over again.

"How does it feel to be Mrs. Liebowitz?" Jacob asked as he sat down on the side of the bed and stroked my hair.

If I heard Jacob say the name one more time, I was going to scream.

"A few more minutes," I pleaded as I dropped my head back onto the pillow. And I now had the same headache that I woke up with yesterday.

"Come on. We have to get going."

As Jacob pulled on my arms, I rotated the wedding band on my finger and knew that this was not a dream.

"Why do we have to leave so early? The brochure said that check-in was not until 3," I said.

"I don't want to take a chance with traffic. Anyway, are you hungry?"

"I am always hungry."

"Ok, well shower and we'll grab something downstairs."

"How about room service?"

I started thinking about fresh strawberries on a high stack of pancakes, muffins, orange juice and some great wake-me-up coffee. But, as if Jacob had a business appointment to keep, he vetoed my idea and we had a quick breakfast in the hotel's coffee shop before embarking on our honeymoon.

Never having left the State of New York, I had always dreamed about going to "paradise" for my honeymoon. I would be sitting by the pool under a palm tree sipping a Mai Tai. And one night my imaginary husband and I would have a romantic dinner on the beach and then take a walk along the shore under the moonlight and make love.

But my prince charming said he could not get that much time off from work. So we settled on the Pocono Mountains in north Eastern Pennsylvania which, for New Yorkers without a lot of time, was a very popular honeymoon destination.

As we started out on our road trip, it reminded me of the original movie "The Heartbreak Kid" with Charles Grodin. The radio was blaring and we were singing along in our best karaoke voice each song that the station played. But by the time we crossed the George Washington Bridge, Jacob lost interest and tuned the radio to an all-news station. So, with no one to talk to, I decided to revisit the hotel brochure.

"Escape to the Pocono Mountains and cuddle with your lover in your own in-suite spa. Or indulge yourselves with a couples' massage in the privacy of your room."

"It would be fun to get a couple's massage. And they will come to our room."

My suggestion got no response.

"Experience the sexiness of the Blush king size round bed with its lush pillow top mattress, layers of luxury featuring satin striped sheets, a plush duvet and silky smooth satin striped pillows that will make you melt, setting the perfect mood. "

"This hotel looks amazing."

"What?"

I lowered the volume on the radio and repeated, "The hotel looks amazing."

"Don't do that," Jacob barked.

"What?"

"Don't touch the radio."

"Well, you didn't hear me."

"What?"

"Like I said, you didn't hear me so I lowered the radio."

"Ok, I am sorry." Jacob softened his tone. "Yeah it does look great. Did I tell you that this guy from work, I told you about him? Greg. He was also there on his honeymoon and had a great time."

"No you didn't. I would remember. How come he wasn't invited to our wedding?"

Again my question drew no response. And except for asking Jacob to stop so I could get out to pee, we had very little conversation the remainder of our way to paradise while I dwelled on how Jacob jumped on me for touching his stupid radio.

The brochure described the bed perfectly. It was lush and felt silky smooth against my skin. And because it rained almost continuously for the three days we were there, we saw very little outside of our room, which for most honeymooners would be the perfect storm.

But other than meals and sex, Jacob seemed more interested in holding his Blackberry than me. And when he did want sex, which I dutifully performed every morning and night, I was at first flattered that someone would find so attractive an overweight girl pushing 30. But that excitement wore off by day three as Jacob did not care whether I rocked his world or not so long as I supplied the receptacle for his sexual release. I felt stupid that I had packed some very sexy lingerie as Jacob could not care what I wore or not or whether my top was on or off. Foreplay did not exist. And no different from when we first had sex, Jacob was unsympathetic to my sexual arousal. All that matter was that he was satisfied.

However, rather than discuss his lack of emotion and our intimate life with him on our honeymoon, I accepted, or fooled myself into believing that it would get better. Besides, we were in paradise, or Pennsylvania, and I was happy to have the time off from work and enjoyed my alone time relaxing and reading magazines.

Chapter Ten

Jacob had purchased a loft in a recently renovated three story building at the base of the Queensborough Bridge on the Queens side, which was ideal for me as it was only a two stop subway ride to my work. I was very excited about moving there, not only because it was my first apartment away from home, but the neighborhood had become a vibrant hot spot with many new restaurants and upscale stores that helped revitalize what was once a place you would never walk around at night. With frequent trips to Pottery Barn and Macy's, in a few short weeks I had transformed our two bedroom home into a very chic abode.

However, Jacob rarely shared my excitement; he only seemed concerned with how much everything cost. Whenever I would suggest that we try one of the restaurants *"that got such great Zagat reviews,"* my suggestion was returned with a lecture that *"had I not spent so much money on decorating, we would have money to go out."* And he would figuratively slam me whenever I reminded him that I work too and that if I wanted to go out for a nice dinner, it did not require an act of Congress to authorize a spending bill. Instead, he would remind me that he was the money manager of our finances and had the final word. He had the only word. And though I thought I had signed up for a shared lifetime, that also meant shared finances, for better or worse. But I was apparently misinformed or did not read the fine print.

The only thing he did permit us to splurge on was TIVO, which allowed me to record and watch my favorite programs. With the Food Network's "Barefoot Contessa" on when I wanted, routine dinners became gourmet delights. However, the rest of our marriage was routine--my nights were spent cleaning and washing while Jacob was immersed in researching stocks and bonds and fondling his cold and unemotional Blackberry.

However, being the good wife, I decided to be patient and see if my lump of clay would turn into a bar of gold. But with the arrival of fall, Jacob's internal weather changed as well. Aside from him being rude, having poor eating habits and often appearing disheveled, he was now finding fault with everything I did. And when he was not tenderly caressing his Blackberry or watching the CNBC stock quotes waltz seductively across the bottom of the television screen, he was often cursing me. He even pounded the table when he was upset. One night after I prepared his favorite dinner, meatloaf, he discovered that I had forgotten to enter a check in the checkbook. Not accepting my explanation, he responded by throwing a dinner plate against the wall. I responded by sleeping in the guest bedroom.

The next morning, as was always his pattern, he tried to justify his behavior as if it were only a "reaction" to something I had done or said to him. It was always my fault; I had provoked him. Oftentimes, he would go as far as saying that I deserved it. And after each and every incident came the well-known remorseful stage, where he would profess his "deep love" for me, and in the next breath he would stage another verbal assault.

The scariest part was that sometimes he wouldn't yell and scream or curse me out. Instead he was quietly abrasive and displayed the most hateful and evil manner while whispering in my ear. But my dad's words kept echoing in my mind, *"He's a good man."* My father had always been such a good judge of character that I wanted to believe that he was right. But as more time passed, I believed no more and realized how stupid and naïve I had been.

Curiously, though, Jacob walked around like a lion in his den. His public image was that of a loving husband, a good provider, well liked and respected by colleagues. He could be personable and sometimes even charming. He was also always polite and respectful to my father and gave my Nana a welcome kiss and always asked how she was. But he could sour honey behind closed doors.

As for intimacy, sex was the only thing I was useful for. But sex with Jacob was no different after the honeymoon than before; very quick and purely for his satisfaction. For me, it had become nasty and sleazy and something to dread. In the first few weeks of our marriage, I kiddingly reminded him that the Talmud said that a husband must provide for his wife's sexual pleasure, but he would remind me that I was not getting any younger and that we should start a family. And so, to avoid arguments, I continued to have sex with him. But I knew he had to see the disgust on my face and hear the sigh of relief when it was over.

By our fourth month of marriage, I lost any desire for an emotional attachment and preferred that he did not hold my hand or even touch me. And on the very few occasions I felt the desire for a sexual release, afterward, instead of feeling good I would hate myself for doing it and I would end up in the bathroom crying on the floor. When I could not hold back the need to scream, I would put a wash cloth over my face and sob without a sound.

My own father could hardly believe my situation. He initially dismissed it as typical marital problems that had gotten out of hand. He even said that he couldn't imagine my husband ever losing his temper. Eventually, I gave up trying to convince him that this was not normal or typical, and that the person he saw for a few hours at a time was not the same person I lived with day to day.

As for Nana, I tried to shield her from my pain. However, Nana was a very wise woman. She could see that I was upset and she conveyed her concern with her eyes.

But Jacob's obsession with getting me pregnant was what I feared the most as he often refused to wear a condom. Since it was against our religious beliefs to use birth control pills, I depended on Jacob to use a condom every time to be sure we weren't accidentally getting pregnant. And even our limited conversations somehow always seemed to revolve around starting a family.

One Sunday morning, I held my mug of coffee while looking out our living room window. The sky was an amazing blue with only a few puffy clouds. I enjoyed walking in the park near our home, which was always littered with young couples and families enjoying the view of the Manhattan skyline.

"I am going to go for a walk. Want to go?" I asked, already knowing his answer.

"No."

"Come on. It is a beautiful day. We can then find a place to get something to eat."

Jacob did not answer.

"Come on. We got nothing else going on today."

"I said no," Jacob barked back with an icy glare.

"Ok. I will be back in a few hours."

But as I started to put on my jogging shoes, Jacob spoke in an ugly tone.

"Good. Maybe you will shed some weight."

This was the first time Jacob had ever brought my weight into a conversation.

"Excuse me?"

"Come on. You have really beefed up. Look in the mirror."

"And you should talk. Take a look at your belly. Do you think that is attractive?"

I thought my comment would have quieted Jacob but he lashed back.

"You won't be doing much walking when you have a baby in your arms."

"Say it again."

Jacob glared at me. "I just said, get all the walking out of your system now. But it will be a little different when you're feeding a baby. And there goes that job of yours."

In the past, when Jacob would bring up my job, I would ignore him. But not this time.

"I don't understand you. You make it sound like it will be punishment to have a child. Don't get me wrong. Raising a child will be my number one priority. But now is not the time. Not yet. And I will let you know when it is the right time. As for my career, I love what I do. And no one, including you, is going to change that." I shouted and slammed the door.

As a result of my unhappiness, work became my substitution for marriage. Going to work was fresh air while being in the same room with Jacob was choking. By our sixth month wedding anniversary, my spirit was dying and Jacob's very presence repulsed me. Foolishly, I had thought that things would get better. I let myself be subjected to some of the worst verbal and emotional abuse anyone could imagine, as Jacob's goal was to break me down and make me his servant and baby oven. Scared and frightened, all I could do was lay in bed each night humming, *"Tumbala, Tumbala, Tumbalalaika."*

Rose's Eighth Diary Entry

The commandant a bitter man in his forties; he was short, stocky, with steel gray eyes and crooked cigarette stained teeth. And every time I looked at him, I caught him staring back at me with his eyes narrowed and mouth pressed into a thin, disapproving line. His expression also reminded me of this nasty, dirty man that worked in the butcher shop in our town. Whenever I saw him, I became very frightened.

But working in the commandant's home afforded me heat from the cold, and three meals per day. When Irene did not have a specific job for me, I spent my days either polishing silverware, dusting, or peeling potatoes in the kitchen.

But regardless of all the hours that I worked, I could never stop thinking about my parents. And when Irene would talk about the conditions in the camp, she did say people were starving. Whenever she had business at the camp, she would smuggle food from the kitchen and put it in a basket with a fake bottom. Once inside the camp, she would go to the infirmary and give it to the sick Jews. She had been doing this for some time but was fearful that someone was watching her. She asked that I pray for her safety. She also promised that she would try to find out any information about my family. I held on to her promise as that was all I had, though I knew it my heart that their fate had long ago been decided by someone else.

Nights were forlorn as when the commandant was home, I was locked in the basement after completing all of my chores. The basement had very low ceilings, making it difficult to stand up. Even if I did, the ceiling was not finished and I often hit my head against the exposed pipes. And my only light was from a bulb controlled by a light switch in the kitchen which often was left in the off position. But when it was on, it gave off very little light. Even more intolerable was that the basement was not heated and the outside cold filtered through the cracks of the stone wall. And just by touching the walls I felt a chill shoot throughout my body.

I also feared the commandant's two German shepherds that roamed the house. One night, one of the dogs ran down the steps when the door was still open and pinned me on my bed. I was so scared.

But on the nights that the commandant was away, I would sit in Irene's room and we would take turns brushing each other's hair. I soon learned that Irene had a daughter, who would now be my age. Irene was not married when the baby was born and she did not really know the father. Her child died of pneumonia and Irene would often tell me how I reminded her of her daughter.

As we brushed our hair, Irene taught me a song:

Tambala, Tambala, Tumbalalaika
Tumbala, Tumbala, Tumbalalaika
Tumbalalaika, shpil balalaika
Tumbalalaika freylekh zol zayn

Tumbala, Tumbala, Tumbalalaika
Tumbala, Tumbala, Tumbalalaika
Tumbalalaika, shpil balalaika
Tumbalalaika freylekh zol zayn

She told me that whenever I was frightened, I should hum this song to myself and it would take me to a place where there were no guns and bullets. She said to think of myself as a ballerina dancing on a big stage. And I would be safe.

Chapter Eleveen

Burying my head in the sand, another month passed. But after being married for what now seemed like a life sentence, and without access to any money to rent my own apartment, I made the decision to move back home. First, however, I needed to speak with my father rather than just showing up at his door with my worldly possessions in tow.

Jackson Heights was still a neighborhood that took working-class immigrants new to America and lifted them into the middle class by providing them the opportunity for hard work. What made Jackson Heights a rarity is that it was an urban neighborhood, based around the subway and elevated train line. And unlike many urban neighborhoods in the 80s, Jackson Heights had not become a slum.

Traveling north, Queens Boulevard was the main artery leading into the Queens-Midtown Tunnel and Manhattan and the asphalt paved street had hardly changed from the time I was a little girl, despite the attraction of the many nearby malls. With both sides of the street occupied by businesses, my father has always said that the people that live in Jackson Heights remained loyal to the businesses frequented by the generations before them. Even a heavy snow storm has little chance of paralyzing the noisy street always crowded with shoppers.

On Wednesdays my father worked until seven so that he could accommodate his customers' work schedules. As I waited to cross the busy street, the all too familiar steam billowing from its manholes gave the illusion that pedestrians were disappearing into thin air as they walked.

My father's store faced the #7 subway line and was only four blocks from our apartment. To his right was my favorite pizzeria, on the left was the dry cleaners, and down the block was Frishman's, our kosher butcher. Standing in front of the store, I read the sign above the window, "Lee's Opticians," and laughed. Mr. Lee was a very nice Jewish man who sold the store to my dad, but everyone always thought that he was Asian.

As I closed the door, I could still hear the muffled sounds of the street permeate inside; the roar of the accelerating buses, the blare of car horns, the screaming ambulance that passed by, and the voices of barking dogs being walked by their owners.

But the most irritating sound came from inside the store. My father's customer, Mrs. Nadel, had apparently stopped by to check on her latest match. She had a very deep and recognizable voice for a woman, like the late actress Bea Arthur. As soon as I heard the caustic sound of her voice, I immediately turned around to leave. But I was not fast enough, and my father motioned with his hand for me to walk to the back of the office behind the display counters. As I approached, I tucked my head into my chin hoping "Yenta the Matchmaker" would not see me.

"Danielle."

I was trapped.

"Hello, Mrs. Nadel. So nice to see you."

"So? How are the newlyweds?"

"Fine," I said, looking down at the floor and wishing I had not awakened this morning.

"He's a good boy," my dad answered.

I shrugged lightly, searching for the strength to form a smile.

"And what's with that bag," Mrs. Nadel asked, referring to my attaché. "It is so full you can hardly close it."

"I take files home to work on. There's not enough time in the day to get all my work done."

"She's going to be the next Perry Mason," my dad remarked assuredly.

"Well, with all that work, there's not a lot of time either to start a family. And you know, it is something you should start thinking about."

Like my husband, all that was ever on Mrs. Nadel's mind was having babies.

"Well, we will when the time is right. But right now we are just getting to know each other."

"*Fe*. Who needs to know each other? I already have four grandchildren and I can't begin to tell you the *nachas* I get from them. Just seeing their faces, oy, what a gift. And someday soon, God willing, your father will know what I mean. But don't wait until he's an old man."

"My brother has two children and Dad sees them all the time."

"Not the same. When your daughter gives you grandchildren, it is different. You'll see," she said, gently stroking the side of my face with her hand.

Her hand smelled like fish but I smiled. "Nice seeing you."

"Come," my father said, walking her to the door.

Rather than taking a chance that she would prolong our conversation, I stayed at the rear of the store.

"Ok. She's gone. Could you have been ruder?" my father said, turning to me.

"Ruder? Is that a word?"

"Ok, so I don't have all the degrees my daughter has. But what does it cost you to be polite?"

"Dad, she is the most annoying person. I don't understand why you don't see that."

"Whatever. So what do I owe for you to come to see your father during the day?"

"Dad, please don't be so sarcastic," I said, following my father as he stopped at the large display counter of women's glasses. "You need to clean the glass top, Dad. It's disgusting. There are fingerprints all over. People don't like that." I reached for the bottle of Windex in the bottom drawer and wiped the counter.

"You came to lecture me on housekeeping? How much do lawyers charge to give cleaning advice?" he said, lighting up his cigarette and taking a nervous drag.

"It is against the law to smoke in offices," I said as I took the cigarette out of his mouth.

My father dismissed my act with a wave of his hand.

"Not funny, Dad. And it is not only your health. I am breathing it in too. So if you really loved me, you would quit. Anyway, you're right, I am not here to clean your counter or lecture you about smoking. But I do need to talk to you."

"She must have looked at twenty different frames after she picked up this one," my father said as he started to put the frames back in their respective spaces on the display. "She touched everything," he said, lighting up another cigarette.

"Dad, are you listening to me?"

"All right, all right." My dad extinguished the cigarette in the ash tray.

"I have one vice," he complained.

"Ok and your point?" I said, exasperated.

"You know that Mrs. Nadel and her family have been coming to me for over twenty-five years. And she has referred plenty of people. This is what you call public relations. You treat your customers right and …"

I finished my dad's sentence, "and they will do you right. I know, Dad. But you're ignoring me."

Upset, my father lowered his head raising his eyes above his half eye glasses.

"I am ignoring you? My daughter walks into my store in the middle of the day when I have a customer and expects me to drop everything and I am ignoring you? You know the money Mrs. Nadel has paid and what others have paid covered your law school and many other things. And you don't have loans. So don't talk to me about ignoring you."

"Dad, please. I appreciate everything you have done. But I don't need a lecture and I did not come in here to disrupt your day. I need to tell you something."

"All right, all right, sit, sit." My father pointed to the chair facing the display counter. "And take off that back pack. You'll soon walk like me." Dad always had rounded, stooping shoulders and walked slightly hunched over. And in the last few years his posture had worsened.

"Sit."

I sat down on the chair facing him.

"So, talk to me."

"Dad, it's about Jacob."

"Jacob? What about Jacob? He just called me."

"He did?"

"What? Your husband can never call his father-in-law? He needs your permission?"

"Not quite, Dad."

"Anyway, his boss offered him two box seats for Sunday's Giants game. They're playing the Rams. That's why he was given the seats. Who wants to see the Rams? But they're good seats. And he asked if I wanted to go with him and his father and uncle."

"You don't even like football. What did you say?"

"I said my daughter invited me for a Sunday dinner so I couldn't go."

"But that was a lie."

"Well, are you making dinner?"

"I wasn't planning anything but …"

"Good. I said yes."

"Well, you should go. But now we need to talk."

"Ok, you're here ten minutes and I still have not heard anything."

I took a deep breath.

"Dad, it's not right."

"What's not right?"

"*It's* not."

"What's 'it's not'? You learned a new language? I thought you wanted to tell me something."

My father started to get up.

"It's Jacob."

"What? What Jacob?" My father sat down again, heavily. "He's not providing for you? Buying you groceries? Paying the rent? What, you need more money? You want to move to a bigger place? I can help you. But your husband works very hard, Danielle."

"Dad. It's not that." I cleared my throat. "It is not working out."

"Stop talking like some code. What's not working out?" Again my father rose from his seat. "You come here to talk to your father about what goes on between a husband and his wife and you make no sense. Either talk to me or let me get back to work."

"Dad, even in the best of marriages, problems don't leave. But I have to."

My voice sounded stiff.

"Danielle, even in the best of marriages, people may grow apart. But they learn how to grow together."

"We're never going to grow together." It pained me to say it out loud.

"What are you saying?" My dad's voice rose.

"I can't stay any longer. I am suffocating."

"You are upsetting me. You go home to your husband and spend a nice night with him. Maybe make something special for dinner. Go to Frishman's and buy some steaks. Here, my treat."

My dad took out his wallet. "And you need to think about what you are saying."

"Dad, I am not here for you to buy us dinner."

My dad looked confused.

"Dad, he's very abusive. He says terrible things. It's not the way a husband--" I paused. "You wouldn't treat a dog this way. And he makes me. I can't, Dad. Don't make me say these things." I started to cry as if like an apple, the core of me had been nibbled away.

My father took his seat again as I reached for a tissue from the box on the display counter, expecting my father to say something. But he remained still.

"Dad. This is not how it is supposed to be between a man and a woman. I don't know this man."

My father raised his left hand and rested it under his chin. He was shaking his head and appeared as if he was going to cry.

"I don't understand. Your mother and I were married for seven years before God took her from us. And during that time we never fought. She may have said things, or done things, but that was between me and her. If we had a problem, we talked and we worked it out between us. And we never talked to anyone else. But to talk to me about what goes on between a man and his wife." He paused. "I am ashamed of you. What? Are you married even a year? What do you know? You are a baby when it comes to marriage. But you are passing judgment. Jacob is a good man. Are you now God?"

Throwing up his arms in disgust, my father turned and started to hang more frames on the display.

"Dad, you are not listening to me. I don't love this man. I am afraid of him and I won't stay with him."

"You will learn to love him, "my father shot back.

"Dad, this is not a class in law school, Jacob 101. I will not learn to love him!"

My father slowly turned around. "Heinech Nesu'ah Tachat Ei'Nei Hashem. You are married under the eyes of God. He is your husband. Now go back to your home and pray for forgiveness." My dad then motioned with his hands for me to leave.

"Dad. You are not listening to my pain. You make glasses and everyone praises you for making them see so well. But you cannot see the pain your daughter is suffering. I plead with you. Hear what I am saying."

My father responded in a very reserved tone. "You are married. Go back to your husband."

We both stood staring at each other. But the awkward silence was broken when the door opened.

"Hello, Mrs. Dotan."

My father went to greet his next customer as I quietly exited the store. Not wanting to go home, I walked to what used to be the candy store that was now a Starbucks. As I looked inside, I saw myself as that little girl standing inside with my father. He would take me to the store to reward me when I brought home an A on a test. I pressed my lips against the coolness of the glass window and I could see my father reaching into his pocket and paying the man behind the counter. As we walked out of the store, he handed me a big candy bar and he had an even larger smile on his face. My dad looked so happy. But then I looked down. There was no candy bar in my hand. And I started to cry as I walked down the block to Frishman's to buy some steaks for dinner.

Rose's Ninth Diary Entry

The commandant had been away for over a week. But he would be home tonight and had planned a dinner party. The commandant also told Irene that he specifically wanted me to assist her in serving the meal.

Irene said I needed something more appropriate to wear and somewhere found a warm woolen dress and very comfortable boots. The dress was of a classic design with a tunic and high collar. It was the first time in months that I dressed in something pretty and I felt like a princess. As I dressed and looked at myself in the mirror, for a fleeting moment I thought I was back with my family and we were having our own party. I wanted to dance!

Wearing the dress also gave me freedom to move about the house as my movement had been restricted to the kitchen and Irene's room. Exploring the home, I noticed that the living room was carpeted with luxurious rugs. On one wall hung old paintings of stern looking officers in battle uniforms as well as women dressed in gorgeous jewels and gowns. On the facing wall was a bear's head, stuffed. The den's wall was also covered with stuffed hunted animals and a gun cabinet. The home also included a music room, a billiard room, a library and fireplaces in almost every room.

The uniformed men began arriving around 8 for some kind of celebration and I heard them all toasting each other from the kitchen. Their raucous laughter was so loud that it rattled the crystal on the table.

I had never worked before as a server and Irene instructed me repeatedly to be very careful. Above all, do not spill. So, very cautiously, I served enormous trays of food including pheasant that looked as if it was still alive, brightly colored salad, and beautiful dessert tarts covered with chocolate and jeweled decorations with ice cream that were carved to resemble beautiful swans.

After we finished serving dessert and clearing the table, Irene said she had a very bad headache and was going to lie down. I thought this was odd as Irene never left me alone for very long, especially when the commandant was home.

But shortly after I heard the last guest leave, the commandant appeared at the kitchen door. His eyes immediately focused on the chopping board in the sink covered in meat juice and the stone floor littered with potato peelings.

The commandant's smell of alcohol and tobacco was overwhelming and I feared I would be punished for the dirty scene. But, instead, as I continued washing the cutting board, he put his hand on my shoulder. As he did, my lower lip quivered and it was an effort to hold back my tears. But I would not let him know I was scared. Instead I prayed that Irene would quickly return.

"Hübsches Mädchen (pretty girl). Hübsches Mädchen," he snarled with his narrowed eyes glaring at me as he brushed his hand across my face before he turned around and left. My heart was pounding as I rushed to finish.

It was also Irene's responsibility to watch me go down the stairs, turn out the light, and lock the door. Nevertheless, I finished my chores and shut the door, making my way in total darkness to my bed.

Moments later, I heard the basement door open and then quickly close. Scared, I pulled the sheets up over my face but the sheets could not filter out the smell from the cloud of alcohol that was growing closer.

A hand pulled the sheet down and I opened my eyes. Sitting on the side of my bed was the commandant. His eyes were icy cold.

"Sie sind meins (You are mine)," he said in a vulgar voice as he put his hand over my mouth and kissed me on the side of my face while whispering that if I fought him I would be back with the dying.

His terrible eyes told me to remain still and not make a sound, Nodding my head in agreement, I followed orders and did not move as he lifted my top shirt, touching my breasts and painfully squeezing each nipple. I choked on the smoky smell of his body .

He then pulled off all the covers and the coldness of the room blanketed my body, sending me into shivers from head to toe. I tried to cry but my body was too cold to form tears as I felt him tug at my underwear. Instead, I tightly closed my eyes as he climbed on top of me and parted my legs with his dirty cigar-stained hands. He pinned my wrists with his weight and strength, repeating that I would be back with the dying if I fought him.

My mind raced as my mind searched for some way to escape the clutches of this demented creature. But if I did not succumb I would probably not live to see another day.

I needed to breathe. When I opened my eyes I looked into the commandant's eyes which had now turned from stone cold to fire and I felt my body being kissed and bitten all over. My head was spinning and aching and I wanted to bathe my face in cold sink water to shower off the smell of alcohol. But instead the commandant buried my face in his hairy chest as he moved on top of me.

"*Sie mögen* (you like)?" he asked but not caring as he inserted one finger up into me and moved it in and out. Then a second finger as I again closed my eyes. But my eyes opened wide as I felt him enter me with one great push. I was about to scream out when he put his hand like a vise tightly over my mouth.

As he moved in and out, it felt like he was tearing me apart and I feared that the springs on the bed would not hold and we would crash to the ground.

Tambala, Tambala, Tumbalalaika
Tumbala, Tumbala, Tumbalalaika
Tumbalalaika, shpil balalaika
Tumbalalaika freylekh zol zany

I hummed to myself and he thrust in and out and in and out.
Tumbala, Tumbala, Tumbalalaika
His movement grew faster.
Tumbala, Tumbala, Tumbalalaika
I dreamed I was in my home. I had my ballerina outfit on and I was performing for my parents and sisters. And the sun was shining so brightly.
Tumbalalaika, shpil balalaika
Everyone was smiling.
Tumbalalaika freylekh zol zany
The thrusting abruptly stopped and was replaced by an awful sound

as the commandant grabbed the back of my hair while the palms of my hands fell limp against the ground.

Finally, the weight of his body lifted and he placed a slobbery kiss on my forehead. I was now a woman but not in the way I wanted to become one.

Daylight could not come soon enough. I could not sleep and lay awake wishing I could wash the smell and taste of the commandant off my body.

The next morning, as the basement door opened, I bolted into Irene's room. Pausing in front of her bedroom mirror, I lifted my top and caught a glimpse of my naked body. I was shocked to see purplish reddish spots all over my breasts and other parts of my body. Turning my head slightly, I was confronted by my reflection; my face was sad, the corners of my mouth were tight, and my eyes were gray and anxious and verging on tears. Also in the reflection was Irene. Seeing her weep, her eyes were asking for forgiveness. But I knew there was nothing she could have done.

Chapter Twelve

It had been bitterly cold for several days with the daytime temperature never getting above freezing. But though I reminded Jacob this morning that today was our six month wedding anniversary and it would be nice to go out somewhere for dinner to celebrate, he texted me later and asked if we could stay in and go out over the weekend. So, like a good wife, I stopped off at Frishman's, bought some vegetables at the market, tossed a salad, set the table and waited for my prince charming to arrive.

"What's for dinner?" Jacob barked as I heard the door open.

"How about hello," I barked back from the kitchen.

Getting no response, I walked into the living room where Jacob was standing with the TV remote in his hand watching CNN.

"Happy anniversary," I said.

"Sorry, happy anniversary," he replied, giving me a peck on the cheek but immediately returning his attention to his other wife, Anderson Cooper.

"Dinner will be ready in about fifteen minutes. I hope you are hungry. I bought these amazing steaks."

Talking to Jacob was like talking to an empty room as there was no response. But animals are distracted when they smell and see food, and Jacob found his way to the table.

"I was watching Ina Gartner," I said, trying again for conversation.

"Who?" Jacob asked, getting up to open the refrigerator door.

"You know. The Barefoot Contessa. On the Food Network."

"Oh yeah, that big fat lady with the gray hair She puts butter on everything."

"No, that's Paula Dean. And she's not fat. She's beautiful."

"All right. Then I don't know who you are talking about."

"Doesn't matter. Anyway, I marinated the steak in a ginger sauce."

Jacob ignored what I said as he found the ketchup bottle on the door shelf.

"The bottle's almost empty," he demonstrated turning the bottle up and down.

"Yeah, but I don't think you will need it," I said pointing out to Jacob the perfect grill marks.

Not impressed, Jacob sat back down holding his almost empty bottle of ketchup and squeezed out a few drops of the red condiment over his steak while I poured myself a glass of wine. Without commenting on the taste, he stabbed the steak and cut a large slice which then found the opening of his mouth as he scrolled through his messages on his Blackberry with his other paw.

"Why don't you put that away and talk to me?" I asked, searching for conversation. But the only sounds heard during dinner were the buzzing of the refrigerator and the clock ticking on the wall.

Finally, as I began to clear the dishes from the table, my prince uttered his first words of dinner conversation.

"That was good."

"Really?" I reacted, surprised to hear a compliment, no matter how slight, roll off Jacob's lips.

"Really good. And I like you, too." And out of character, Jacob got up and grabbed my belly with his hand.

"What are you doing?" I asked, pulling his hand away as I moved the plates from the table to the sink.

"It is our anniversary, isn't it?"

"Yeah."

"And I was just checking to see if there was an anniversary present in there."

"What? What do you mean?" I asked moving his hand away again.

"I wanted to see if there is a baby in there."

"What, I would tell you if there was." I said, annoyed. "And we are not even trying."

"Well, I don't know."

I looked confused and wished he was not in the room.

"We have been married for six months and people are starting to talk."

"People. What people?"

"Mrs. Nadel."

"She should worry about herself. Besides, we had this conversation before. Most couples wait a few years before they start having a family. It is called the honeymoon phase of the marriage. Something you don't know anything about."

"So that's what you are mad about?"

"Whatever," I said, borrowing my dad's favorite phrase as I started to load the dishwasher.

"Well, I just need to get things settled at work. And I may be in line for a promotion. Then we can plan to go to somewhere."

I did not respond but started to clear the dishes from the table.

"We should go away. Maybe Miami? Anyway, our honeymoon was too short. Miami is nice and warm and we can get away from this cold," Jacob said as he grabbed the box of chocolate chip cookies that was on the counter and shoved one into his mouth.

"I don't know. Sounds nice."

"We can swim, sightsee. Go to some good restaurants."

"What a joke," I snapped back. "We don't go to restaurants here. Within two square miles of where we live, we have some of the most diverse restaurants. But how would you know."

"Yeah, but when you're away, you don't have the pressures. Besides, we can splurge a little," Jacob said as he put his arms around me and kissed me on the neck before returning to the box of cookies.

I was surprised and confused by Jacob's attempt at being romantic.

"So, what do you think?" he asked.

I started to load the dishwasher as Jacob shoved two more cookies into his mouth. "Well I have a few days off in the middle of March, so maybe."

"You are."

"What? I can't understand you. Your mouth is full. Chew and swallow. It's like I am talking to a baby."

Jacob cleared his throat.

"I said you seem quiet tonight."

"No, just tired. I have a big case coming up and I haven't had the time I need to prepare," I replied.

"Bigger than me?" Jacob grabbed my butt and grinded his groin into my side.

"You're disgusting."

"Maybe I am. But you should take a break from work. Maybe it is too stressful."

Outraged and insulted, I shut off the water in the sink and turned to face him. "Well, you don't take a break from a job. And I love my work," I answered very sternly as I returned to loading the dishes.

"Fine, fine, I married a modern woman," Jacob responded, licking the fudge from the cookie that was on his finger. "But that doesn't leave a lot of time to raise a family."

I turned again to Jacob. "You talk about a family. How about making me feel like I want to have a family?"

"What do you mean?"

"Well. Did you send me flowers, or even a card? Or did you even think about it? I would have even been happy with a text message from you. And if I didn't say something, would you have even remembered? And do you ever make me feel romantic? Do you ever do anything special that shows that you care and look at me as something other than your cook, your maid and your future baby oven?" I slammed the dishwasher door closed and turn on the dial. "And haven't you had enough cookies?" I asked pulling the box from his hand."

The phone rang and I picked up.

"Hi Nana. Ok, don't worry. I will go to Walgreens and pick it up for you. I can bring it on Friday."

As I talked, I was hoping that Jacob would rejoin Anderson Cooper. But instead he decided that the refrigerator needed support and positioned his back against the door, grabbed the cookie box from my other hand and munching away as I spoke.

"I love you too," I said to Nana. "Goodnight."

"Nana says hello."

"How is she?"

"She sounds fine. She was tired and was going to bed."

"Well maybe we should take a hint from Nana."

I ignored this last remark. "I don't want to talk anymore tonight. You have ruined whatever small moment there was. I think I am going to do some reading and try to get ahead, so happy anniversary," I said. As I walked passed Jacob he grabbed my arm.

"What are you doing? You're hurting me," I cried.

Jacob looked at me stone cold.

"Let go."

"I want a baby," he said.

"You are crazy. How can we have a baby if we don't have a marriage?"

"Who are you listening to? Those stupid talk shows?"

"Take your hand off me. You are hurting me." In response, Jacob tightened his grip. "Jacob, you use me. You don't love me. I am just an outlet for your needs. And you want to turn me into a baby maker so I can pump out little Jacobs. Then you will proudly show off your litter of children."

"How dare you," Jacob shouted, pointing his finger in my face. As he spoke, I saw a fire in his eyes that I had never seen before.

"Move away, you're scaring me."

Jacob did not move.

"I am tired." I walked into the bedroom but Jacob followed me.

"What?" I asked, turning around.

"I want a baby," he said in a low voice.

"A baby," I laughed. "When you are not belching or farting and during the little time that we ever have any conversation, all you are consumed with is having children. Well this oven is not accepting. And I suggest that if you are that horny, then go in the bathroom and jerk off. Just don't get near me," I said as I opened the bathroom door. But before I could step in, Jacob pulled me by my hair and threw me onto the bed, holding me down by pressing his hands against my shoulders.

"Get off me. Get off me," I pleaded but Jacob did not respond, just staring at me with the eyes of the devil.

"You are really scaring me," I said but Jacob did not move. "Please get off me."

With that, Jacob shot me that famous shit eating grin of his and patted my tummy with his sticky cookie fingers.

"You're going to get so fat and ugly when you get pregnant. And that's going to start tonight," he said as he pulled down my gray sweats below my knees. Keeping his right hand against my shoulder, he moved his left hand over my panties.

"Oh, you're getting ready for me. You want it so bad," he said as he ran his index finger inside the top of my panties.

"You are disgusting," I said, pushing my fist into his upper body and causing him to roll off me.

For a fleeting moment, the room felt still as I kept my eyes shut, praying that he would leave me alone. But I was wrong.

"Tell me how bad you want me," he shouted, standing at the side of the bed.

"I don't want you. I want you to leave," I pleaded.

"No way Danielle, the mother of my baby." With that, he yanked off my my sweats and underwear.

"Look at you. Naked. And you're mine," he said as he dropped his pants, exposing his erection. "Tell me you want me," he bragged as he parted my legs and climbed on top of me.

"I don't."

"Tell me you want me," he answered back.

I tried closing my eyes. But he stared at me; those flickering coal dark eyes taunted me and I felt my heart miss a beat.

"I don't," I shouted as I felt him try to push inside me but I was very dry. It was a deep soreness that only intensified as he tried again to drive in further. "It hurts. I am not ready," I yelled as he continued pushing and pulling and making deep heavy grunts while holding on to me. Finally, he reached into the night stand and grabbed the tube of KY Jelly.

"You know a young wife should always be ready for her husband," he said as poured the lubricant onto his middle and index finger and then shoved them up inside me, working them in and out like a mechanic working on a car.

"Now you are ready," he smiled as he glided inside me. "Do you like that?"

"Please Jacob. Please. Put something on. We're not ready for a baby."

It was clear that Jacob had no intention of using a condom tonight. Ignoring my request, he pushed again. This time he rested inside me as I grabbed with my right hand the piping on the mattress and held it tight as I anticipated his next thrust.

"Does that feel good?" He slowly pulled out and then thrust harder pounding his fat belly against me and again pausing.

"Please stop," I cried.

With each thrust, he delayed the ending by stopping again as if this was his sick way of torturing me. I wanted this to be a nightmare so I could wake up. But it was no nightmare and each further thrust was accompanied by another ugly grunt that sounded as if it came from an animal.

"Now we are going to make a baby," he proudly announced as he began to thrust in and out and in and out. I wanted to yell and scream but knew that my plea for help would go unanswered.

"We're making a baby," he shouted as his pace quickened. And as I felt my feet dangling over the edge of the mattress, I could see his blood pooling in what was the whites of his eyes.

Tumbala, Tumbala, Tumbalalaika

I hummed. With each further thrust, my body seized while my heart froze.

Tumbala, Tumbala, Tumbalalaika

"Come on, you want to cum, let me feel you cum," he demanded.

Tumbalalaika, shpil balalaika

Finally, as if a gunshot exploded in the air, his body arched and he made the most disgusting sound before crashing back on top of me, leaving me bare of all normalcy and sanity.

Tumbalalaika freylekh zol zany

He rolled off me and I lay motionless but crying uncontrollably inside as a police car stormed past our building, sirens screeching. I wanted to jump from our bedroom window hoping the car would stop and help. But suddenly, as if someone had traded places with Jacob, a new voice had entered. It sounded calm and remorseful.

"I am sorry. I didn't know," Jacob said, placing a kiss on my forehead.

Jacob's eyes were trained on the bed sheet that was loosely draped over my leg.

"What?" I asked again, staring into his eyes of fire.

"Your period."

I opened my eyes and glanced down at the fresh red clot of blood that was on the sheet.

Disconnected, Jacob stepped away from the bed as if anticipating that I was going to slap him. I immediately felt nauseous and ran into the bathroom to put a cold wash cloth on my face. Sitting on the toilet with the seat cover down, I quietly cried, trying to catch my breath between each heavy sigh. Finally, I had to remove the taste of Jacob from my body and turned on the shower. When I came out, Jacob was fast asleep on the mattress, having pulled off the stained sheet. I did not want to crawl under the sheets that smelled of lubricant and Jacob. So I grabbed a pillow and blanket from the closet and lay down in the guest bedroom. It was colder in that room, but at least I was alone. *Tumbala, Tumbala, Tumbalalaika,* I hummed myself to sleep.

Rose's Tenth Diary Entry

The next few nights I slept very poorly, always fearing that at any minute the basement door would swing open again. But by the fifth night, exhausted, I fell into a deep slumber. And I dreamed. I was sitting in the garden with my mother in our home. It was spring time and the smell of our sweet roses filled the air. My mother and I were laughing as I was telling her about this boy who liked me. But my mother said he was too short and he had big ears.

Suddenly, I heard the slamming of truck doors followed by shouting and screaming and I did not know if I was still dreaming. The door to the basement opened with a loud bang and the sound of heavy boots grew louder as I pulled the covers over my head fearing the worst.

"Raus, Raus," the soldier shouted, pulling on the leash of his German shepherd whose nose was pressed against my face and only separated by the bed sheet.

"What is it? What is it?" I asked but the German did not answer me as the weight of the dog's paws was pushed in the mattress.

I grabbed my sack that was on the window sill containing all my worldly belongings and picked up my shoes as the soldier pushed the barrel of his gun into my back.

"Schnell, Schnell," he shouted in my ears.

As I walked up the steps, I looked for Irene but she was not there. So I ran down the hallway to her bedroom but was stopped by the soldier who grabbed the back of my neck and threw me to the floor. With his gun pointed at my head, I slowly rose to my feet, begging for my life.

The soldier pointed to the open front door where a truck was parked in the road. As I walked, praying I would not be shot, all I wondered was where was Irene?

"Erhalten Sie innen," (Get in) another soldier ordered as I was lifted and pushed into the back of the truck. Crying in the dark corner was Irene. I tried to reach her outstretched arms but the soldier riding in the back pushed me away and spit into Irene's face.

"Sie ist ein Judegeliebter," (She is a Jew lover) he announced with a gun pointed at her head.

"Be brave," Irene whispered, her lips quivering. But as I starred at her kind sweet face, I sensed how frightened she was.

As the truck started to move, the soldier lit up a cigarette and started a conversation with the driver. Irene determined it was safe now to talk to me. She said that someone saw her bringing food to the Jews in the infirmary and turned her in.

"Why did you do this?" I asked.

"Save a life, seed a generation," she poetically replied with tears in her eyes.

A few minutes later, the truck came to a screeching stop. The soldier pulled back the tarp that had covered the back of the truck, and I recognized the large wooden doors to the camp.

"Erhalten Sie weg, erhalten Sie weg," (Get off, get off) he shouted and I was dragged by my shoulder from the truck and pushed to the icy ground where another soldier's gun was pointed at my face.

"Weg," (Walk) he shouted.

I took a few steps toward the camp's opening gates and turned around to see the truck pulling away with Irene in it. I never saw her again. But her last words stayed with me: *"Save a life. Seed a generation."* Those words gave me the strength to stay alive.

Chapter Thirteen

Tumbala, Tumbala, Tumbalalaika.

I could not fall asleep and kept humming the song as I tossed and turned, fearing that Jacob would awaken any second looking for me. As I lay in the spare bed wrapped in my afghan blanket trying to stay warm, I was scared and wanted to run. But I had nowhere to go.

Tumbala, Tumbala, Tumbalalaika.

I must have dozed off for a few minutes but was awakened by the sound of snow plows working throughout the night trying to clear the roads for the morning traffic.

I checked the clock again; it was three in the morning and I had to pee. So I quietly got up and tiptoed into the bathroom without turning on the light. As I sat on the seat, I could hear Jacob snore and thought how pathetic it was that he was having a peaceful night's sleep while I lay awake and tortured. I thought of harming him like that woman who cut off her husband's penis. But could I really do it? What knife would I use? Would the police believe me? And what would my father say?

I didn't flush and quietly lay back down on the bed. *Tumbala, Tumbala, Tumbalalaika* I hummed as I gripped the blanket, tucking it under my chin and once again closing my eyes. Finally, I fell asleep.

Jacob was gone when I woke up and I was too upset to go to work. All I wanted to do was shower again. But with my hands trembling from fright and the cold, I had difficulty finding the strength to turn the shower knobs. I cursed out Jacob's name waiting for the water to turn hot.

I turned my back on the shower head and let the water pound my shoulders, hoping to release the tension from inside. But I could not relax and raced through the shower, forgetting to shampoo my hair until I was already out and drying off. I looked into the bathroom mirror and saw the image of a woman who had had the ultimate violation committed against her.

I was feeling lightheaded and needed to eat something. But I could not concentrate. Instead, I threw on some sweats, pulled my hair back, and wrapped a scarf under my coat to brave the weather.

The sidewalk was shoveled but navigating by foot was very hazardous as the surface had already been covered by ice from the previous days' freezing rains. As I walked in the bitter cold around the corner to my Nana's building, I was upset that I had forgotten to wear gloves.

"Nana, its Danielle."

"I am coming sweetheart," she said in her broken English voice.

I heard her feet shuffle towards the door as she turned the three dead bolt locks.

"What a surprise. You never come by this early. Come in, come in. Are you hungry?"

Nana was wearing the pink fleece robe that I gave her for her last birthday. I followed Nana into her bedroom.

"Do you want some tea? I can make some tea. And Bessie brought me some fresh cookies from Schwartz's. No work today?"

"No Nana. It was cancelled because of the weather," I said as I took off my coat and put it on the couch. I hated to lie to my Nana, even if it was a white lie.

"No one should go out in this weather. But it's warm in here. The heat works good."

Normally I would have corrected Nana, saying *the heat works well.* But I was too upset.

"Yes it does, Nana."

Nana sat down in her rocking chair near the window.

"How is Bessie?" I asked as I sat on her bed facing her.

"Not well. Her knees are so bad and she can hardly walk. They shouldn't call it the golden years. It should be called the tarnished years."

I smiled.

"What sweetheart? You look sad," Nana said putting her hand on my chin and tilting my face. "You have been crying."

I did not answer.

"Talk to me. You can always talk to your Nana."

I looked at my Nana's sweet, kind face and started to cry.

"It's Jacob."

"*Vus?*"

"Nana. He is a bad man."

"Did you talk to your father?"

"I can't talk to him." I said, ashamed. "I tried but…"

"Your father doesn't always understand," Nana said, finishing my thought. "But you need to let him know. Sweetheart, look at me. Did he hit you?" she said, examining my arms for bruises.

"No. He didn't hit me."

"Then what?"

I hesitated. "It is worse, Nana."

Nana clutched both my hands in hers.

"He made me. He forced me," I said turning my head.

Nana looked confused.

"I don't understand. What could he force you to do?"

I wiped my eyes and slowly began to recount want happened last night, leaving out the most horrid details. But as she heard my painful words, my Nana's face stiffened and her eyes were fixed with fright as if she had lived this story before.

"I can't stay with him anymore," I said, breaking out into a loud sob. As I cried, my Nana covered me in her arms and I fell to my knees. And as I rocked with her, she sang *Tumbala, Tumbala, Tumbalalaika.*

"Nana, he's my husband. And the Talmud says that a wife is the property of the husband."

"Ahf Gever Ei'No Yachol Le' Hachrichech Benigood Le'Retzonech," she replied.

"Nana, in English."

"No man can make you do anything against your will."

As Nana spoke, she grew very upset and then stoic.

"A long time ago, I, no, I can't talk now."

Nana stretched her arm, revealing the tattooed numbers on the inside of her wrist, and I turned my head away as I always have done.

"Don't be afraid. That's my number. The mark of something awful.

An eyewitness account that is irreplaceable. I never wanted to remove it so that when someone sees it, they will remember and never forget."

Nana rarely hid her tattoo from my brother and I but always refused to talk about it. But my revelations of Jacob seemed to remind her how fragile her life once was.

"What, Nana?"

"No. I can't. It is not safe. But you have to go."

"I don't want to move back in with my father, but…."

"No, far away. Jacob will only come looking for you. You have to go far away so he can't ever do that to you again."

"Nana, I can't run. Where can I go?"

Nana's eyes were filled was fright as if she has seen a ghost.

"Where am I going to go, Nana? Except for the meager allowance that Jacob gives me, I have no money. I give him my pay check. I don't even have a credit card since Jacob insists that we pay everything by check. My name is not even on the checking account. And where am I going to live?"

"Shh. Open my closet."

"What?"

Nana pointed. "Go."

I opened the door.

"On the top shelf. You see a black beaded purse?"

"Nana, what am I doing?"

"Stop asking so many questions. Please bring it to me."

I handed the purse to Nana but she fumbled trying to open it.

"My hands hurt. Here. Open it."

I twisted the metal clasp.

"Take out what's inside," she instructed.

Folded neatly inside were five one hundred dollar bills.

"Here, take this."

"Nana, I can't take your money."

"You have to take it. And you need to go far away."

"Where? Everyone I know is here. You're here. My brother is here. I work here. Where am I going to go?"

"What about your friend Marcia?"

"In California? I've barely left New York. I have never flown on a plane."

"That Marcia, she is such a sweet girl. And you were so close with her in law school. Maybe you can stay with her?"

"I don't know. I can't think right now. But I can't leave you."

"I will be fine. Your brother is nearby and I have my friends and… And take this," she said, handing me her hair brush.

"Nana!" I pushed the brush away.

"I insist." Nana spoke sternly, pushing the brush back into my hands. More tears flowed from my eyes.

"Give while your hands are warm," she recited.

"Nana."

"Sweetheart. I don't have much. I am an old lady. But while I am still here, it is better to give while your hands are warm. So please. Please your Nana and take this. And when you hold it, you will always think of me."

"Nana, don't talk that way," I begged.

"Danielle. You must promise me," she replied firmly.

Walking home from Nana's apartment, a terrible thought came over me. What if I was pregnant? The blood could be from my period or from Jacob's thrusting so hard that he tore me. And if I was pregnant, Jacob would be granted his wish, as I knew I could never terminate the pregnancy.

My heart was pounding as I entered the Walgreens. I had read about this pill. And as I walked up and down each aisle, I kept counting. Adding and subtracting. Figuring and refiguring. When did I get my last period? And then I counted 28 days ahead. I counted again and again and again. And today was day 26.

I walked on past the shampoos and conditioners, the skin crèmes, deodorants, and toothpaste. And then I thought I found it. It was just past the array of contraceptive products; the two sitting end to each other like an exhibit demonstrating the law of cause and effect.

As I read and reread the product in search of what I had heard of, an elderly man with yellowed eyes was examining toothbrushes, holding them up in the store light as if they were going to turn into something else. Another woman was opening the lids of moisturizers and smelling them. And she kept turning her head toward me, making me feel very uncomfortable. It was as if I had done something wrong.

Finally, a young woman, close to my age, asked if she could help. Embarrassed, I told her what I was looking for and she took me over to the pharmacy window. I was given a small package labeled Plan B.

"Take this now and the second pill 72 hours later," the pharmacist said, nodding her head that everything would be all right.

I paid and thanked her and quickly walked past the lady who was passing judgment on my life. If she only kn

Rose's Eleventh Diary Entry

I have lost track of how long it has been since my last journal entry. I remember back to the last few weeks in the camp, after the guards had fled but before the liberators arrived. I was so tired and hungry. I spent most of my days with three other girls. But though the guards were gone, I was too weak to lift my body and run.

The last few days were been especially difficult as I could not remember too much of what happened. I think I was fading in an out of consciousness. When I did wake up, I had a terrible headache. Sleep had become the only form of relief. But in my dreams, the horrors of the past appeared with such starkness. And I could not turn on a light to drive the nightmares away.

It was still cold at night, though winter had slowly melted into spring. To keep warm, we slept huddled against each other. Sadly, we didn't even asked each other our names. But names do not matter; survival does. To survive, we even peed on each other to stay warm. One night, as I turned, the smallest girl's body felt cold. She had had a fever for days and wouldn't drink any water. When we woke up, she was dead. As weak as we were, two of us managed to pull her limp, exhausted body outside and we laid her to rest by the side of the building.

Still fearing that there might be some guards remaining, we only searched the camp at night for food. Another night, walking inside what looked like a storage room, we saw that the ceilings were covered with blood. Suddenly an old man appeared. He offered us a piece of a loaf of bread but told us that he had seen guards earlier in the day and told us to go back to our bunk, which we did. He also said that the Americans and Russians were coming soon and we would be liberated. But that had been a rumor for weeks.

The next morning, we explored the clothing warehouse, which was stocked with coats of all sizes. For a short time, we made believe we were in a Paris fashion show as we modeled for each other. Amongst the piles and piles of clothing, we stumbled on what looked like a sack of flour. Thinking she could make some cereal, one of the girls mixed the contents in the sack with some well water which we found outside the abandoned kitchen. But almost instantly upon tasting it, she threw up. Only after examining the writing on the bag did we realize that the sack contained naphtolene, which is used to make moth balls. As the day wore on, the girl became sicker and sicker and was gone by nightfall. Ironically, she had survived all the hardships and horrors up til then but died before the camp was liberated.

When the Americans entered the camp, they gave us bread, cereals, soup, canned beets and tuna, salami, milk and cheeses. But I only ate cereal and bread. I later discovered that this was the best thing to do. People who overate all the things they had hungered for died because their bodies could not handle the richness and needed time to readjust gradually.

A few days later, I was moved to the hospital in which I am now. And I thank God for my safety but fear for the fate of my family and Irene.

PART

TWO

Chapter Fourteen

The sunlight struck me in the face, momentarily blinding me as I pushed open our apartment building door and stepped outside. Taking my first step, my shoes made a crunching sound as they disappeared into the snow drift that had formed on the top landing.

"Careful, Danielle. It is slippery," shouted a familiar voice.

"Is that you Sammy?" I said as I shielded my eyes from the light. "Why aren't you in school?

"It's a snow day. School's cancelled."

I extended the retractable handle of my luggage and carefully navigated down the four steps.

"Do you need help?"

"No, that's kind of you. I am ok."

"Where are you going?" Sammy asked as he tossed a snow ball into the air and watched it fall, making an impression in the snow covered ground.

"I have to get a cab," I said, slowly walking to the curb. We both stared in amazement as a jogger passed us by.

"That guy must be crazy. Does he not know how cold it is?" I tilted my face to the sun.

"He must be. So, when will you be back?"

I did not answer Sammy's question. "So, where is Raj?"

"He's sick."

"Well, that's too bad," I replied, frustrated as a cab filled with passengers drove by.

"Maybe you should walk to the corner. There's more cabs going by on Elm Street."

"You know Sammy. You are so right," I said as I gave him a kiss on his forehead. "Now you take good care of yourself, ok?" I rubbed my hand through his thick hair and started to walk toward the corner as I heard the thud of another snow ball falling to the ground.

Sammy was right. Within moments, a driver saw my outstretched hand and stopped.

"Los Angeles," I said as I stepped inside.

"I am sorry, ma'am, I don't leave New York." The driver chuckled in a heavy Middle Eastern accent.

"Sorry. I am little nervous. I meant Grand Central Station."

Grand Central Station was only a twenty minute subway ride providing that the connections were on time. But waiting to change trains was the last thing I wanted to do this morning so I had decided to take a cab. As we pulled away from the curb, I turned to look out the back window at the neatly arranged identical buildings.

"Could you turn up the heat?" I requested.

The cab was freezing and I so wanted my morning cup of coffee.

Turning onto Queens Boulevard, the number seven train had just left the subway station and we were about to pass my father's store.

"Could you stop here?"

"Did you forget something?" the driver asked as he slowly rolled to a stop.

I looked through the window of the cab and saw my dad waiting on a customer. For a split second, I thought about darting from the car and running into my father's arms, knowing that a big hug would be waiting for me. But if I did that, I would never leave.

"No, that's ok."

The cab drew away. And after a few minutes of attempting to make conversation with me, the driver turned up the volume on his news radio station and left me alone with my thoughts.

Grand Central is cavernous and no matter what time of the day, it is always filled with bustling crowds. As you enter the main concourse, you immediately noticed the large American flag that was hung in the terminal a few days after the September 11 attacks.

And in the center of the concourse is the famous four-sided marble and brass clock designed to look like a pagoda which sits on top of the information booth.

As I waited at the ticket booth, a young woman with one hand holding her daughter and her other hand holding the handle of a small tattered suitcase stood in front of me. In front of her was an older gentleman who was arguing with the woman behind the yellowed glass window.

I looked down at the very pretty little girl who was saying something to her mother. But I could not understand her as track announcements of arriving and departing trains were being broadcast through an overhead speaker that was making a horrible crackling sound.

Finally I heard, "Next in line."

I moved up my rolling suitcase and it was my turn.

"Next in line," repeated the robotic voice.

"Where to?" was the next programmed phrase she uttered.

"Los Angeles," I said.

The ticket agent mumbled.

"I am sorry. Could you repeat that?" I leaned forward to hear better.

"Sleeper car?"

"Ah, no."

"ID."

"What? I am sorry I cannot hear you." Another track announcement muted everything the ticket agent said.

"Your driver's license or some other form of picture identification," she replied rudely.

As I fumbled through my wallet, the voice behind the window grew impatient as did the other passengers waiting in line behind me.

"Return?"

"Excuse me."

"What is your return date?" the agent sounded annoyed though I suspected that was her usual demeanor.

"Oh. I am sorry. I don't have a return date. Just one way."

"One hundred ninety five dollars and forty cents."

"Let's go, lady," a voice piped up from behind.

I reached into my wallet and gave her the money as my ticket popped through a small metal slit in the counter.

"Track 23, boards at 11 a.m. Next in line."

I tucked my ticket in the front zipper section of my backpack and followed the signs to track 23. But as I did, I quickly found myself in the middle of a human stampede.

"This is a track change for train 195. The Baltimore train will now leave from track 32. The train is now boarding on track 32. All aboard."

In true New York style, I bullied my way through the crowd and found an empty seat in the waiting area. Stuffed in my backpack was a banana. As I peeled it back, my cell phone rang. It was my father. I didn't want him to worry. But if I told him what I was doing, he would call Jacob. So I let it ring until it went to voice mail.

Another announcement was followed by another and another. My train, once listed near the bottom of the second column, had now worked its way up to the middle of the first column. Tired, I decided to close my eyes for a few minutes.

"Anyone sitting here?"

I was startled. The voice sounded like Jacob's. But it couldn't be. He left for a work. Unless he followed me? I kept my eyes shut as my body tensed, fearing who was next to me. But after hearing the rustling of a paper, I opened my eyes slowly and saw a man reading the New York Post. Relieved it was not Jacob, I closed my eyes again, resting my head against the back cushion of the seat as my mind took me back to this morning.

Jacob and I had not spoken the next night after the attack, though he had made several attempts to engage me in conversation. His apologies ran the gambit from almost sincere to childish. But I kept telling him that I wasn't ready to talk and I slept in the guest bedroom while I plotted my escape.

Finally, on the third night, to promote a quieter evening, I lied and told him that he was forgiven. I also returned to our bed only to have a miserable night's sleep.

"It's cold," I shouted as the alarm clock sounded. "Please turn on the heat for a little while."

"When I come out," Jacob answered as I heard the bathroom door close behind him. And instead of getting out of bed to prepare Jacob's breakfast as I usually did, I turned on my side facing the closet doors.

"Heat's on," I was startled to hear. I must have dozed off for a few more minutes.

As I opened my eyes, I saw Jacob standing naked by my bed side.

"Aren't you getting up?" he asked.

I quickly turned on my other side. "I don't feel good. I have cramps. You know. That time. I think I am going to call in sick. Can you get your own breakfast?"

"Sure," he said as he walked out of our bedroom and into the kitchen.

"I'll put on some coffee," he called out.

"Thanks," I said as I pulled the covers up higher. But moments later, I was awakened again by the feel of Jacob's hand on my forehead. Pushing it away, I turned again facing the closet.

"I told you. I am not feeling good. Please," I said, moaning in discomfort.

"I can make you feel better."

Jacob was now standing with his erection inches away from my mouth and I wanted to start a tirade about how he raped me and how could he possibly believe that my few words of forgiveness now gave him carte blanche to have sex. But I also feared that if I began a verbal attack, there could be a repeat of the other night.

"Please Jacob. I will make it up to you tonight. I promise," I said in my most sensuous way.

"But what about taking care of this guy right now?"

Jacob held his erection in his hand and moved towards my mouth.

"Please Jacob," I said turning my head again seeing the fire in his eyes.

"I will warm you up," he said wearing the most repulsive grin on his face.

As he pulled the sheets off me, I remained turned on my side. But with his left hand, he pushed me over onto my back as he moved his right hand between my legs.

"Wait." I opened the night stand drawer and reached for a condom.

Jacob took it from my hand. I closed my eyes and prayed that he would put it on. Seconds later, Jacob pull down my panties and moved on top of me, spreading my legs with his hand.

Tumbala, Tumbala, Tumbalalaika,

I hummed.

And with one great thrust, he entered me as I cried silently in pain.

"Please, Jacob. It hurts me. Please go slow."

Tumbala, Tumbala, Tumbalalaika

Chapter Fifteen

"Ma'am. Ma'am. Are you all right?"

I opened my eyes and saw a young girl with the most beautiful dark brown hair smiling. She was no more 10 years old.

"I must have fallen asleep."

"You had a nightmare."

"Oh."

"You were singing."

"I was?"

"Tumbala, Tumbala," the girl repeated as an announcement was made.

"Train # 407, the Starlight Express, is now boarding on track 23. All aboard."

"That's my train," I smiled. "But thank you."

A line of passengers apparently anticipating the announcement had already formed and extended outside of the boarding area as I took my place.

"Tickets only, no ID required," the man in a gray uniform announced.

There was another train agent directing passengers on the train platform.

"Sleeper cars are the first five cars only. All others cars are open seating."

The agent repeated himself over and over and over and I mused what would he do for work if he ever lost his voice?

Stepping aboard, the train car was dimly lit and I took the first window seat I could find. But waiting for the train to move, I started to panic. I imagined that the car doors would any second swing open and Jacob would enter. He would call my name but I would not look up. Then, he would approach me with his shit eating grin and stand by my seat. He would command me to follow him off the train. But I would not go. And he would start pulling me out of my seat. I tried to control my breathing by taking deep breaths. I then turned my face outside the window and counted the dim lights as we passed through the tunnel. One, two, three. I was barely holding on. Eight, nine, ten. My breathing was still labored. Fifteen, sixteen, seventeen.

Tumbala, Tumbala, Tumbalalaika

As I repeatedly told myself that I would be all right, something warm flashed across my face. And another flash and another. Finally, there was this constant warm feeling. The sun was shining brightly through the train car window and I kissed the glass. We had crossed through the Hudson tunnel from New York into New Jersey. And I was safe.

"Good morning, tickets please," I heard.

I smiled and handed the agent my ticket.

"Los Angeles! Visiting family or going to become a star?"

"Huh?"

"You know. Hollywood."

"Oh no," I laughed. "I am seeing a friend."

"Well, you have a long way to go," he said as he punched my ticket. "Change in Chicago."

Newark was our first stop. As the rail car slowly pulled out of the station, it made a strange rattling sound. Looking out the window, I thought the train had run over one of the many rusting cars and old appliances that littered the area near the train tracks.

Surprisingly, no one was sitting next to me and I wished that I would have the seat to myself for the whole trip. But no luck. The front door of the train car opened and revealed a very tall, good looking man in his late twenties. He was wearing a blue suit, crisp white shirt and tie. And as he walked down the car aisle, he stopped at my seat.

"Is this seat open?" he inquired.

"Ah, yes."

The man was holding an attaché case and the NY Times. After we exchanged smiles I returned to my window view of what now looked like a graveyard of rusting cars and appliances.

"You would probably be more comfortable if you put your suitcase up on top," he said pointing to the suitcase I was clutching.

"Oh, well."

"Would you like some help?" he asked with a very sweet, kind smile.

"Thank you."

"My name is Cliff," he offered.

"Hello."

"And yours?"

"Mine?" I stared at him.

"You do have a name?"

"I am sorry. Danielle. My name is Danielle," I replied, flustered.

"Beautiful day."

"Yes it is."

"So where are you going? Washington?"

"Ah, no a little further."

"Well this is the Chicago train."

"Keep going," I laughed.

"Well, I don't know."

"Los Angeles," I said.

"Wow, long ride. Haven't you heard of airplanes?"

I did not respond.

"I am sorry. That was presumptuous on my part."

"That's ok. And you?" I asked.

"I work in Washington. I was just in New York on business and my parents live in New Jersey so I saw them last night before returning today," he said.

"What kind of work do you do?"

"I am a researcher at the Holocaust Museum in Washington."

As he spoke, the light shining in from outside the train made his soft, brown eyes sparkle. And he had such straight teeth, square jaw, a beautiful nose, and long tapered fingers. Even his fingernails were nicely trimmed.

"That must be interesting work," I observed.

"It is. Very rewarding."

"How did you get into that?"

Curiously, I showed no interest the first time Jacob recited his résumé, I thought.

"Well, I graduated college as a history major and of course there were no jobs. I thought about going on for my Masters. But why put off the inevitable? And I liked doing research. So I answered a job opening that was posted at my school, and well, here I am."

"That is great."

"And what is your story? Are you still in school? "

"You are very flattering," I said as I touched my ring finger which was now bare, since I had left my ring on the kitchen table when I left the apartment.

"I am an attorney. I work in the DA's office in Queens."

As we continued getting to know each other, I felt a sense of comfort; here was someone who actually listened to what I said.

"Would you like a cup of coffee? I need my morning fix. I am going to go back to the snack car. Can I bring you a cup?" he offered.

"I know what you mean. I would love that," I said as I reached for my wallet.

"Please, my pleasure."

Cliff was back in a few minutes holding what looked like the bottom of a shirt box. Inside were two cups of coffee, two muffins, and a few packages of cream and sugar.

"What's this?"

"I didn't have time to get breakfast this morning. Are you hungry?"

"I am always hungry," I laughed.

"Well, I hope you like muffins. They're blueberry and blueberry."

"Wow. Well I think I will have a blueberry."

"Good choice. So what are you going to do in Los Angeles? Are you starring in some movie?"

I laughed. "The conductor asked me the same question. So is everyone who is going to Los Angeles wanting to be star?"

"I don't know."

"Well, it's kind of a vacation. I am staying with a girlfriend from law school," I explained.

Not wanting to give any more details, I changed the subject.

"My grandmother is a Holocaust survivor."

"Oh, what camp?"

"She was in Austria. Ah, I can't pronounce the name."

"Mauthausen," he said with assurance.

"Yes, that's right. But she never talks about it."

"Most of them don't. Did anyone else in her family survive?"

"No, all we ever heard was that, when they arrived at the camp, she and her sister and mother were separated from her father. I never got the story straight, but somehow she survived. She never talked much about it except that there was this very nice person in the camp."

"From time to time, I come out to LA. My office works together with the Simon Weisenthal Center."

I must have had a blank stare on my face.

"You know, the Nazi hunter. They built an amazing memorial and research center in LA. And Steven Spielberg established the Shoah project."

Again, I gave Cliff the same look.

"You don't get out much. Spielberg. *E.T. Schindler's List.*"

"Of course."

Cliff and I chatted for the next few hours without running out of things to say. And as we talked and talked, it felt as if I had known Cliff forever.

"Next stop, Union Station, next stop," The announcement blasted through the speakers.

"Well this is where I get off. Sure you wouldn't reconsider and spend some time in Washington? I know the Smithsonian museums really well. And we could continue our conversation," Cliff said.

"Sounds nice. Perhaps another time," I replied.

"Well, here is my card. It also has my e-mail address on it. If you ever want to ask something about your grandmother or, well."

I read the card. "Clifford Warner. That's a nice sounding name."

"My parents thought so. Goodbye, Danielle."

Cliff smiled and walked toward the front of the car. But before he exited, he turned around to wave, flashing that very sweet smile.

Over the next three days, like a time elapsed photo, my seat partners changed. And it was like watching a play though I was also in it. There was an older man who sneezed a lot, the Rabbi with a crutch who told too many stories. And a grandmother who was traveling with her granddaughter. She was taking her home to care for her because the girl's mother was ill. Approaching Phoenix, we even celebrated the girl's fourth birthday.

And though the scenery was ever changing, the images from my immediate past remained. But for now, contacting my work, terminating my marriage to Jacob, and explaining my flight to freedom to my father was the furthest from my mind. Instead I chose lost in time as my state of consciousness.

Chapter Sixteen

My feet felt a little wobbly as I rode the escalator up out of the train station in Los Angeles. But that sensation quickly disappeared as my face was gently kissed by the warm rays of the California sun that greeted me atop the train platform.

"Danielle." A familiar sounding voice called my name. But I could not find the face to match the voice as the crowd around me was pushing and shoving to claim their luggage. But then, like Moses parted the red sea, a path opened and I spotted a waving hand quickly moving towards me.

"Marcia," I yelled as the two of us embraced.

"Hello, girlfriend. Sure didn't think I would see you again this fast."

"Thank you, I think."

"For what?"

"For being a friend," I said, smiling into her eyes. "I am so sorry, I was going to call but my phone died soon after leaving Chicago."

"It's ok. I knew if something had changed, you would have let me know. So where's your stuff?"

"This is it," I said, gesturing to my small suitcase and backpack.

"Are you crazy? You traveled across the country with one little rolling suitcase?"

"I just threw in whatever I could. I really didn't have any time to...." I trailed off, too pained to elaborate.

"No need to go into details. And now we have an excuse to go shopping. Anyway, I am just glad you are here," Marcia said.

"Thanks. This really means a lot to me."

Marcia's car was parked only a short distance away. And as we walked, I marveled at all the people wearing shorts and sleeveless tops in the month of January.

"You won't be needing that winter coat in this weather," Marcia reassured me.

"I can't believe I am here. Everything is so beautiful," I marveled.

"Sweetheart. You're only at the train station," she smiled. "Come. You have a lot to see."

After a few minutes of driving, we were bumper to bumper in heavy traffic.

"This is something you never get used to and just accept it as a way of life," Marcia said.

"Well I don't drive and don't plan on anytime soon. So I won't have to be worrying about that," I said confidently.

"Danielle, everyone drives. This is not Queens. Anyway, are you hungry?"

"I am always hungry."

"Good. Ever have Indian food?"

"I don't think so."

"Well, you are in for a treat. And their beer is amazing!"

Chapter Seventeen

Unlike the summer like weather that greeted me upon my arrival in January, it seemed to rain almost every day in February. Being new to the city of angels, I was unprepared for the downpour I experienced as I stepped off the bus. Running the four blocks from the bus stop to Marcia's apartment, I was drenched and could not wait to get out of my wet clothes. But as I opened the outer screen door, the key slipped between my fingers and I fumbled putting it into the lock. Finally, after two attempts, I turned the lock and pushed the door wide open. I stepped inside and sighed with relief as I found shelter from the deluge.

"Hey, I am home," I shouted as I removed my soaked shoes and placed my wet jacket over one of the chairs in the kitchen. "I have been in blizzards. But I have never seen rain come down this hard before," I said as I took a paper towel from the kitchen counter and blotted the water on my face. As I spoke, I remembered Marcia saying she had a doctor's appointment and realized that with the rain she was probably stuck in traffic.

"Danielle," a male voice responded.

Already chilled from the rain, the sound of that voice sent me shivering from fear.

"Danielle," the voice sounded louder.

I momentarily thought of leaving but instead walked slowly into the living room like a cat preparing to attack its prey.

"I couldn't stop him," Marcia said. "He practically pushed the door in."

Jacob was seated on the couch by the window.

"Hello Danielle."

My face was still dripping from the rain. And without answering, I walked back into the kitchen to get another paper towel. Returning to the room, I found Jacob now standing with his arms crossed. I saw his mouth moving, but the only sound I heard was that of the rain pounding against the window panes.

"How did you find me? My father?"

"Don't blame your dad. He only had your phone number. But I was able to Google Marcia's address."

There was a long painful silence as I stared at the floor.

"You did not call. You just vanished." I said nothing.

"It has been over a month. I have been worried," he said accusingly.

I still did not respond.

"You are my wife," Jacob announced as if he had judged a pie contest and picked the winner. "I have come to take you home."

Jacob's voice was cold steel. And as he said those frightening words, I noticed my black suitcase next to the couch and with my eyes I pleaded with my friend for some explanation.

"He went into your room. What was I supposed to do? He opened the closet and started grabbing your clothes."

I finally summoned the nerve to speak. "I am not going anywhere." My voice was now ringing out loud and harsh. And as I spoke, I looked squarely into his eyes. "This is where I now live and I want you to leave," I said, walking toward the apartment door.

"I am willing to forget everything," he replied.

I smirked. "You are what? You are willing to forget? You don't even have a clue. So I suggest that you leave right now or I will call the police."

Marcia nodded in agreement as she joined me at the apartment door. But to our surprise, Jacob sat back down on the couch.

"Let's talk. Can we go someplace to sit and talk?" Jacob's tone softened. "I have already imposed enough upon your friend," he said looking at Marcia. "Please. For just a few minutes."

Marcia moved away from the door as I stepped toward Jacob with my arms crossed against my chest. As I began to speak, I took another step toward Jacob. "Jacob, I don't love you. And I surely should not have married you. I married you only because my father wanted me to. But we don't have a marriage."

"Perhaps we should be talking in private."

"No, Marcia knows everything. I don't keep secrets. And I am not ashamed and I am not embarrassed."

Once again, Jacob rose from his seat and approached me, reaching for my hand. But Marcia stepped in front to block him. Noticeably frustrated, Jacob clenched his hands into two fists and thrust them into his pants pockets.

"Don't touch me," I shouted. "You will never touch me again. And I am filing for divorce."

"Divorce," Jacob uttered as if he had never heard the word said before. "The Talmud teaches us to work things out. And I want to try."

"You should leave now," Marcia said and this time she opened the door. "Before there is any trouble."

"There is nothing I can do? And you make it seem so simple. I travel thousands of miles to find my wife. And I am asking for the opportunity to open a dialogue with you but all I am getting is a door that is about to close."

Frustrated, Jacob walked toward the door but stopped before exiting.

"Danielle."

"Go," I said, turning away from him.

As he left the apartment, he shouted, "You are my wife," pulling the door shut behind him.

"Please make sure he leaves," I said to Marcia. She walked over to the window and pulled back the curtain. Seconds later, I heard a car engine start.

"He's gone. He drove away. And I am so sorry I put you through…"

"That's all right. You did not know. But I have to end this."

But I knew in my heart that it would not be the last time I would have to confront the devil.

Chapter Eighteen

After Jacob's startling visit, my new life in California was slowly beginning to settle down. I began studying for the July California Bar examination and took a part time job at Barnes and Noble as a sales associate. Also on my radar screen was to lose weight and get in shape. But I could not escape the smell of the freshly baked apple turnovers every time I walked by Cantor's Deli on the way home from the bus stop.

Seeing a dentist was something that I had been putting off as it was difficult to chew anything tough on my right side. Not surprisingly, soft foods like apple turnovers caused no problem. And with it being Good Friday, no work, and no bar study class, I made an appointment with Dr. Crial.

The waiting room was airy and spacious, and very different in appearance from my dentist's office in Queens which was probably last decorated in the '50s. Suspended from the ceiling was a flat screen television. And on the screen was Oprah chatting with four other women. I had grabbed a fitness magazine and was reading an article about starting to get in shape when I heard one of the women refer to the *"Mauthausen concentration camp."*

As I lifted my head, Oprah was holding a photo of a Jewish camp survivor who was near starvation. And I listened intensely as Oprah spoke with the daughter of a woman named Irene. She told how her mother worked in the home of the camp's commandant as his housekeeper. And when the officer was away, she would take scraps of food and smuggle them into the camp's infirmary and feed them to the sick prisoners. She also spoke about a beautiful young Jewish girl whom her mother saved from almost a certain death by selecting her to be her helper.

I held on to every word that Irene's daughter said. And as she spoke, I thought about Nana's response whenever I asked her about the Holocaust. All she would ever say is that *"someday, after I am gone, my story can be told."* Until then, she feared that those who protected her would be harmed.

I repeatedly told her that such thoughts were foolish. Regardless, she stood firm in her beliefs.

Two cavity fillings later, I was back on the bus. And though I was excited that I could chew without pain, I thought about Irene and wanted to call Nana as soon as I got home.

"Hey Marcia, I am back," I said sorting through the mail that Marcia had left on the kitchen table. "You are right. Dr. Crial is really nice. I didn't see a wedding ring. Is he married? I know this girl that I work with. I think she would really like him. Where are you?"

I kept sorting the mail and opened up a circular from Target. "We should go to Target. They're having a great sale on towels. Hello," I shouted, "Where are you? Anyway, do you want to get some Indian food tonight? Dr. Crial said that I can chew but just should wait a few hours. And I really feel like having one of those beers."

At that moment, Marcia walked into the kitchen holding the phone and wearing a worried look.

"Hold on," she said into the phone, "Danielle just got home."

"It's your brother," she said as she held out the phone to me.

"Hi David, you probably tried my cell but my phone is dead. I forgot to charge it again. What?"

My brother paused.

"Just tell me. NOOOOOOOOOOOOOOOOOOOOOOOOO!"

The cabin doors were closed for more than thirty minutes and I had already flipped through every magazine stuffed in the seat pocket in front of me when the loud speaker overhead squeaked.

"Folks. This is Captain Williams speaking to you from the cockpit. Kennedy is reporting severe thunder storms in the New York area so operations here at LAX are keeping us on the ground a little longer than expected."

I strained to hear what he was saying as the obese passenger sitting on my left was shouting across two rows to his friend.

"I hope to have an update for you shortly. Meanwhile, sit back, relax, and we promise to get you to New York as quickly as possible," the captain concluded.

Sit back and relax, I mused. I had never flown before and had always imagined that my first flight would take me to someplace exotic. Instead, I was now sitting in a long metal cylinder, alone with my thoughts and petrified. And except for an energy bar that I had grabbed from my kitchen and my morning coffee fix, I had not eaten anything and was facing six grueling hours on a plane that I just discovered no longer served meals.

As I readjusted the Kleenex box-sized pillow behind my head, my row mate selfishly took possession of the arm rest that separated us. Feeling claustrophobic and searching for something to do, I reached again for one of the magazines. Another twenty minutes had passed when the loud speaker vibrated again.

"Folks. Captain Williams here. The weather in the New York area has improved and we should be getting off the ground shortly."

The captain went on to inform us of the route we would be flying. As he spoke, I wondered why he thought we needed to know this information. Was someone planning to stop along the way and needed to know when to get off? My only concern was getting to New York and I really didn't care what route we took as long as we arrived safely.

Finally, we were next in line for take-off. And as the plane roared down the runway, I thought about what I might have forgotten to pack. Did I bring the right shoes? Did I remember to pack my hairdryer? Had I unplugged the iron? And then I thought about my life. Less than a year ago I was walking down the aisle for what should have been the happiest day of my life. Instead, the next several months proved to be a nightmare. And now, I was going back to New York to face my father, who still believes that Jacob is a good man.

Soaring through the clouds that hugged the coastline, the captain navigated a slow left turn and my row mate mumbled something about being able to see Catalina Island through my window. But I was too busy hugging my seat and feeling every turn the pilot made.

As the plane turned left again and leveled off, the sun cast an oblique shadow across my face and I felt kissed by the sun. I closed my eyes but I was too wired up to sleep. Instead, I imagined being a little girl again. And my Nana slowly rocking me in her chair.

_____

"Ma'am."

I felt a tap on my shoulder.

"Ma'am, we're getting ready to land."

Startled, I opened my eyes.

"Ma'am. You need to bring your seat back up to its upright position for landing."

"Ok."

"You were sleeping pretty good," my row mate said.

I am usually never able to take a nap, so I was very surprised that I was able to fall asleep on the plane. Perhaps, I reasoned, I was so nervous about flying that my mind shut down my thought process and allowed me to fall into a deep sleep. Regardless of why, I was anxious to land.

Darkness had now filled the view from my window as I felt the plane begin its descent. Moments later, the wheels touched down and I thanked God that we had landed safely.

After making a quick bathroom stop, I found my way to the baggage claim area which was already crowded with passengers from other flights. And despite all the pushing and shoving that was so typical of New Yorkers, I firmly stood my ground in the space that I had staked out behind the moving conveyor. But by the time my suitcase rolled down the belt, almost all the passengers had already claimed their luggage.

As I walked toward the exit, I passed a receiving line of private drivers holding up signs with names of arriving passengers. Even though my brother had told me he would be waiting outside of the terminal, one sign caught my eye. It read: "My precious angel."

Holding the sign was my dad, dressed like a limo driver in a black suit complete with a white shirt and black tie. Other than some very brief conversations, we had not seriously talked since I left for California and I feared how he would accept me. But just seeing him, I knew we would be able to work things out.

"Oh my God! I can't believe you came," I said as we hugged.

"Where else would I be? I missed you so. Are you hungry?"

"I am always hungry."

"Great. I know a nice place to go."

We drove silently with only the sound of the night air blowing through a small crack in the window my dad opened on the driver's side. And though I wanted to tell my father, every time I began to open my mouth, a tear would start. So instead, I made small talk about how nervous I was when the plane took off, that there are palm trees in Los Angeles, and that southern California gets all of its annual rain fall in one month.

Finally, as my dad pulled into the parking lot of Benjie's Deli, he reached across the seat to grab my hand. It was a familiar gesture and one that I missed. As he did, I thought about how all through the years, my father was always there for me. He was so easy to talk to and depend on. And though we many times agreed that we disagreed, I knew he was always looking out for me.

I put my hand over his, gently. And then I lifted his hand to my lips. "I love you, Dad. And I never meant to hurt you or worry you. Can you ever forgive me?"

"How can I not?"

We shared the best onion rings in all of Manhattan. And My dad ordered his favorite corned beef on rye sandwich, extra lean, with coleslaw on the side while I warmed up from the cold New York air with a big bowl of chicken and matzoh ball soup. For dessert, what else, we each had apple turnovers which, as my dad announced, *"were not as good as Schwartz's."* And after hearing my dad's new repertoire of jokes, it was if we had turned back the clock; I was once again that little girl having dinner out with the only parent I had ever known. Life was simple. And I decided that the conversation that I needed to have would wait for another day.

March in New York is the cruelest month. It teases spring time long enough to have you fooled. And then it casts its shadow for several more weeks before finally yielding to the changing season.

Our car joined the hearse that was waiting at the cemetery gate and we followed it a few hundred feet where the narrow road ended. My brother and sister-in-law exited the car first and waited by the door for my father and me.

I took my first steps carefully, avoiding the scattered puddles of mud. But as I did, the heels of my shoes sank into the soft wet grass.

"Careful. It has been raining for several days," my brother said as I slowly started to navigate down the hill while searching the horizon for the distant skyline of Manhattan.

Normally, it is visible on a clear day but today was blurred by thick gray clouds that were threatening to rain again. And the branches on the trees were bare and black and dripping. I felt a drop of rain on my head, and then another and another. My brother opened an umbrella for me but I wanted to feel the rain.

"You're gonna get wet," he said nudging me under the umbrella but I smiled.

"I've gotten soaked at least one before," I mused.

Nana was opposed to a *"fancy, shmancy"* "service in a sanctuary and often told my brother and me that "*it was foolish to spend so much money just to put you in the ground. And that someday, but hopefully not too soon, I want a simple service like we did for my Abraham."* (My grandfather)

In response, I would say how I hated that kind of talk and that "you will live forever.*"*

At the grave site, there were twenty-four white plastic chairs set out in four rows with the open grave covered by artificial turf. Greeting our arrival were my father's and brother's friends and Mrs. Nadel as well as a few of Nana's friends that I recognized from her building. At one time, my Nana had had a rather large circle of friends, but now that circle could barely surround a small chair.

As the Rabbi stood beside the casket and began to read the 29th Psalm, I turned to my father and reached for his hand. He in turn put his arm around my shoulder and it felt so comforting. I had missed the feeling of security being in my father's presence.

"The Lord is my Shepherd, I shall not want. He maketh me lie down in green pastures. He leadeth me beside still waters. He restoreth my soul; he leadeth me in the paths of righteousness for his name's sake. Surely good-

ness and mercy will follow me all the days of my life, and I will dwell in the house of the Lord forever."

Once Nana's casket was lowered, the Rabbi took a shovel of dirt and tossed it into the grave. A flume of dust rose from the ground as the dirt hit the casket. He next passed the shovel to my brother and to me so that we could repeat the ritual. I then handed the shovel to my father who became very emotional as he lifted a shovel of dirt. His eyes were noticeably teary and bloodshot and he whispered to me, "I loved your Nana."

As the Rabbi recited the Mourner's *Kaddish*, the sky became a gray, glistening curtain and a steady rain began. Within moments, the sky was spitting rain with big drops falling. The sensation invoked all my senses from childhood as I was always intrigued by the thunderous roar that preceded a storm. I had always loved how the purest of water cleanses everything in its path, always leaving behind a sweet scent when it stopped. But the rain was falling thickly now and drummed on my head as I took my brother's offer of shelter under his opened umbrella.

"Nana always said it was good luck when it rained on the day of a funeral," I whispered to David, remembering that when I was a little girl she said the rain was *"God's message that the doors of heaven were opening to accept the recently departed."*

He smiled. "I do remember."

As the last shovel of dirt was tossed onto the grave, I looked up at the sky. In the Jewish tradition, death is not a tragedy; death is simply a part of the process as there is a firm belief in an afterlife where the soul continues on. And, as if God had turned a page, a small patch of blue sky appeared. It was rectangular in design. As I gazed, the patch grew longer. It was as if a pathway through the sky was opening within the dark clouds. And just as quickly, the patch faded away, leaving behind the dark sky, and I knew Nana was now in heaven.

"Come; let's go before it starts to rain again," my brother said. But I wanted one more moment alone with Nana as I stepped to the fringe of the mound of dirt that now covered her grave while my brother waited behind me.

"I love you Nana. You will always be with me," I said as I kneeled and touched the dirt with my hand.

As I slowly rose, I looked at what seemed like miles of headstones and thought I saw Jacob a few rows over. But I looked again and the figure was gone.

Chapter Nineteen

Except for my niece who kept asking *"are we home yet?"* it was a silent drive from the cemetery. And whenever my brother tried to engage my dad in conversation, Dad motioned with his hands that he did not want to talk, appearing in an almost hypnotic state. He seemed mesmerized by the sight of the splashy streaks that merged into vertical pools of water and the sound of the metal wiper blades on the Cadillac that flicked away the countless tears falling from heaven.

For the next three days, I stayed in my dad's apartment where we sat Shivah, the Jewish morning period where friends and relatives visit to pay their respects. And by the end of each evening, I would politely say to my dad "good night" as I disappeared into my room. But by the end of the third night, and after all of our guests had left, it was apparent that one more night would not pass without my father talking to me about why I left my marriage.

"Sit down. Don't go running away," Dad requested on that night.

My father had seated himself in his favorite chair facing the television but the set was not on.

"Dad, I am tired. I am going to go to bed. But tomorrow morning I am going to make a run to Schwartz's just to fill in. David said some of his friends from work are going to stop by so I want to make sure we have something to feed them."

"That's it? Nothing else to say?"

"What, Dad?"

"All of a sudden, we are strangers. Roommates talk more to each other."

"Dad, it is between me and Jacob."

"No, I am your father. And I raised you to come to me when there is a problem. I did not raise you to run away."

I sat down on the couch next to him.

"Dad, all I will say is that I had no choice. So let's leave it there."

"You had no choice. You couldn't talk. A husband and wife all of a sudden lose their tongues. Your mother and I talked about everything. She was my best friend. I could…"

I stopped him before he finished.

"Dad. See, that is what I mean. You just assume that we had some difference of opinion but one of us was too lazy to try to work it out. So your daughter took the easy way out and just ran away. Ok, believe what you want."

"Then tell me how I am wrong." My dad paused. "Talk to me. Please sweetie. I lost sleep at night first worrying where you are. And then feeling like a failed father because I am not there to help you."

"I tried to tell you."

"Well, you didn't try hard enough. Instead you run off and…"

I started to cry.

"It is something terrible," I cried, my voice shaking.

"What could it be? So terrible that you leave your job and travel across the country? So terrible that you forget that you have family here? So terrible that…"

Before he could finish, I shouted, "He raped me."

As I sounded that four letter word, my father picked up his head, looking confused. And I was not sure that he heard what I said or could process what he heard. So I said it again.

"Raped. He raped me."

My dad took off his glasses and looked suddenly exhausted as he rubbed the bridge of his nose with his fingertips and gave me the sorriest look.

"Raped. Who would do this? And you don't tell your husband?" As he spoke, I watched my father's face grow stony and pale.

I started to cry.

"Rape. Danielle, I would never have known. But who is this animal that could do this to my precious angel? I want to murder him. Who is he? Tell me. Who is he? Who? Who? Tell me. Who?"

I was crying and shaking my head, "No, no, I can't."

"Danielle, it's your father asking."

"I can't. I can't," I pleaded. And then I spit out his name. "It's Jacob. That's your animal. He raped me, Dad. He raped me," I sobbed. "And I couldn't stay." I reached for my father and cried in his arms. And I felt a sort of peace come over me.

"Does anyone else know?" he asked.

"Only Nana. I told her. And she was so frightened for me. She gave me $500 and told me to go as far away as I could."

My dad took my hands and I put them against my cheek. I felt his fingers grow wet with my tears. But I kept his hands tight against me.

"And Jacob. Have you?"

"I am taking care of it, Dad. I am filing for divorce. And please don't do anything and don't say anything if he tries to talk to you. Have you talked to him?"

He was silent.

"Dad, talk to me. Have you talked to him?"

"He's called me. And I told him Nana died. But I promise. I won't talk to him anymore. If he calls, I will hang up."

"Please, Dad. You must promise. I need to handle this myself."

"I promise."

"I am so sorry I did not hear your pain. Can you ever forgive me?" he asked.

"I already have, Dad," I said as I kissed him on the forehead. "I am tired. We'll talk more. I love you," I said as I walked out of the room, leaving my father staring at his blank television screen.

I felt uncomfortable about going alone to Nana's apartment and asked my brother to go with me.

"How much chicken soup could they be cooking?" David joked, referring to the distinctive smell of the hallways.

Nana kept her apartment very clean and she would boast that "*you could eat off my floors.*" But as we entered, it smelled musty and felt drained of air. I went quickly through each room opening the windows. The sounds of the street quickly filtered through, but without Nana the apartment was eerily quiet.

"Are you ok?" David asked.

"Yeah. But I can feel Nana's presence though she is no longer with us. It is just a little weird."

"I know what you mean."

As I walked through the apartment, I saw her favorite cup that she would drink her coffee from sitting on the pie-shaped mahogany table next to the frayed suede arm chair by the window in the living room.

"When she was alone, Nana told me that she would sit in her living room admiring her things," I said as I sat in her seat and panned the room from right to left the same way my Nana would. "She would sit, drink her coffee, and read her newspaper. This was like her throne," I said, looking out the window.

"I know," David replied. "Except it took her forever to answer when the phone rang. And I wanted to get her a cordless phone but she refused. So every time I called, the phone would ring and ring and when she finally picked it up, she would remind me that *I am not a young lady. It takes me time to get to the phone.*"

"That was Nana." I moved off the chair and looked at her plants on the window sill.

Wow, these plants are freezing," I said, touching the limp petals.

"Sure. I am surprised they are not all dead."

In the kitchen was Nana's old AM radio that was shaped like a train car. She would listen to the news each morning. Next to it was a basket of bananas that had turned black. I held on to the enamel of the sink and saw a few dirty dishes that were in the sink. The only movement in the room was the anniversary clock covered by a glass dome as the pieces whirled around knowing they too would die if they were not wound soon. As I stood motionless, I thought I heard Nana's tea kettle boiling. But the sound was coming from the apartment next door.

Returning from the kitchen, I asked, "Who is going to take care of these plants? She gave them life."

"I'll knock on Sid's door. Maybe he'll take them," David offered.

"All right," I replied.

Nana had apparently died in her sleep and was discovered by her neighbor Sid after he noticed that she had not taken in her newspaper for two days. Fortunately, Sid and Nana had exchanged apartment keys and he immediately called my brother.

As David left, I walked into Nana's dining room and admired, like I always did, the tall, silver Shabbos candlestick holders. They were beautiful and so intricate. Each one was as long as my forearm, gleaming silver with a wide claw foot base, two slender stems that swelled into a large blub covered in silver leaves before ending with the candleholder large enough to take a candle that would burn for 24 hours. And Nana kept them well polished.

"Sid said he would take the plants," David said as he re-entered the room. "He'll come by later."

"Ok," I said, holding one of the candlestick holders. "David, remember how Nana would cover her head with a shawl, and with you and me standing by her side, she lit the white candles and waved her hands over the flames and then covered her eyes and prayed?"

"Of course, how I can forget?"

While I continued to examine the candlestick holders, my brother picked up a few pieces of unopened mail that were sitting on the dining room table.

"She must have sensed something. There is unopened mail here from the last couple of weeks," said David.

"It's funny," I replied. "I spoke to her only a few days ago. She sounded fine but said she was tired. I think she knew."

"Yeah, it's sad."

As my brother continued to go through the mail, one by one I picked up each picture frame that was set on the dining room server.

"Look at Mom. I wish I knew her. She was so pretty," I said.

"She was," David agreed.

"And it is so sad. There are no pictures of her parents. All killed by the Nazis."

"It is amazing she survived. But she said someday we would know."

As I looked at each picture, I remembered how Nana would pick up each frame, look at the photo, and tell me a story.

"Danielle," David interrupted my reverie. "I really should be getting on the road. I don't want to be stuck in traffic." My brother had finished the mail and was growing impatient.

"Ok, just a few more minutes," I said as I walked into Nana's bed-room.

Against the window was the plain slat back rocking chair under a standing lamp so Nana could read. On an end table beside the rocker was a crystal bowl that was always filled with candy. In front of Nana's bed was a mahogany hope chest covered with a lace shawl. Nana always said that *"the chest was filled with a treasure of memories."*

Opening the center dresser drawer, I admired the pearls that she wore to my wedding.

"I found Nana's pearls," I shouted.

"Take them."

"Maybe Denise would like them."

"You're the granddaughter. They should go to you."

"All right. I am just going to look in her closet."

Sitting on the top shelf along with a few pair of shoes was a box that would fit a man's shirt.

"How did Nana ever put anything up here?" I wondered aloud. "She was so short."

"What did you say?" David called.

"There's this box on the top of the closet."

"Do you need help?" he asked, entering the room.

I stood on my toes, reaching for the box, but I could not grab it.

"Yes, please," I admitted.

"What's in it?" David asked, handing the box to me.

It was fastened with some fancy tooling.

"I think the bow was from Nana's 80th birthday. She received so many gifts and it looked like she even kept the gift wrapping. She never threw out anything."

"Maybe Nana had a lover? And she kept all of his love letters," my brother quipped.

I rolled my eyes. "You're disgusting. I don't think so."

"Ok. It probably contains birthday cards. Nana saved everything. Come on. You can read them later. Anyway, I need to get going. So, if there is anything else you want, take it. Otherwise, let's go.

"All right," I said, putting the Shabbos candlestick holders in a grocery bag along with the pearls, some photo frames and the shirt box. But on our way out, I took one more look at the apartment before my brother closed the door on a lifetime.

Chapter Twenty

By tradition, the seven day mourning period of Shivah concludes with walking around a block, symbolically representing the circle of life. But life had not returned to the trees that lined the street as they had long shed their leaves and looked barren against the gray buildings as I took the symbolic walk. Fortunately, it was a glorious, crisp day, with sharp fresh air and a stark blue sky much welcomed after three miserable days of torrid rain.

Walking past the identical rows of apartment buildings that made up my neighborhood, I saw some familiar faces. There was the mailman who waved to me as he walked up the steps to the building next to ours. How ironic that I never knew his name though he has delivered our mail since I was a little girl.

As I turned the corner, I saw Mrs. Fleischman hobbling along with her cane. She was walking her dog Charlie, or vice versa, and I wondered how old Charlie was; Mrs. Fleischman had been walking her adorable collie for as long as our mailman had been delivering our mail.

I waved to Mrs. Fleischman as Charlie visited the fire hydrant and I pondered how fragile our lives were; neither the mailman nor my neighbor knew that Nana passed away. Yet life goes on.

With the steps to our building in sight, I thought I saw Jacob. But was my mind playing tricks? I looked again but the figure was gone. Feeling scared, I quickened my pace. But as I reached the top step of my dad's building I heard a haunting voice.

"Danielle."

Rather than turn, I froze.

"Danielle," the voice said again.

This time, I slowly turned around as the voice approached the first step.

"Stop," I snapped, raising my hand like a police officer directing traffic.

"I want to talk."

"I said stop. Do not come near me."

I backed away as Jacob pleaded. "Please give me five minutes. You owe me that." Steam from the cold poured from Jacob's mouth as he stuttered each word.

"I owe you? I don't owe you anything," I said, raising my voice. Fortunately, there was no one else in front of the building to hear us.

Jacob lowered his voice. "I am sorry. I did not mean that. But please, hear me out," he said, taking another step forward.

We were now separated by only two steps.

"Don't," I said holding up my hand like a stop sign.

"Five minutes. That is all I ask."

I looked at my watch. My plane back to Los Angeles was not for several hours.

"All right. I am going up to the apartment but I will be right down."

"Can I…."

"No, stay here!"

I had to use the bathroom and grew tense as I entered the building. Perhaps if I stayed long enough, Jacob would leave. But what if he found his way into the building?

Upon returning, I found Jacob standing at the base of the steps as rigid as a statue. It looked like he was afraid to move for fear that he might break into a thousand pieces.

"I will talk to you. But not here. Let's go to the park," I said.

Victory Park was called a park but was really only a small patch of grass and a few benches that made up the courtyard surrounded by the six identical apartment buildings. And though the area was not big enough to throw a ball, it did offer some escape in the summer from the concrete landscape that made up our city neighborhood.

It was bitter cold as we walked in silence, though I could listen to the winter wind that swept through the narrow alleys that divided the apartment buildings. As I stepped on the frozen pavement that was covered over by snow and frozen rain from the night before, it was difficult to walk. But I took each careful step over the previously undisturbed snowflakes that were now marred by my footsteps, and I rehearsed in my mind what I was going to say.

Jacob walked a few steps ahead of me and his feet made whooshing noises trampling through the snow. His posture, which I had always complained about, had not improved as he walked with his head bent swinging like an elephant from side to side.

As we approached the park, the long and bitterly cold winter left the few trees naked with long skinny branches reaching eagerly toward the fading afternoon sun, which had now turned pale as the end of another day quickly approached. And the ground was littered with dead leaves. I bent down and picked up a lifeless leaf and held it in my hand. It was a sycamore leaf, brown and brittle. With my thumb and forefinger, I tore a piece of it away and ground it into dust between my fingers as Jacob watched like a condemned person about to face his executioner.

"This is what you did to my soul. You broke me open and ground me away," I said as I took a seat on the concrete bench.

The gray stone of the bench with a brownish moss decorating its sides yielded to no body and soul and its coldness sliced through my clothes and seeped into my bones. But inside, I was radiating heat as I prepared my words for Jacob while he looked at me like a young child seeking permission to sit down.

"Sit."

Jacob obeyed.

"You were at the cemetery yesterday?"

"I was," he confirmed.

"I knew I wasn't crazy. Why didn't you come over?"

"I didn't want to make a scene."

"Well, that's the first smart decision you made."

"I also stopped smoking," he offered.

"Good for you," I said.

"But how did you know I would be at the apartment? Wait, let me guess. My father?"

"Yes, I called him."

"He lives in a fantasy world."

"He only wants to see you be happy."

"I am happy. It's just taken him a little longer to get the message."

"I was very worried about you," Jacob said.

"You said that when you showed up in California," I reminded him.

"Well, I was."

"Thank you for your concern but I have been fine. And you look well, so you must be eating. So now that we have established each other's state of health, is there anything else you want to say?"

Jacob looked up to the sky.

"I have changed."

I looked at him, confused, and said, "Is that it? Is that your statement? You have changed. Well, let's call a press conference. Jacob Liebowitz has changed. Alert the media. Did you post it to your friends on Facebook?"

Jacob bowed his head and I continued.

"Changed? What does that mean? No, let me rephrase that. Are you now saying that you're a different person than the man I married? You no longer...."

"I should not have, well, ah."

"What, raped me?" I shouted, fearless if anyone would hear me.

"Keep your voice down," he said. But except for two pigeons who had braved the cold weather and were oblivious to our presence as they searched for food, there was no one else in the park to hear us.

"Why Jacob? Did you do something wrong? Are you afraid someone might hear about how you raped your wife?"

In front of the bench, I noticed a blade of grass that had somehow found its way to the surface through a crack in the pavement. It now stood naked twisting in green and brown amid the concrete.

"You see that blade of grass," I said, pointing. "That was my life with you. Struggling to stay above the surface but fearing any minute you would snuff out my life by stepping on me. But 'you have changed.'"

"Please lower your voice," he pleaded.

"Why? Are you feeling guilty that you raped your wife?"

Each time that I have used that word, Jacob reacted like someone had hit him with a Taser gun.

"I came here to talk," he insisted.

"Did you also want to talk to Tristan after you attacked her?" I asked. Jacob looked bewildered.

"You sister clued me in. And it was easy to figure out the rest. But I had a friend in the DA's office do some checking and she found the police report."

"That was different."

"The only difference, Jacob, is that she had the balls to call the police. So you said you wanted to talk. So I am listening," I said, glancing at my wrist watch. "And then I will talk."

"I have sought help. I am in counseling. What I did, I know you cannot forget. But I ask you to forgive. I am sorry. And I want you to come back to me so we can start over." Jacob again lowered his head, staring at the cold pavement.

"Are you done? Is that it? Is that your big speech? And you think you can just waltz back into my life?"

I had wanted Jacob to break down, to cry, to show some form of emotion so perhaps his tears would help wash away my pain. But Jacob's performance was robotic.

"Did you think what happened between us was some moving storm, and a rain cloud burst but now the sun is shining?" I continued. "Do you really think I will do the nice wifely thing and throw away my new life to come home to you?"

Jacob did not respond but his eyes widened and he looked confused.

"Well then it is now my turn," I said.

I gave him a long, penetrating look and then abruptly rose.

"First of all, forgiveness isn't on my timetable and I don't see it ever being scheduled. I was 29 years old when we were married. I didn't have a lot of experience but I knew what was supposed to feel right. But on our honeymoon night, instead of being tender and loving, you climbed on me like an animal. And it hurt. It hurt very badly. And I cried. But you were deaf to my tears. Afterwards I said to myself, maybe this is the way it is supposed to be. And I was a good wife. I cleaned your clothes and cooked your meals, and gave you of myself, thinking it would get better. But it never did, as you only saw me as an outlet for your needs. When you wanted me, you were indifferent to me. It never got better but got worse. And despite my objections, you ruled. Oh yes, I was your wife. I was your property and you could have me anytime you wanted. Well guess what. I will never let anyone ever touch me again against my will. So now what do you have to say?"

As I was talking, the two pigeons walked by oblivious to my discord in search of a handout while Jacob sat stiff. And despite the cold, there appeared to be perspiration on his forehead.

"Now you say that you have sought counseling. What a joke. And how ironic. You want us to try again? You want another chance? Jacob, the one thing you have never said before, not even today, is that you love me. So you have not changed. You are incapable of change," I finished.

"You are still my wife," he insisted.

His voice was bitter as he rose to his feet. But I stopped him before he could continue.

"I am filing for divorce when I get back to California. You can have whatever is in the apartment. I don't want to have any memories. I only pray that if you ever meet someone again and do what you did to her what you did to me, that you are prosecuted like the criminal that you are. My regret is that I did not do something about it."

Jacob continued standing in silence.

"I have to go," I said as I stood looking at the gray smoke rising from the chimneys.

Jacob also did not move but stared at me like a wounded animal. I felt a soft wind cascade through the naked trees and the sun released its remaining rays of light before disappearing into the horizon.

"Wait," he said.

"I have nothing more to say," I said calmly.

Jacob reached into his pocket.

"Here."

In his hand was Nana's brush.

"You left this."

As I took the brush from his hand, the metal handle was cold like the air. But I could feel the warmth of my grandmother as a tear rolled from my eye.

"Thank you. That is the nicest thing you have ever done."

With that, I got up and walked away, never turning around to say goodbye.

Chapter Twenty One

I was delighted that the two seats next to me were not occupied on my flight back to Los Angeles. And with the extra space, I arranged my day planner, attaché case, and magazines on the open seats.

Learning from my first flight that meals are not served prior to boarding I had purchased a chicken Caesar salad. But after eating the bland tasting wilted lettuce, I was feeling tired and raised my arm to turn off the overhead light. As I did, I looked at my ring finger and remembered the moment Jacob placed the wedding ring on my finger. The thought upset me. So, I took out my legal yellow pad and numbered the sheet from one to ten of the things that I needed to do once I returned to California.

Number one on the list was to file for divorce. Not having any children or property, I knew that it would be a simple procedure. But until I began the process, I was still married to Jacob and I needed to finally terminate that part of my past.

Number two was to go on a diet. I had been struggling for my entire adult life with what my father still referred to as baby fat. And I knew that unless I cut out the apple turnovers and the other garbage food I was eating, I would never lose the weight.

Related to going on a diet, the third item was exercising. And since Marcia was always begging me to go to her gym, I would use her as my motivation and join.

Number four was to pass the California Bar exam which I was taking this July. And my boss had already authorized me to have the month before the test off so that I could study.

Number five was to cut my hair. I had had the same haircut since high school and it was time to lose the bangs and join the 21st century.

Number six was stay on a diet, which was self-explanatory.

Everyone drives in Los Angeles and I was tired of taking the bus or asking Marcia or a friend for a ride. So number seven was to get my driver's license.

And to further establish my independence, it was time that I lived on my own. Therefore, my eighth entry was to get my own apartment.

Growing up, my father would never allow my brother and me to have a pet. He always made up some nonsense that we were allergic to animals. But how did he know if we never had a pet? So number nine was to adopt a pet.

Struggling to find an entry to place next to the number 10, I kept reading and rereading the list and asking myself what was missing. What would complete the list?
Suddenly, as I doodled a heart on the notepad, the answered appeared in my mind and I drifted off into a peaceful slumber.

The next day on my lunch hour, I walked over to the family law clerk's office and obtained the forms to file for divorce. In checking the boxes, I laughed as the only two choices for seeking a divorce were incurable insanity or irreconcilable differences. Knowing that the court would want proof of Jacob's state of mind beyond what I could offer, I checked the second box. I also requested that that the court restore my maiden name. I had never liked how Danielle Liebowitz sounded anyway.

Upon completing the forms and paying the filing fee, I mailed a copy to Jacob. Since there was nothing for Jacob to contest, I knew that my nightmare would soon be over.

Chapter Twenty Two

The California State Bar had posted on their web site that the test results from my exam were going to be released at 10 a.m. the Friday before Thanksgiving. Yesterday, I told my boss that I would not be coming in tomorrow. And this morning, restless from a poor night's sleep, I got up early and made a mushroom and cheese omelet only using egg whites and low fat cheese. But with my legal career as a practicing attorney on hold for almost a year, I was too nervous to eat.

Looking at the wall clock as it counted down to the 10 o'clock hour when I would learn my fate, I found the remote that was buried in the couch cushions and turned on Regis and Kelly. But after a few minutes, my nervous energy prevented me from sitting still. So I decided now was a perfect time to break out those pant hangers that I had bought on sale at Bed, Bath & Beyond. Leg by leg, I neatly hung each of my pants before moving on to my tops, which I arranged by color starting with white, followed by black and then the other shades of the rainbow.

Getting lost in time, and surprisingly enjoying what I was doing, I was jolted back to reality as I heard the TV announce the ladies of "The View" -- that meant it was ten. So, hurdling over the two piles of clothes that I had made on the floor outside of my closet, I raced to my laptop and typed in the State Bar's web site as I felt my heart race. After entering my name in the sign-in box, I was prompted for my password.

"ROSE"

And then, the message that I was praying for appeared:

"Congratulations, you have successfully completed the test requirements of the State Bar of California."

I read it again and again, just to make sure, before I jumped for joy and let out a large shrill. But Marcia was at work and there was no one else there to share my excitement. I picked up the phone.

"I passed, I passed," I shouted into the phone.

"That is wonderful my sweetie. I am so proud of you."

"Dad, I wish you were here."

"I promise. I will make plans."

I wanted to talk more but my dad said he was busy with a customer. And after calling my brother and Marcia, the one person who I wished I could call was Nana. So I held her photo frame and told her the good news. And she sent me a sweet smile like only Nana could.

Chapter Twenty Three

While most of the Northeast woke up on New Year's Day under an arctic blanket with daytime temperatures barely above freezing, I felt guilty giving my dad the weather report.

"Dad, it is so beautiful. Remember, you said you would make plans."

"I know, sweetie. I will. And I think your brother is also planning a trip to LA. Did he mention anything?"

"Nope but knowing David, until he works out everything, he we won't say. But you would love this weather."

"What's the temperature?"

"It has been in the high 80s."

"It looked warm. I watched the Rose Parade."

"Dad, I want you to come out here."

"Ok. We'll see."

"No, I am serious."

"Alright, alright. So how's my LA Law attorney?"

"Well, I have exciting news."

"What? Something about the Dodgers. They're moving back to Brooklyn?"

"No Dad, nothing like that. But…. I am getting my own apartment."

That weekend was even warmer. I worked out at the gym, feeling energized that I was up from barely two minutes on the treadmill when I started nine months ago to thirty minutes, with 25 pounds lost. After my workout, I borrowed Marcia's car and set out to my find my new residence.

Unlike New York where city dwellers depend on the subway system, working in Los Angeles often means that you are a slave to the freeway, spending a good part of your day in bumper to bumper traffic at 20 miles an hour. I did not want to have a long daily commute, so I looked for places that were within a short drive of the Santa Monica courthouse.

By noon I had seen four apartments and was feeling frustrated as their online descriptions were greatly misleading. *"Charming"* really meant old and small. And *"breezy"* was code for no air conditioning. After viewing two more apartments that sounded amazing but were not, I was really angry and mad that I had not accepted my friend's invitation to go to the beach. But I had one more listing. And though I was unable to confirm an appointment, I decided to take a chance and stop by.

"Hi, I am here to see the apartment," I said, smiling at the young boy who answered the door.

"Hold on. I will get my grandmother," he said before running back inside.

As I waited, I noticed a *Mezuoth* mounted on the door post. Seconds later, an older woman appeared.

"Hello. Can I help you?"

"Yes, I was wondering if the apartment was still available? I tried calling but…."

"My grandson knocked off the phone. I am babysitting." The woman spoke with a very distinctive New York accent. "My daughter is working. Anyway, you're in luck. Someone looked at it two days ago and was supposed to come back with a security deposit but never showed. So, if you like it, we can talk. I am sorry. I didn't get your name."

"It is Danielle."

"Nice to meet you, Danielle. That's a pretty name. I am Beatrice. Let me get the key."

The apartment was actually a separate guest house behind Beatrice's home and was accessible by walking up the driveway.

"I just had it painted so you may smell…."

"That's ok," I reassured her.

"And the carpet is new," Beatrice boasted as she opened the door and immediately went to the front window and opened the drapes. "The apartment gets plenty of sunlight and is very cheery. I had the nicest couple living here for the past three years. But the husband got a transfer out of state. They were good people. Always paid on time. That's what I like."

I cringed when I heard Beatrice say "cheery" as from the other listings I learned that the word really meant "depressing." But the apartment was bright and cheery and spacious with a large bedroom and modern kitchen. There was even a small patio in the back with a barbeque.

"Do you live alone?" Beatrice asked.

"I do."

"And what do you do?"

Ordinarily, I would be annoyed when a stranger asked me so many questions. But Beatrice seemed very sweet and I did not mind.

"I am an attorney with the LA District Attorney's office."

"Oh. And so young."

Beatrice seemed impressed.

"The listing said that you allow pets," I said.

"What kind of animal do you have?" Beatrice asked.

"Oh, I don't yet but I am thinking about it."

"Well, when you do, there is an additional security deposit. But we can talk about that later. So what you do think? Do you like it?"

Beatrice would have made a good car salesperson as she was pushy to close the deal. But the apartment was really nice.

"I think it is amazing," I said as I opened the large guest closet in the hallway. "I'll take it."

"Mazel Tov," Beatrice shouted. "That means good luck."

"I know."

"You do. You're Jewish?" She seemed surprised.

"I am," I replied.

"Even better. Do I know a nice boy for you! Come inside. We'll sign some papers and you can give me a check. You hungry? "

"I am always hungry."

A week later, I moved into my own apartment. I could now check off number eight on my to do list.

Chapter Twenty Four

My apartment was wonderful and I was enjoying living on my own. Even when I would start to feel lonely and miss my family, my case load at work kept me very busy. In fact, after only six months of being sworn in as a deputy DA, I had handled two felony trials that ended in convictions, which went a long way to gaining the respect of my colleagues my boss.

With the little free time that I did have, however, Beatrice did her best to set me up with who she thought would be my next husband, though her idea and my idea of a perfect match was not the same. There was Aaron the geologist, who was as exciting as a rock. Then there was Henry. He and his father imported tile from Italy. After one date, I thought he would be a perfect match for Aaron.

And there was Brian. Brian loved me and all but proposed by the end of our third date. But, as Nana once said, he didn't make my heart go pitter patter and I gently led Brian away.

But my rejections did not stop Beatrice. One night, as I was getting out of my car, she was waiting for me.

"Sweetheart, let me help you."

I had a banker's box filled with files in one hand and my purse in the other.

"Thanks, Beatrice. How are you?"

"I am fine. But I am worried for you. Such a pretty girl and you work so hard."

"It's ok. I love my job."

"But you should also be in love. Come. Put your things down. I have enough dessert to feed Coxey's Army. Unless you have plans?"

I had been so good on my diet. But it was Friday and I was going to the gym in the morning.

"OK, let me just freshen up and I will come over."

Visiting with Beatrice in her home always reminded me of sitting in Nana's apartment. And tonight, with her Shabbos candles lit, I especially missed Nana.

"Good Shabbos," Beatrice said, giving me a hug as I entered the kitchen.

"Good Shabbos to you," I replied.

"Come. Sit down. I have something good."

"I really shouldn't."

I had now lost 25 pounds and was being very careful.

"What? A little piece. You're shrinking away! And I will make some tea."

I didn't want to insult Beatrice, so I promised myself to spend extra time tomorrow morning on the treadmill and took a bite out of the most amazing apple turnover I had ever had.

"My dad would go crazy over this," I exclaimed.

"Sure. Everyone goes crazy for Benishe's turnovers."

"And this is even better than Cantor's."

"Cantor's," Beatrice scoffed. "They don't know how to bake. Here, eat more! So, the Ryan guy. He didn't work out?"

"I think you mean Brian," I corrected her.

"Whatever."

"That's alright. That Mr. Special is out there. Here. You need a little sugar in your tea. You look pale."

I smiled and reached for the Sweet and Low and again thought about tomorrow's workout.

"So, I think I know someone for you. I was speaking to my friend Marilyn in the Valley who told me about her friend who has a grandson. Anyway, the boy just got a divorce. Thank god there were no children. But can you imagine. He was only married six months and the *zona* (bad woman) he found in bed with his best friend. You think you know someone. So he wants to meet a nice girl and I thought of you."

"Well, thanks, Beatrice. But I think I am going to stay away from married men."

"You're smart."

"But I do have a new man in my life."

"Voos. You did not tell me?"

"Well, you'll meet him tomorrow."

"What does he look like? How did you meet him? Tell me."

"All I can say is that he is purrfect!!!"

Chapter Twenty Five

Number nine on my list of things to do was to adopt a pet. And from the moment I first held this cuddly ball of fur with the loudest purr, we had an immediate connection. Cabby was a male gray Persian cat with the biggest blue eyes. He was wandering the streets when he was lucky enough to be found by the rescue shelter and I was lucky enough to have found him.

It was very easy for Cabby and I to adjust to living together; he had his routine during the day and I had mine. And at night, we would review our day--though I would trade for Cabby's life anytime.

One night, upon arriving home, I could not wait to crawl into bed. I had had a terribly hectic day that started with a preliminary hearing in the morning that did not finish until the early afternoon. That caused me to be late for my 1:30 arraignments. Not surprisingly, judges don't care about your schedule and Judge Faust scolded me when I finally arrived in his court. But before we could get started, the building had to be evacuated because someone called in that there was a bomb set to go off. Fortunately it was a hoax. But now the cases that were set for today were added to tomorrow morning's calendar. And with two attorneys out this week, my work load just doubled.

"Hi Cabby," I said as I put the key in the door. "I hope you had a better day than me. Do you want some treats?"

All I had to do was shake the purple package of kitty goodies and Cabby was brushing against my ankle.

"Ok, here they are," I said as I placed three chicken flavored treats in his bowl. "Now what am I going to eat? Hmm," I said, surveying the shelves of my refrigerator. "Is tonight going to be a leftover Chinese food night or should I go wild and order a pizza? Thinking about my waist line and the last five pounds I had recently lost, I settled on the Moo Goo Gai Pan.

"Do you want to watch some TV, Cabby? Ok, let's see what Mr.

TiVo recorded."

The program guide recorded episodes of "The Bachelor," "Gray's Anatomy" and "Oprah."

"I don't think so. Let's see what else is on."

After a few minutes of channel surfing, I could not concentrate and decided to unpack the box that I had placed in the hallway closet when I moved in.

"Let's put the box on the bed." As I sorted through its contents, I found old bank statements, paid bills, and restaurant menus. But on the bottom was the shirt box that I had taken from Nana's closet. Cabby seemed interested and jumped onto the bed. But like my brother had thought, the box contained old birthday cards that Nana had saved.

"Oh my God, I must have been five years old when I made this card. Look, Cabby. I drew a picture of me and Nana."

Cabby's ears momentarily perked up.

There were dozens of other cards and a few recipes that Nana had saved. But on the bottom of the box was a bound composition book. It was no more than a quarter of an inch wide and had ruled pages. The entry on the cover was smudged but I could still make out Nana's maiden name: Rose Melhman.

Opening the cover revealed yellowed, brittle pages that were written in German or Yiddish; I was only able to read a few words. Some of the pages included calendar entries of dates in the margins and it appeared that Nana had kept some type of diary.

As I massaged the top of Cabby's head I said, "Cabby, Nana wrote this many, many years ago. But I think I know just the right person who can make these pages come alive!"

Chapter Twenty Six

I had wanted to call Cliff. But each time I would start to dial his number, I got cold feet and hung up. Now, after discovering Nana's diary, I finally had an excuse. So the next day at work, with my desk covered in files, phone messages and post it notes, and my belly growling for lunch, I picked up the phone. On the third ring, a voice answered.

"Hi, this is Cliff Warner."

"Cliff, you may not remember me. But we shared a train ride to Washington."

"Danielle?"

I was very surprised Cliff remembered my name since it had been almost a year.

"Yes."

"How are you?" He sounded pleased to be talking to me.

"Well, ah fine," I said nervously.

"I have thought about you."

"You have?"

"Sure. Have you gotten your own television series yet?"

"I think you may have me confused with someone else."

"No, I definitely remember you. And I remember telling you that you would be a star."

"Well that's sweet. But I am not a star. So will you still talk to me?"

"Of course."

"I did call to ask you something."

"Oh."

"My grandmother passed away," I said.

"I am very sorry. Was she ill?" he asked.

"No, she just went in her sleep. I guess it was her time."

"I suppose. But I don't think there is ever a time to go."

I paused and thought how sensitive he was.

"Anyway," I continued, "after her funeral, I went through her apartment and found a journal. I can only make out a few words as they are in German or Yiddish. But from the dates it looks like she wrote it after she was, ah..."

"Liberated," he said helpfully. "I remember you told me that she was in Mauthausen."

"Wow. You have a good memory."

"That's part of my job description, but thanks. And it was a common practice to ask survivors to write about their ordeal. Most did not want to because, well, their life was hell and who would want to remember. But the ones who did, their stories were amazing."

"Well, I was wondering if I could get the diary to you? Perhaps you have someone at work who could translate it. I would be happy to pay for any expenses."

"Danielle, this is what we do. We have an entire staff that speaks and reads German and Yiddish fluently."

"Oh, ok."

"But I have a better offer.'""

I listened.

"How about dinner? I know this very authentic Mexican restaurant in Santa Monica."

"Santa Monica? I thought I was calling you in Washington."

"Oh, well, you called my cell number. I never changed it. I need to do that but I have been so busy. Anyway, I took a job about six months ago with the Simon Wiesenthal Center in Los Angeles. So I now live in LA."

"Wow. That's great," I said, regretting I had now used the word "wow" twice in sixty seconds.

"So how about it?"

"Well, I don't know." I had very bad Mexican food shortly after moving to LA and was not anxious to repeat the experience. But my friends kept telling me that I had to give it another chance.

"Come on. You have to eat, right?" he said encouragingly.

I hesitated. "You are very kind."

"Then your answer is yes."

"Well, sure. It's yes."

"Great. Let me get the exact address and I will text it to you. Will tomorrow night at 7 work?"

"Ah, sure."

"All right. See you then."

For the rest of the afternoon, I could not think about work and I was guilty as charged for being on the government payroll at the taxpayer's expense. That night, I pulled out every item of clothing in my possession trying to decide what to wear. In the process, I discovered that I owned over three dozen shirts and blouses including eight white ones. Tossing all of the clothes on to the floor did not make Cabby happy either.

I arrived a few minutes late to the restaurant and I was hoping to freshen up. But Cliff was already standing by the hostess stand when I opened the door. As I extended my hand, he moved in to give me a polite hug and I looked a little startled.

"Hey, come on," he said. "We don't need to be so formal. We're veterans of the Starlight Express. And if we can survive a three hour train ride, we're passed the handshake stage."

"Ok," I giggled. "I am sorry I am late."

"You're not late. I just got here myself. Come, let's sit down."

The restaurant's décor was a decorator's nightmare with green, fire truck red, and orange painted walls and even more colorful paintings. In addition to the loudness of the walls, there was also the deafening mariachi music blaring on tape. We were immediately seated opposite each other by a window that looked onto the ocean. Seconds after we sat down, a waiter brought a bowl of chips with two bowls of orange colored sauce.

"I told you it was authentic. But customers don't come here for the atmosphere. They come because the food is incredible."

"Oh," I said looking at the two bowls.

"It's salsa," Cliff explained. "Try it," he said as he dipped a chip into one of the bowls and handed it to me.

"All right," I hesitated before shoving the chip into my mouth. "Wow, that is hot."

"Drink some water. You'll get used to it. I promise."

I had now said "wow" three times and feared that Cliff would think that my vocabulary was extremely limited.

"Margarita?" he offered.

"Sure," I nodded affirmatively, as I knew that would put out the fire.

"Señor," he called to our waiter. "Two margaritas with salt. Gracias."

Along with our drinks, chips and salsa, Cliff had placed that all too familiar Blackberry on the table and I was fearing it would be dinner for three. But to my welcomed surprise, he had set it to vibrate and ignored all his calls. However, when it buzzed several times in quick succession, I asked him if he was going to answer it.

"I am with you," he said. "And it is never that important."

I almost said "wow" again but caught myself and smiled.

"Your hair is different."

"Yeah, it was longer. Do you like it?"

"Very cute. Frames your face."

"Thanks."

I blushed and raised the multi-page menu to cover my face. The menu had more pages than the average short story and I must have looked a little bewildered.

"Can I suggest the chicken enchiladas? Do you like chicken?"

"I'm Jewish. What Jewish girl doesn't like chicken? We ate it every Friday night."

"Well, this is a little different. But it is the best."

Cliff was right about the food. At the end of the dinner, I proclaimed, "This was the best Mexican food I have ever had."

As we talked, I found Cliff to be just as charming as when I first met him on the train. And even better looking than I remembered.

"Please, let me pay for my share," I offered.

"Absolutely not," he said. "It is my pleasure. But I was hoping the evening was not going to end here. Would you like to take a walk on the pier?"

I gladly said yes.

"I wanted to call you," he said as we strolled down the pier.

"Why didn't you?" I asked.

"Well, I thought you were married."

"Why?"

"Well, it was the way you touched your ring finger. I did not see a ring but I did not want to pry. And I did not think it was my business to ask."

We sat down on a bench and I told Cliff that I had been married but I left out the most horrid of details. And as the pigeons walked between our feet searching for crumbs, our relationship was born.

"Come with me," he said, pulling my hand.

"Where?"

Across from where we were sitting was an instant photo booth.

"Remember I said you should be in pictures?"

"Yeah."

"Well, here's your chance."

We walked into the photo booth and posed for the silliest of photos. Afterwards, we continued our walk toward the end of the pier.

"So, how do like living in California?" Cliff asked.

"I miss the snow," I said.

"It snows here."

"It does?"

"Yeah, not too often. But you know the Hollywood sign? That's where it snows."

I accepted Cliff's explanation.

"So how about a ride on the Ferris wheel?" he suggested.

"Huh?" I replied.

Cliff pointed to the huge neon lit ride that was rotating. "Have you been on a Ferris wheel?"

I had never been on an arcade ride before and I was feeling my nervousness build inside me.

"Actually, I haven't."

As little kids, when my brother and I begged Dad to take us to Coney Island to go on the rides, my father would try to ask us why normal people would eagerly trade in their serenity of the ground for a chance to be tossed into the air like a vegetable in a blender. So we listened to him and stayed far away from amusement parks.

"Until tonight," Cliff said.

"What do you mean?" I said nervously.

"Come on." Cliff grabbed my arm and within minutes I was sitting in the "Wonder" wheel as we lifted and ascended to the stars.

Cliff was my tour guide. "That's Malibu. And see the planes? That's LAX."

On the second trip around, Cliff gave me his jacket. And as he put his arm around me, for the first time in a very long time I felt safe.

"Where did you park? Are you in the parking lot on third?" he asked as we alighted the ride.

"No, actually I took the bus. I don't have a car," I explained.

"Who in LA doesn't drive?"

"You're looking at her."

Cliff drove me home. His wonderful sense of humor meant I laughed like I had never done before. That night I fell in love with the kindest, gentlest man I had ever met.

"Goodnight."

I stared into Cliff's enchanting brown eyes as he kissed me. I found his aroma intoxicating. More importantly, my heart melted and for the first time in my life, I felt the pitter patter in my heart that Nana had always talked about.

The next day at work, my secretary Ellen came into my office with a package. It was from Cliff.

"Open it," Ellen said.

It was a snow globe of the Hollywood Hills and sign.

As I shook it I said, "He was right. It does snow in Hollywood."

Chapter Twenty Seven

Cliff and I had been dating almost four months when Thanksgiving arrived. I thought about Nana and how this would be the first year without her. Fortunately, I have all those wonderful Thanksgiving memories. I had talked to my father about going back to New York for the holiday, but by the time I looked into traveling, the price of plane tickets was sky high. My father was understandably disappointed but in the end understood.

Cliff had also thought about traveling east to be with his family and invited me to join him. But because of his work schedule, he too decided not to go. Fortunately, we would not be completely alone as a friend from his work invited us to her home. After a day of stuffing our mouths, it was after eleven o'clock in the evening when we arrived back at my apartment.

"I am so tired," I announced as I opened the door. Cliff nodded his head in agreement and immediately sat down on the couch. Cabby jumped up to join him.

"Must be that tryptophan in turkeys that makes people sleepy," Cliff mused as he picked up the remote and turned on the news.

"I am going to check if there are any messages. I'll be right back," I said.

"Hi Sweetie. Sorry I missed you. Hope you didn't eat too much. I went to your brother's house. Your sister-in-law made an attempt at cooking a turkey but nothing compares to Nana's. I was thinking about you. Say Hi to that nice boyfriend of yours. Maybe we can all be together next year. Love you."

"My dad left a message," I started to tell Cliff as I walked back into the room, but he had already nodded off on the couch.

"Come, lay down in the bed." I put my arm under Cliff's shoulder and woke up him up long enough to walk to my bedroom. Seconds later, he was covered with the thin top cover of my bedding and I watched him fall into a peaceful sleep.

But unlike Cliff, I was not tired. Perhaps I did not eat enough turkey. So I changed my clothes, covered myself in my green Afghan blanket, turned on the TV and settled into bed. To my delight, there was Rachael Ray as energetic as ever making a five course, thirty minute turkey dinner that would take me all week to prepare.

But after a few minutes of watching chopping and dicing, I too felt tired. So I pulled the top sheet below my chin, folded my hands behind my head, closed my eyes, and replayed the day beginning with the delicious food that was served and how my Nana's apple spiced cookies were such a hit. I next kissed Cliff on the forehead and stared at this precious being before I drifted off to sleep.

The morning sun was poking through the white shutters and as I tilted my head to meet the sun's rays. At the same time, Cliff raised his head looking somewhat lost.

"Did you sleep well?" I asked.

He did not answer but instead moved toward me, not quite touching, but I could feel his body.

"Did anything happen," he asked with a boyish grin.

Cliff and I had not had sex and this was the first time he had ever slept over.

"No. I took off your shoes and put you into bed and you went right to sleep."

"I was tired."

"You were."

"But I am not tired now."

Putting his arm behind my neck, I turned my head into his shoulder and he softly stroked the curve of my neck from ear to ear. It was ticklish but I did not move or speak. He then ran his hand along my arm, brushing the delicate hair gently. I remained perfectly still as he moved a little closer; his stomach was now against the small of my back and I felt the hardening of his manhood pressed into my thigh. He then slipped his hand under my shirt, circling his thumb around my navel as I shifted a bit to look at his face.

Cliff was so calming. As he moved closer, he circled my belly with his middle finger and I uttered a sigh as he placed his lips against mine. After that moment, we both knew we had transgressed. There was no turning around and I closed my eyes and felt the sensation of his fingers passing over the tips of my breasts, hardening, wrinkling the skin like a whisper of wind. His fingers teased my nipples and I moaned and sighed with each touch. As I shivered in delight, he ran his fingers slowly down my spine from the nape of my neck to the curve of my butt.

"One moment," I said as I reached for the condom packet that I had placed on my nightstand before I went to bed.

He smiled as he took it from my hand and tore the foil packet.

"As you already know, I am a very detailed person."

Cliff smiled again and moved on top of me, gently parting my legs as we both looked at each other. He was asking me for permission. And with my returned smile, he entered me, huge and fierce. The sensation that took over my entire essence was so piercingly pleasurable that I thought I would scream. He thrust slowly at first with deep measured strokes and I felt a throbbing fullness as he began to move inside me. But, without a sound, I was soon moving with him as he thrust deeper and withdrew, and then deeper. I became even more aroused as my body seemed to float and fall only to float again as Cliff positioned his right hand under my butt, allowing him to thrust even deeper. And with each movement, I arched my bottom to meet him as we moved rhythmically as one, ever faster and faster. I was moving with him like two figures locked together on a speeding carousel.

I moaned uncontrollably as his thrusting increased in speed. He then withdrew from my tightness almost to the tip, and then plunged back in as deep as he could possibly go and I cried silently with the sound of utter passion, sliding helplessly into the fire of my desire, so tightly woven. I then thrust my body up to meet his downward strokes, running my hands down his back.

"Harder," I begged, not wanting to utter a single word as I was losing all control of my body and mind. And over and over he drove into me.

"Harder." I repeated the word only to be heard by myself.

"Harder," without a sound I cried one more time as my body tightened. And I felt myself losing control, being swept away in a sea of blinding desire. My body was pouring its sweetness onto the throbbing head of his manhood as I cried out my desire with his name on my lips. With one more plunge, I crashed against the shore as my climax tore through me, sending rolling waves of pleasure throughout my body. I was unable to bear anymore as I cried out my passion. But I had one more wave to ride as Cliff erupted into me; his orgasm powerful as a rocket and sending his warm rush deep inside me.

"Wow," Cliff said as he rolled onto his side and we both giggled like little children at his choice of words.

I felt goose bumps from head to toe trying to wiggle my toes. And as Cliff spoke, his face was alive with love and I gazed into his endless brown eyes. For me, never before had I realized that such closeness could be a beautiful experience instead of one fraught with pain and terror.

PART

THREE

Chapter Twenty Eight

It had now been almost a year since I joined the LA District Attorney's office. Because of my trial experience as an assistant DA in New York, along with budget cuts which did not allow the department to replace attorneys who left, my seniority rapidly ascended.

Our office was headed by Ryan Preston and each Wednesday morning we met for calendar assignments. We also took turns bringing donuts.

"Ah, bear claws," Ido said with delight as he grabbed the artery clogger and took his seat. Ido was a second year DA like me. "Those are from B and B. I drive by there all the time."

"Yeah, my friend said the place has been on Olympic forever!" I said.

Ido joked, "I wonder if they cater?"

"Good morning everyone," Ryan said, grabbing a chocolate frosted donut as he took a seat at the head of the badly chipped and worn conference table.

"God's gift, these donuts, aren't they?" he said, taking a big bite. "Thanks, Danielle."

"Good morning," all of us responded in unison.

Despite the hectic work load and the responsibility of managing ten attorneys as well as a work staff, Ryan was surprisingly always in a great mood, which made him a great boss.

"Everyone here?" he asked, looking at Rochelle who was our court calendar coordinator.

"Tina is in 73 with pre-trials and Mike is doing the Watson prelim," Rochelle replied.

"How is that going?" Ryan asked.

"He says ok but the defense attorney is pushing hard for a deal. Otherwise, his client is looking at three strikes."

"Well, his client should have thought about that before he held up that liquor store and knocked around the clerk with the barrel of his gun. He should spend the rest of his life in jail. Ok, let's move on," Ryan said as he dumped dozens of manila files on the table that had been neatly stacked in a banker's box. He began to assign cases that were going to trial.

"People vs. Hartinger, case number SM-078675633," Ryan announced as he opened the file and read from the notes. "Defendant is charged with PC459. He was offered a first time plea with 60 days, credit for time served, three years' probation and declined. Prelim found sufficient evidence to bind him over. Plea offered again but defendant refused. Now set for trial on 11-14, Department 38. That is Judge Wilson. How's your calendar?"

Ido had just reached for another donut and cleared his throat. "I am open. I can take it."

"It's yours," Ryan announced and launched the file like a hockey puck into Ido's waiting palms.

"All right, moving on, People vs. Feingold, case number SM-076542084. Defendant is charged with shop lifting and," Ryan paused as he reviewed the file, "well, it seems Mrs. Feingold has good taste as she tried to walk out of Gucci's with a belt and blouse in her purse. And," he paused again, "her attorney is claiming his client had just returned from a vacation and was suffering from jet lag and therefore was soooooo tired that she was not in her right frame of mind and did not know what she is doing. He therefore wants the charges reduced to a trespass. Well, Mrs. Feingold, the People of the State of California don't buy your defense. Ok, Joe, this will probably end up with her taking the plea but I want you to handle this one."

"What's the date?"

"11-15."

"Yeah, no problem. Send it down."

Another file was launched down the middle of the wobbly conference table.

Ryan continued through at least twenty more cases before announcing, "People vs. Robbins, case number SM6767554444. Defendant charged." Ryan paused to read the notes in the file. "He was originally charged with PC 273.5. And later charges were enhanced to PC 262, Marital

Rape. Why do I know this case, Rochelle?"

"He's the son of some studio head and the dad's publicist keeps trying to keep it hushed up."

"Oh yeah, I remember now. This case is old," Ryan flipped through at least an inch of paper in the file. "The recommendation by the arresting officer was to file the case as a rape. But when the wife was later questioned, she said she did not want to testify. So it was filed as a domestic violence. We have had two pre trials, the offer is the standard first time but the husband isn't biting. We made a few offers but it looks like the victim is wavering."

"And the wife has now filed for divorce," Rochelle said.

"But they were still married at the time of the attack?" I said.

"Yeah, but I think they were separated. Anyway, marital rape is a tough one," Ryan commented as he read the file notes.

"Ryan." I held up my hand.

"Yeah, go ahead, Danielle." Ryan momentarily lifted his head.

"I would like a shot at it."

"I am not sure. You have a lot of…"

I interrupted. "A woman just doesn't throw out the word rape. That is what she told the police."

Ryan looked over his half eyes. "Yeah but there are no pictures, no bruising, no rape kit."

"When I was in law school, I wrote a paper on marital rape for my law review. And I remember some crazy statistic that over 70 percent of married women never report that they were raped."

Ryan continued to flip through the file as I rattled off some more statistics.

"But in this case," Ryan said, "the parties were separated. They weren't living as husband and wife, and I'm not sure we can get a jury to buy the marital rape."

"But neither party had filed for divorce. So, they were still married."

"It's a tough one, Danielle," he warned. "This is an election year and I'm not sure we should be spending taxpayer money on…."

"Let me work the file up and talk to the victim," I requested. "Besides, just because she took off her ring, doesn't change the fact that she was forced to do something against her will."

"Allegedly."

"Allegedly. But let me talk to her. If we can't get her to cooperate, then I will recommend that we dispose of it. But maybe she needs some encouragement. We owe her that much."

"Fine," Ryan said, sliding the file to me, which stopped midway because of its size. "Make contact with her and report to me next week."

That night, I took the file home. I wanted to be completely prepared before I called the victim the next day.

_____

"Hello," the voice answered hesitantly.

"Hi, is this June?"

"It is."

"My name is Danielle Landau. I am with the district attorney's office. Is this a good time to call?"

June was an elementary school teacher. At first she was resistant to my suggestion that we get together to talk. But after a little prodding, she agreed to meet the next day at a Starbucks near her school.

"Hi, you must be June," I said when she entered the café.

It was our office policy to have pictures of all witnesses and I recognized her from her photo.

"Can I buy you a cup of coffee?"

"Thanks. Ah, decaf. Otherwise, I will be up all night."

"I know what you mean. I will be right back."

Waiting on line, I observed June over my shoulder. She seemed nervous as she kept touching her hair and looking at her watch. I knew that I needed to quickly put her at ease or this would be a very short meeting and her husband would end up getting the break of his life.

"Here you go. I brought you some cream and sugar."

"Thanks."

"First off, thank you for agreeing to meet with me," I started.

The coffee shop was noisy but I sensed a bubble of silence between June and me.

"I know this is difficult," I continued.

"It is. I just did not want to relive this and wanted it to go away," June replied.

"I understand. But your husband is charged with a very serious crime. And you must have felt very angry about what he did or you would not have called the police and told them what you said."

"I did, I mean I do. But."

"Well, I have read your file and I feel you have a strong case. But we can't prosecute it without your cooperation."

"I know. I have been told that. But there's no evidence of the attack," June said in a defeatist tone.

"That's right. Other than your word against his, we have no independent evidence."

"And we were, I mean, we still were married. But I knew if I didn't do something, I would end up like that girl."

"Girl. What girl?"

"You know," June said. "Laci Peterson. They found her body. She was in her ninth month."

As June said that name, a chill rushed through my body and I froze as I thought about Jacob.

"Are you all right?" June asked.

"I am sorry," I apologized. "I am. I just remembered something I needed to do at work. I am sorry. Please continue."

"Well, I need to move on. I have filed for divorce but I don't think I could do this. And his family is very powerful."

"June, you used the word rape when you spoke to the police. That means that you were forced to, against your will. And just because there was a wedding band on your finger did not give him the right to do that to you."

June scrutinized every word I said with her eyes roving over my face.

"I know."

"By you not doing going forward, you are opening the door for him to do this again. And next time, there could be even greater consequences."

"I don't know," June looked away.

"June. I need to tell you something. I was where you were several years ago." Her eyes were again focused on mine. "But I was scared."

As I continued, June set her cup of coffee on the table.

"And I didn't do anything. Instead I ran away. Please don't follow my mistake."

My eyes provided her a reflection.

"I need to think about it," she said, reaching for a tissue from her purse to wipe the tear that was about to roll down her cheek.

"I understand." I covered her hand with mine.

"It is so hard. And I want to do the right thing, but…"

"I know." I flipped open the file. And we do have another pretrial hearing on the 26th, so perhaps he will take our offer."

"I wasn't aware of that date."

"You wouldn't be," I reassured her. "The court schedules hearings to allow the defense to meet with the DA and try to negotiate a deal. So far, his attorney is still holding out that we will drop the charges. And, well, without you, we may have to. And your husband will get away with what he did to you. But at this point, we're holding firm. So, if you do decide to testify, and I hope you do, I promise you, I will do everything in my power to bring you justice."

"I know you will," June said.

"But, please understand, I will need your answer before the next hearing so I can advise the court that we are ready to proceed with trial." I handed June my business card. "If I am not available when you call, because I am in court a lot, please leave a message. I check my messages every day and will return your call. I promise."

"Thank you for your help."

"I do want to help you."

The next afternoon I received a message from June. And after obtaining Ryan's approval, I immediately began preparing for the trial of my life.

Chapter Twenty Nine

The wheels of justice were turning even slower today as Ido was out with the flu. As a result, I had double duty trying to cover his and my hearings. I had just walked out of Department 33 rushing to my next appearance when I heard my name.

"Ms. Landau."

"Yes," I said, slowly turning in the direction of the towering radio announcer sounding voice as I balanced my attaché over my shoulder and at least a dozen files in my hands.

"May I have a word?"

Without offering me an opportunity to say no, he proceeded.

"My name is Michael Pontrelli."

Pontrelli was a very tall, tan and dapper gentleman dressed in what I was sure was a very expensive custom made suit, flashy cufflinks, and a neatly pressed handkerchief that complemented his bright red tie.

I juggled the files to reach his outstretched hand.

"Hello. Do I know you?" I asked even though I did.

"No but you will soon," he responded with confidence. "I am the new attorney on the Robbins file."

Pontrelli had handled many high profile criminal clients and loved the media attention. But I did not want to give him the satisfaction of knowing that I was familiar with him.

"Oh, well I wasn't aware that he had changed attorneys. Have you…"

Again, he interrupted. "Yes, I filed a substitution on the case. I know my secretary sent you a copy. It should be in your office."

"Well, it probably hasn't reached the file yet. Anyway, I am sorry. I am really late," I said, straining to expose my wrist so that I could see my watch, and I started to walk away. As I did, he stepped in front of me.

"I would like to set a time to sit down and go over the file with you and see if there is some middle ground."

"Middle ground?" I asked curiously. "Your client is charged with a very serious offense," I reminded him as I walked towards the direction of my next courtroom while he tried to slip his business card into my hand, which was losing the battle of trying to juggle all of the files.

"I am sorry. As I just said, I am late. But call my office."

"I was hoping I could buy you coffee or…"

This time I interrupted before he could finish.

"Mr. Pontrelli."

"Michael."

"Mr. Pontrelli. When you want to talk to the DA, you come to our office." Knowing I had won the first battle, I walked away. But I also knew the next encounter would not be that easy.

The next day, Pontrelli called my office to make sure I would be there when he stopped by.

"Counselor."

I looked up and there stood Pontrelli, who had perched himself at the doorpost. Today's outfit consisted of a double breasted suit, blue shirt, white collar and cuffs, and a red tie that would light up a room, and even flashier cufflinks than what he wore yesterday.

"Did we have an appointment? I didn't see anything on my calendar," I said matter-of-factly.

I was also embarrassed by the look of my office as it was a study in clutter. The first thing you noticed when you entered was the many stacks of files scattered on the floor. My desk was littered with post it notes and phone messages. There were also two dented metal file cabinets with draws that would not close next to the window separated by a rubber plant that I have nursed back to life so many times. My desk was walled in by more piles of files and behind my chair was a large cork board covered with all colors of more post it notes which I used as my calendar to keep track of my courtroom assignments. In front of the desk were two unmatched chairs which were barely recognizable as they too were covered in files that almost completely obscured the seats. There was also my Nike gym bag. And a sweater that sat all alone on the hook behind the door which I would wear because they could never regulate the air conditioning.

"No, but your secretary said you might have a few minutes," Pontrelli said.

"Well, have a seat," I said, clearing a chair so that he would not have to stand.

"Thank you," he answered as he slowly lowered himself to the chair.

"I did find the substitution of attorney in the file."

"By the way, some of my colleagues who have sparred with you in court said that you are very impressive."

I was warned that he would try to patronize me and I ignored the comment.

"So how can I help you?" I asked.

"Well, it is really how we can help each other," he began.

"Interesting. So how is that?"

"Ms. Landau, I am not one to skirt the issues so let me get right to the point."

"You have my full attention."

"My client is very sorry for what happened that night."

I was surprised by his choice of words as I remembered Jacob's version of his sorry speech.

"I am not the one he needs to deliver that message to. There is a victim. I am only the prosecutor."

"Please let me finish."

"Go ahead."

"And he has sought counseling."

"I am aware."

"And as you know, the parties have filed for divorce."

"Yes, I know that too."

"But he does not want this to haunt him the rest of his life."

Haunt him. Another interesting choice of words. I became outraged but contained my emotion.

"Considering all the facts, and the people's questionable evidence, my client would be willing to plead to a trespass," Pontrelli offered.

"Trespass?" I repeated the word in disgust, no longer able to contain my outrage. His now demanding tone of voice reminded me of how Jacob spoke to me.

"Yes," Pontrelli explained, "that way, your client would be spared the stress of testifying and they can both go on with their lives. Plus the county will save a lot of taxpayer money which I am sure your boss will be happy about since this is an election year."

Having made his pitch, Pontrelli moved back in his chair and crossed his arms behind the chair back.

"So what are your thoughts, counselor?"

I had always hated when anyone referred to me as counselor as it came off as so condescending.

"Mr. Pontrelli."

"Michael. My friends call me Michael."

"Mr. Pontrelli, we are not friends and I would prefer to retain a professional relationship. I know you have your job to do. But let me first say that if the district attorney did not think that we had a strong case, we would not being going forward. And we have made a reasonable offer to your client to plead to charges and we would seek only probation. That being said, what your client did was a crime."

"But they were married."

"Let me finish. Yes they were married but that marriage license does not give your client the right to sexually assault his spouse. "

Pontrelli leaned forward in his chair. "Ms. Landau, are you going to tell me that you are going to try and convince a jury that she had nothing to do with this?"

"What are you implying?"

"Come on." Pontrelli's tone of voice had now taken on a threatening sound. "It takes two to tango. It will all come out. Your client has a history of exaggeration. I will eat her up alive on the witness stand. And then, at the end of the day, you will have a weeping client who will be stuck in therapy for years trying to put her life back together. So let me ask you. Is that what you want on your conscience? Or should the DA's office be spending the taxpayers' money going after criminals, instead of a husband and wife who decided to rub one out for old time's sake?"

"Mr. Pontrelli, please don't lecture me and tell me how to do my job."

"I am just saying…"

"Mr. Pontrelli, your attitude is disgusting. And the only offer on the table is for your client to plead to PC262. Take it or I will see you in trial."

Seeing that he was getting nowhere, Pontrelli tried using a legal argument to persuade me.

"Counselor, there is a presumption in the law. That is, since the parties were separated at the time, the court will consider Mrs. Robbins' state of mind. And since she later filed for divorce, she had the state of mind that she was no longer married. Therefore I will argue that it is not marital rape. Also, because she did not file for divorce immediately after the alleged attack, perhaps she thought the marriage could be saved. The jury will need to ponder her state of mind."

"Mr. Pontrelli. June's father died the next week of a massive heart attack. So I think she had other things on her mind besides running to the court to file for divorce."

"I am sorry. Very sorry. I did not know."

His show of emotion lasted only seconds as he went right back to arguing his case. But not wanting to hear any more I said, "You know, you are really good. For a moment, albeit a very brief moment, I thought you actually cared!" I got up from my seat and walked toward the door. And just when I thought our conversation was over, Pontrelli pulled out one more card.

"I know what the DA pays and you could be making bigger money working for a firm. Think about. I can help you if you help me."

"I think we are done here," I said pointing to the door. "I will see you in trial."

Chapter Thirty

Unlike an attorney in private practice where you are in trial with one client at a time, the district attorney's office does not allow for such luxury. Instead, we are involved in many cases at different stages of the court process at the same time. Fortunately, with the start of the Robbins rape trial only two weeks away, Ryan was considerate of the time I needed to prepare as well as the importance of obtaining a conviction, and he eased up on my work load.

In organizing my case, I knew that my biggest challenge was overcoming the so-called "he said, she said" argument that Pontrelli would make by trying to show that June was not believable. To defeat that argument, I had to carefully craft questions to ask my client that would leave no room for doubt in the minds of the jurors as to what actually happened that evening.

Sitting at my office desk, I was starting to fall asleep when my Blackberry rang.

"Hi Cliff. I was thinking about you. Are you upset that we are not going away this weekend?"

As a surprise, Cliff had bought tickets for a wine festival in Santa Rosa. I had been looking forward to going away together for the first time but the trial had taken over my weekend plans.

"I was never upset," he said. "And we'll make other plans soon. I just want you to put that bastard away. So how is it going?"

"I am still here," I said, staring at my desk which had now become a sea of paper, files, notes, paper clips, yellow highlight markers, and a service of six coffee mugs. "I am going to leave soon. I just wanted to get some more work done."

"Sweetie. It is 7 o'clock. And I don't like you sitting there alone."

"I am not alone. The janitors just came in to say good night."

"That's great. I hope you are on a first name basis."

"I am only going to work another hour and grab something on the way home."

"Ok. But I want you to look at something. Are you near your computer?"

"I am chained to it. Ok, hold on. I need to fine my mouse. It is buried here somewhere. Ok, I see your message."

"Open the attachment. It is a picture."

"All right. I just clicked on it. Damn."

"What?" Cliff asked.

"It is that stupid hour glass," I complained. "We have such a slow connection at work."

"Be patient."

"Ok, ok. All right. It is starting to load. What is it?"

"It is not what but who."

"I see a nice looking older lady. But, ah, who is she? Wait. Oh my god, look at that hair. Oh my god. You found Irene!"

Chapter Thirty One

Two days before trial was to start, Pontrelli made another attempt to bully me into offering his client a reduced charge of trespass. When that was not successful, he charged forward calling the District Attorney for all of Los Angeles. Fortunately his calls were not returned which I interpreted as a sign of the confidence that my boss had in me. Of course, I now had the both the legal burden of proving that I was right as well as the professional burden of preserving my reputation.

Along with the relentless efforts from Pontrelli, the son of a movie studio head in Los Angeles about to go on trial for rape created a lot of interest in the media. As expected, our office received several inquiries from reporters seeking interviews. However, it was the DA's policy to decline such requests. Not getting the cooperation that they wanted, the media ran free with their portrayals of my client as a vindictive, gold digging soon to be ex-wife seeking revenge and a big payoff in a civil trial that would most likely follow the criminal case regardless of the outcome.

Having the media cloud overhead caused me great concern as I feared it would be difficult to empanel a jury that would not already have been poisoned by what they had read in print or online. However, after five days of arduous jury selection, I felt confident that we had found 12 jurors and four alternates who were not biased and would objectively consider all of the evidence before making their decision. And so, after a full day of opening statements, I was ready to call my first witness.

I arrived very early that morning. Except for Jennie, the clerk who was just turning on her computer, there is was no one else yet in the courtroom.

"Good Morning. How are you?" I asked her.

"I am fine, Ms. Landau."

Jennie was normally very chatty but she seemed disengaged this morning as I went about organizing my files on the counsel table.

"There should be fresh water in the pitcher," Jennie pointed out.

"Thanks."

I told June she did not need to arrive until a few minutes before nine. And as I sat alone at the counsel table, I gazed at the courtroom. The walls were dark paneled, the seal of justice hung on the wall behind the judge, two rows on the right side of the courtroom made up the jury box, and in front of the judge was the seat for his clerk.

But from my experience in law school, I learned that a courtroom is more than just furniture and fixtures. I remembered how one of my professors so eloquently described where many of us would be spending the greater part of our professional lives.

He said that, in many ways, the courtroom resembles a church or a synagogue, or at least a place where people assemble to pray. Its benches look like pews. The man who presides is robed in black. He renders judgment from a sort of sanctuary from a large table, usually elevated, set apart many times by what looks like an altar rail. The bailiff functions as his acolyte and the jury could be his choir. Proper reverence must be maintained in the courtroom; when the judge enters, the people stand. To speak with him, you must ask to approach the bench. People always dress respectfully for the courtroom and, if they must speak, they do so in hushed, whispered voices.

And the judge has the power to silence people in the courtroom and even to hold them "in contempt of court." He knows that the tension in the courtroom is healthy because it focuses everyone on the serious business before them. It is where life and death issues are decided, where a man's future hangs in the balance, where fortunes are won or lost, debts are settled, and guilt is proven or not. The judge knows that if he dilutes this tension, he lessens the importance of his role, his words, and his courtroom. The judge also understands a basic paradox: if the courtroom has the atmosphere of everyday life, then it no longer has any relevance for everyday life.

"Hi, Danielle," June said as she sat down next to me.

To add dramatic flair, Pontrelli staged his arrival to enter with his client, which was most unsettling for June. Upon seeing his entrance, I instructed her not to look at the opposing counsel's table. When all the parties and their respective attorneys were in place, the room took on its own unique sound of silence as the judge took the bench.

"Good morning, ladies and gentlemen," announced Judge Faust.

Judge Faust was a man in his early sixties with a sharp wit. I was very pleased when he was assigned the case as I had always found him to be fair and objective. He was also a master at controlling his courtroom.

"Good morning, your honor," the room responded in unison.

"Are you ready to proceed, Ms. Landau?"

"I am, your honor. The people call June Robbins."

Part of my extensive trial preparation included educating June about the ways in which our judicial system is riddled with double standards for women as opposed to men. This especially applies to cases involving rape. June would be judged not only by her testimony but by how she expressed herself. The jurors would also form opinions by how she looked and dressed. Anticipating that the actual trial would last at least four days, I told June that I had to approve each outfit she would wear.

For her first day on the stand, June was dressed in a dark blue suit and a white blouse with her hair softly swept back so as to not cover her eyes. As her name was announced, my client pushed her chair back from the counsel table and walked slowly to the witness box. I followed her but stood a few feet to her side so as to not block the jury's view.

"Do you solemnly swear to tell the truth, the whole truth and nothing but the truth so help you God?"

A juror's first impression of a witness is critical and it was so important that June convey that she was friendly, kind, and most importantly, believable. To this end, I had instructed June to look into the faces of the jurors and modestly smile before she even spoke her first words.

"I do."

June also spoke softly and I was concerned that the jury would not stay concentrated on her testimony if they had to strain to hear her.

"You will need to speak up," the judge admonished her.

"I am sorry. I will," she smiled.

"Go ahead, Ms. Landau," said Judge Faust.

The first part of questioning a witness is known as laying a foundation. After establishing June's education and employment, I began my questions about her relationship with her husband.

"Were you renting or buying where you were living with your husband?"

"It was a condominium so we were buying."

"Please, if you will, identify the source of the down payment to purchase the condominium."

"Well, soon after we were married, my husband's parents helped us."

"For the record, is that where you were living when the assault took place?"

"Objection," shouted Pontrelli, bolting from his seat. "Counsel has chosen the word 'assault' which implies a crime has been committed. Your honor, my client has been charged but has not been convicted. I ask that the record be stricken and that the jury be instructed to disregard counsel's question."

Pontrelli was dead on right in his objection. And if the jury was instructed as Pontrelli requested, I would appear as a novice and out of my league for making an error that even the most inexperienced attorney would not have made.

"Your honor, I will rephrase the question," I said.

"Thank you Ms. Landau."

"Ms. Robbins," I continued, "for the record, is that where you were living where the alleged incident occurred?"

"Yes," June replied.

"And how long after you were married did you separate?"

"Not quite two years."

"And if you could tell the court, why did you separate?"

"Well, Steven had a gambling problem. He is a writer and did a lot of freelance work. He was also working on his own screenplay. But when he was not working he gambled."

"Can you elaborate?"

"Yes. He would bet online on the horses, on football, anything that he could place a bet on."

"With what money?"

"Well, that was the problem," June explained. "He didn't earn much and was using our credit cards to make bets. We talked and talked about it and he always said he was going to quit and get help. But it never happened. Meanwhile, the credit card bills would come in every month and we did the best to pay them. But we could never pay in full and we got behind and it was ruining our credit."

"So what did you do?"

"A few times, his parents helped us out but I was embarrassed to keep going to them. And after Steven had told me that he had quit, I believed him. But then one day, I came home early and opened the mail. Usually he beat me to it. But on that day, I found bills from credit card companies I didn't even know about. He had apparently opened these accounts without my knowledge. Anyway, we had a big fight and I told him I could not continue living with him."

"What was his reaction?"

"He said again said that he would get help."

"How did you respond?"

"I told him that I had heard it before and was tired and didn't want keep going and I wanted to separate."

"Did he say he would move out?"

"He wasn't happy but I wasn't budging. And a few days later, when I was at work, he texted me that he had moved in with a friend of his."

"After you separated, did you stay in touch?"

"We did. But only by text. Usually, something came in the mail for him and I let him know."

"Did you text him for any other reasons?"

"I did. When we got married, we received a lot of beautiful gifts.

And many of them, well, we never took them out of their boxes as we had no room to put anything. So they stayed in the second bedroom which we weren't using. But when we separated, we thought about selling the condo but the market was bad. And I couldn't afford the mortgage payment on my own. So I texted him that I wanted to rent out the second room."

"Go on."

"And I asked him if there was anything that he wanted. There were so many presents from his family and friends and I just didn't feel right keeping everything."

"And did you get a response to your text?"

"Yes. He said that there were a few things that he wanted and he asked if he could come over."

"And how did you respond?"

"I told him my schedule. That I had been working a lot. But he should give me some times that might work."

"Did you at any time consider getting together as a chance at reconciliation?"

"No, absolutely not."

"And did you get the impression from anything that your husband said or wrote that he saw this opportunity to see you as a chance of reconciliation?"

"Objection," Pontrelli called out. "Asking for an opinion."

"Withdrawn," I said.

"All right, go on Ms. Landau," the judge confirmed.

"When did you next hear from Mr. Robbins?" I asked.

"I think it was about a week later. I got a text that he wanted to come by that night."

"And what did you do?"

"I texted him back that I had a meeting after school but seven o'clock would work."

"Did you prepare in any way for your husband coming over?"

"I am not sure I understand your question."

"Well, did you tell him to come for dinner? Did you put out any food? Did you do anything that would make it feel inviting?"

"No."

"All right. Go on."

"Well, it was a few minutes before seven. I knew this because I had just looked at my watch. And I received another text from Steven. He said that he was on the 10 freeway, there was a lot of traffic, and that he would be about 15 minutes late. So I started to grade some papers and a short time thereafter, the doorbell rang."

"Do you remember what you said when you opened the door?"

"Yes, I was surprised to see that he was holding a bottle of wine. And I asked him what that was for."

"And what did he say?"

"He said something about extending an olive branch. That he did not want to fight. He only wanted things to be amicable."

"Go on."

"I said that I also did not want to fight. I took the bottle from his hands and put it on the coffee table."

"Did you open it?"

"No, it just sat there."

"Then what?"

"Well, we made some small talk. He asked how my dad was. My father had recently had surgery and I thought that was nice that he cared. And then he asked if we could go into the other room."

"Where the wedding presents were?"

"Yes."

"Was there a bed in the room?"

"No, from the time we moved in we kept the room as a catch all. It was filled with boxes and we never really unpacked the room. When we got married, we kept many of the gifts there that we were not using right away. I think I already told you that."

"That is ok."

"And then?"

"Well, I picked up a yellow pad that was on the floor and I was going to make a list of anything that he wanted. There were a few boxes that were not marked with what was inside and he opened them."

"And what happened next?"

"Steven said that he really didn't want anything. That he had no room either. And I could keep everything. He then got up and asked if we can go into the other room."

"What room?"

"The living room. So I said ok and walked into the living room."

"Did Steven join you?"

"No. He walked into the kitchen. I thought he was getting a glass of water. But instead he came out holding the wine bottle opener and two wine glasses. And he sat down on the couch."

"Where you were sitting?"

"I wasn't."

"All right, and then?"

"Steven asked if we could have a glass of wine and that he would then be on his way."

"Go on."

"But I was a little reluctant. I just did not think it was right and did not want to give Steven the wrong impression."

"So what did you say?"

"I told him that I had a lot of papers to grade."

"And how did he respond?"

"He said something about it is only one glass of wine and again repeated that he would then leave."

"How did you answer him?"

"I said ok."

"What happened next?"

"Steven sat on the chair facing the couch where I sat. And he poured us each a glass. And we started to talk and he reminded me of when we first met, and our first date and he was being very nice."

"Did you finish your wine?"

"I did."

"And did he pour you another glass."

"He poured both of us another glass of wine. And we talked some more and then he looked at his watch and said he should be going but wanted to make a toast. But when he raised his glass, he asked if he could join me on the couch."

"And what did you do?"

June took a long breath before answering.

"I was stupid. I thought he was going to leave so I said ok."

"And did he make a toast?"

"No."

"Why not?"

"Well, as he sat down, he put his arm around me and said that he did a lot of thinking and that he thought we should get back together."

"What did you do?"

"I did not respond and moved towards the other end of the couch."

"And what did he do?"

"He moved again towards me and leaned in to kiss me."

"Did he kiss you?"

"He tried to but I blocked him with my hand."

"Ms. Landau," Judge Faust interrupted. "This is sounding like a soap opera. I assume you have some point you are trying to make?"

"Yes, your honor. I just need a little leeway."

"Very well. Proceed."

"And what happened next?" I said, returning my focus to June.

"I told him it was over. That he was upsetting me. That I had work to do and he needed to leave. And I got up and started to walk towards the door."

"Then what?"

"He stayed on the couch and did not move."

"What did you do?"

"I walked back over to him and tried to take the glass out of his hand and I told him he needed to leave.

"You said you tried to take the glass out of his hand."

June started to cry.

"Take your time."

June cleared her throat. "That's right. As I reached for the glass, he pulled my hand towards him and sat me in his lap. And then he kissed me on my mouth and held me very tight. I could not pull out of his grip."

"Did he say anything?"

"It was disgusting."

"I understand. But you need to tell the court what he said."

June was silent.

"Ms. Robbins," Judge Faust said. "Do you need to take a break?"

"I am ok."

"Very well, proceed."

"He told me that I wanted him and he was ready to give it to me."

I turned to face the jurors as I asked June to continue.

"Go on."

"He kissed me but this time with my free hand I pushed him in his chest. And as I did, he spilled the glass of wine all over his shirt. And this made him very angry."

"Did you say anything?"

"I shouted 'please leave.' And he started to get up. And I thought he was going to walk out the door. But instead he came towards me with this look of fire in his eyes."

In all the sessions that I had prepped June, she had never used this expression before. And as I heard June use those words, images of Jacob flooded my mind.

"I had never seen this look before. He grabbed me by the hips and pulled me against him as he licked my neck."

"What did you do?"

"I said 'what are you doing? What are you doing? Please stop. It's over.' But he didn't hear me or did not want to hear me and he pushed me in the bedroom and threw me down on the bed."

"At this point, how much had you had to drink?"

"Just the one glass."

"And how much had he had?"

"He had finished his first glass but the second glass was full when he spilled it on himself."

"So would you say your husband was under the influence of alcohol?"

"Objection," Pontrelli said. "No foundation has been made that the witness can offer such an opinion."

"Sustained," said Judge Faust.

"I will rephrase the question," I said. "On prior occasions, had you ever seen your husband acting under the influence of alcohol?"

"Yes."

"And this time, would you say his behavior was like those other times?"

"No."

"Why not?"

"Whenever we were at a party, and he had had too much to drink, Steven would get silly, or very quiet. And if I drove, he would fall asleep in the car."

"So how was this time different?"

"This time he was on fire. He was mad."

"Ok, so he pushed you onto the bed. Was he on the bed with you?"

"No, he stood at the foot of the bed staring at me."

"And what did you do?"

"I slowly moved to the side of the bed and tried to get off. But he moved in front of me and put his hands on my shoulder and kissed me again on my neck."

"Go on."

"I was scared. And he continued to kiss me. And then he put his hand under my chin and raised my face so that I was looking directly at him. I told him that he was scaring me but he just grinned. He then put his hands under my top and squeezed me."

"Where did he squeeze you?"

"My breasts.   He had both hands on my breasts and he held them tight as he stared into my face."

"Did he say anything?"

"He went on that I was the only one he had ever loved and…' June paused.

"And what?" I prompted her.

"That I had a degree and he was not as smart as me and I wanted to cry but I held back. I knew I needed to stay calm," June said.

"Why?"

"Because of the way he looked at me. Steven weighs probably twice as much as me and he worked out and was very strong. I thought he would hurt me if I resisted."

"What happened next?"

"He lifted my top over my head and started kissing me over my bra and kept asking do I like that, do I like that but I did not answer. He then turned me over on my stomach, unhooking my bra, and quickly rolled me over again and started to kiss my breasts."

"What did you do?"

"I was pleading, 'please stop. Please stop.'"

"And did he?"

"I thought he did. My eyes were closed and I felt him get off the bed. So I slowly opened my eyes but…."

June sobbed.

"Ms. Robbins. Do you need to take a break?" Judge Faust inquired again.

Without answering the judge, June composed herself and raced to finish her next thought.

"He was standing completely naked at the side of the bed with his hands on his hips like showing off and I closed my eyes again."

"June, I know this is difficult," I said gently. "But I have to ask you a few more questions. And you have to tell the court everything that happened."

"I understand," she stammered through her tears.

"Why didn't you run out of the room?"

"I told you. He was strong. I feared he would hurt me."

"All right. What did he do next?"

I could sense June was anticipating this part of her testimony as she pulled her shoulders back and rearranged herself in the chair.

"I felt both his hands around my neck and I felt his penis pressing against my mouth. My mouth was closed and he yelled 'suck on it, bitch.' So I opened my mouth and his penis slipped inside. He then jerked with his hands my head back and forth. And he kept saying, 'You like that, I know you do.'"

June's cheeks turned beet red.

"And I wanted it to be over but he yelled 'your lesson is not over, bitch.' And with his hand pushed into the center of my back, he climbed on top of me. He continued kissing my breasts and I remember tears streaming from my eyes. 'Don't cry,' he said as he blotted my tears with his fingers. 'I am going to make you sleep so well tonight,' he said as he pulled down my pants and threw them across the room. I turned my head to my side but he jerked it back.

"'Look at me,' he shouted. 'Look at me.'

"More tears trickled down my cheeks and I was trembling beneath him as I felt his hand slide down between my legs as he pushed one finger inside me and then another. I winced. But again he ordered me to look at him as he squatted on his knees between my legs. He then spread my legs as he jabbed me."

"You mean he started to have intercourse with you," I clarified.

"This is so embarrassing," June's voice quivered.

"I know it is. But I need you to answer the question."

"Yes, he started to have intercourse."

"And what did you do?"

"I cried 'please stop, please stop' but he looked at me with an obnoxious grin."

I handed June the box of tissues that was on the clerk's desk.

"All right. Please continue."

"I felt him enter me again like you would stab someone with a knife. He pushed into me with such force that I saw stars. And then he stayed in me without moving. And then he pulled out and jabbed me again with even more force."

As she spoke, my mind recalled in vivid images the night I was attacked. In silence, I mirrored June's testimony.

"He picked his head up and said with disdain, 'Do you like that?' and he jabbed me again and repeated the phrase "Do you like that?" And he kept asking me over and over, do you like that, do you like that."

"Does that feel good?" He slowly pulled out and then thrust harder, pounding his fat belly against me and again pausing.

"And after three or four more jabs, he grabbed my hips and then the back of my knees and held my legs up in the air. And as I looked through my legs, all I could see was his face and his eyes were on fire. And then he began thrusting."

"And as I felt my feet dangling over the edge of the mattress, I could see his blood pooling in the whites of his eyes."

"He moved inside me slowly and then stopped and slowly and then stopped and his hands were gripping my hips so tight. And then he moved his hands to my breasts and again squeezed them as he picked up his pace and this time he trusted harder and harder and he squeezed me harder and harder.

"And with each further thrust, my body seized while my heart froze."

"And his breathing got louder and louder and he was squeezing me so hard I thought I could feel his pulse through the palms of his hands. He was so strong. And from the weight of his body, I could not move."

"I could not breathe."

"His pace quickened and I wanted it to end."

"And I wanted it to end. Tumbala, Tumbala, Tumbalalaiku."

"He thrust one more time and made this horrific sound."

"Finally, as if a gunshot exploded in the air, his body arched and he

made the most disgusting sound before crashing back on top of me, leaving me bare of all normalcy and sanity."

"Ms. Landau, are you all right?"

Tumbala, Tumbala, Tumbalalaiku."

"Ms. Landau?"

I heard the judge call my name but my body was frozen and I did not respond.

"Ms. Landau," he repeated again.

I took a deep breath. But still the words did not come out.

"Ms. Landau."

"I am sorry, your honor. I just need a minute."

I took a deep breath and collected my thoughts. "Ok June, I know this is very difficult. But please tell the court what happened next."

June continued, "I wanted so badly for him to move off me but he rested his head on my shoulder and I could feel his heart pounding through his shirt. I kept my eyes closed. I could not breathe. His weight was making it difficult for me to breathe and I pleaded, 'please get off me.' But again, he lifted his head, smirked, and said, 'I know you want more.' And for I don't know how long, I laid there motionless and said nothing. I must have blacked out because when I woke up, he was gone."

Chapter Thirty Two

It was almost noon when I completed June's direct examination and Judge Faust recessed the court until 1:30.

When we returned to court, the judge said, "Mr. Pontrelli. You may proceed."

Pontrelli was wearing a dark blue, pinstriped suit, blue shirt, and gold and diamond cufflinks that were large enough to broadcast his initials from the front to the back of the courtroom.

"Thank you, your honor."

As Pontrelli slowly rose from his seat, he turned briefly to his left and sent a smile from his multi-thousand dollar veneers to the jury.

"I call Ms. Robbins to the witness stand."

I patted June on her wrist and whispered "remember what we talked about" as she slowly walked to the witness stand where she had already spent all morning.

"Good afternoon, Ms. Robbins."

"Good afternoon."

"How are you feeling?"

"I am fine. Thank you."

"I know this is difficult. But you do understand that we are out to find the truth."

"I do."

"And you have made a very serious charge against my client. And that is why it may at times be difficult for you to sit here and answer my questions. But, at the end of the day we cannot allow the truth to elude us."

"Your honor," I said rising to my seat. "Mr. Pontrelli is lecturing my client and I am not sure where he is going?"

"I agree, Ms. Landau. Mr. Pontrelli, please make your point and move on," Judge Faust admonished.

"I will, your honor." Pontrelli paused and then turned to face the jurors as he asked his next question. "Do you ever have difficulty sleeping?"

"I don't understand," June said, confused.

"Well, when something from the day is bothering me, I sometimes have difficulty falling asleep. Does that ever happen to you?"

"Your honor. I object. Again, where is Mr. Pontrelli going with this?" I asked.

"My apologies, your honor. Please strike my question. I know this morning's testimony was probably at times very uncomfortable. And it is extremely uncomfortable to have to provide intimate details to a room filled with strangers."

June nodded.

"But you do understand that there are penalties in the law for not telling the truth."

"I object," I shouted, jumping to my feet again. "Mr. Pontrelli is again lecturing to my client."

"Sustained. Mr. Pontrelli, would you please direct your remarks so that the witness can respond."

"I understand, your honor. Very well," Pontrelli said, momentarily returning to his counsel table to refer to his notes.

"Ms. Robbins. Were you ever married before your marriage to Mr. Robbins?"

Pontrelli had a reputation for being very aggressive towards witnesses. And, as June was easily intimidated, I was concerned how she would do on the stand. My fears came true as he began his cross-examination.

"No I was not," June responded in a very soft tone.

"Were you ever engaged?"

"Only for a short time."

The court reporter interrupted.

"Could you repeat that?"

"Ms. Robbins. The court reporter is making a recording of everything you said. If she cannot hear, there will not be an accurate record. So you need to speak up."

"I am sorry, your honor. I am a little nervous."

"I understand. All right, Mr. Pontrelli. You may continue."

"Thank you your honor. Could the court reporter please read back my question?"

"Were you ever engaged?"

"Thank you."

"Only for a short time."

"The question calls for a yes or no," Pontrelli said.

"I am sorry. Yes I was," June confirmed.

"For how long?"

"Six months."

"And that was to a Mr. Bruce Silverman?"

"Yes, that is right."

"How long did you go out with Mr. Silverman before you became engaged?"

"I don't know. I am sorry. Probably about a year."

"And why didn't the two of you get married?"

"Objection, your honor," I protested. "There could be a myriad of reasons why people don't end up married. But what does this have to do with this case?"

"Your honor. It is foundational," Pontrelli argued.

"Go ahead. Objection overruled," the judge allowed.

"We weren't getting along," June said.

"You weren't getting along?" Pontrelli said. "Well, that doesn't seem like enough of a reason to break off an engagement. There must have been more to it than that."

"He was very controlling."

"Like asking you to make him dinner? That kind of controlling?"

"No, more than that. I couldn't do anything on my own. It was like I had to ask permission for everything. And I called it off."

"So you broke up with him."

"I did."

"Had you already set a wedding date?"

"No, we had talked about sometime the following summer, but nothing was ever definite."

"And after you broke up, did you ever see him again?"

June hesitated. "I think I did."

"You think?"

"No I did."

"Why?"

"We had received some presents when we got engaged. We were living together. And they were still at his apartment. And we got together to discuss how we would divide up everything."

"So a similar situation like you had with Mr. Robbins."

"Objection."

"Strike the comment. Ok, so you went to his apartment."

"Yes."

"And this was after you had already ended your engagement."

"Yes."

"And did you have sex with your ex-fiancé that night?"

"Objection. Irrelevant." I protested.

"Overruled," said Judge Faust.

I remained standing. "I don't see…"

"Ms. Landau."

"Yes, your honor."

"You will have your opportunity to re-direct."

Judge Faust was now lecturing me.

"But I have already ruled," he continued. "So please take your seat. Go on, Mr. Pontrelli."

"Thank you your honor," Pontrelli said, turning back to June. "Please answer. Did you have sex with your ex-fiancé that night?"

"We did."

As June answered, I observed the jurors taking notes.

"But you had already broken up."

"Yes."

"Well, if you could please tell the court how you ended up having sex with your ex-fiancé that night after you had broken up?"

June looked at me for guidance but I could only remain still.

"He had made me dinner. We had some wine. It was just one of those things. But I never saw him after that."

"So, one last time for old time's sake."

"Objection," I said.

"This time I am going to sustain the objection," said Judge Faust. "Mr. Pontrelli, I admonish you to refrain from interjecting your personal comments, which I find offensive."

"I am sorry, your honor," Pontrelli replied.

"The court will disregard what Mr. Pontrelli has just said. And this is a warning to both counsels," the judge said severely. "Stop playing games. I have been on this bench for too long and know what you are doing. And I won't tolerate it. Go on."

June looked worried and I could see from my counsel table that her lower lip was quivering.

"I wish to explain," June said turning to the judge.

"No need to," Pontrelli replied immediately in a very condescending fashion.

Again June looked at me. But all I could do was to sit powerless awaiting Pontrelli's next lob.

"Now, you were married for approximately two years when this alleged incident occurred?"

"He raped me."

"Your honor," Pontrelli smiled at the judge already knowing what the court would do in response to June's testimony.

"Ladies and gentlemen," the judge turned to the jury. "The witness's last comment was unresponsive; that is it was not made in response to a question. You are to disregard it."

"Thank you, your honor," Pontrelli said. "Now Ms. Robbins. I repeat. Is it true that you were married for approximately two years when this alleged incident occurred?"

"Yes."

"And you testified this morning that you separated from Mr. Robbins because he had a problem with gambling."

"Yes. Over gambling. He was addicted to gambling."

"And on the night of the alleged incident, you said, and let me refer to my notes, that you saw *'fire in his eyes.'* Is that correct?"

"Yes."

"Had your husband ever, prior to that night, had this look of fire in his eyes?"

"No."

"Had your husband ever been violent with you before?"

"He had yelled."

"No, what I mean is did he ever become physical with you. Did he ever hit you or threaten to harm you?"

"No."

Pontrelli again returned to his counsel table to refer to his notes.

"On the night of the alleged attack, did your husband wear a condom?"

"Objection. Irrelevant," I said.

I was surprised by Pontrelli's question and had not prepared June for this question.

"Did you husband wear a condom on that night?" Pontrelli repeated.

"I don't know," June said.

"Your honor, I request that you order the witness to answer the question," Pontrelli said.

"Ms. Robbins," Judge Faust said. "You are instructed to answer Mr. Pontrelli's question. Do you understand?"

"Yes, I do. Yes, he wore a condom," June said.

"Thank you," Pontrelli nodded. "Now you have previously testified that your husband became violent that night. And you were afraid that if you did not cooperate, you said that you thought he would hurt you. And you were scared."

"That is right."

"And if I remember correctly, you testified that he '*had you pinned down.*' Were those your words?"

"I believe so."

"Then tell me, Ms. Robbins. In the heat of this sexual act, how is it that your husband managed to place a condom on his penis while he had you pinned down?"

"Do I need to answer," June begged me.

"Your attorney is not asking you the question," Pontrelli warned. "I am. She cannot help you. So let me ask you one more time. How is it that your husband managed to place a condom on his penis while he had you pinned down?"

"I did not want to get pregnant."

"Go on."

"And I asked him to put on a condom."

"Where were the condoms?"

"In a drawer in the night stand."

"So, let me understand. You testified that your husband had pulled down your underwear, that he was straddling you between your legs, that he was aroused, that he had you pinned down, that he was about to have intercourse with you, and then, and then, he stopped because you asked him to put on a condom."

"Yes but...."

"Thank you, Ms. Robbins."

Pontrelli again returned to his counsel table and flipped through his yellow pad of notes.

"Just a few more questions. You testified that after the incident, you and let me quote you." Pontrelli hesitated, as he searched his notes, "you said *'I must have blacked out because when I woke up, he was gone.'*"

"That is right."

"Did your husband come back that night?"

"No."

"And after he left, what did you do?"

"I took a shower and went to bed."

"Why didn't you call the police?"

"I did."

"But not right away. "

"I did the next day."

"But Ms. Robbins. You have testified that your husband raped you. Yet you did not call the police that night."

Helpless, I watched as June cried in her seat.

"For the record, your honor," Pontrelli read from the police report, "let it show that Ms. Robbins placed a phone call to the police on June 13th, which is two calendar days after the alleged attack occurred."

"Very well, counselor. The record is so noted."

"So why did you wait two days?"

"I did not think it was so long."

"Well, when someone cries rape, it is a crime. And it would seem that if a crime occurred, you would want the police to be involved sooner rather than later."

"I was scared and I needed time to think."

"Think about the story you were going to invent?"

"Objection," I cried.

"Sustained," the judge confirmed.

Pontrelli waltzed back to his counsel table. And, as if we were watching a play, the courtroom waited for him to recite his next line.

"Thank you, Ms. Robbins, I have nothing further. Ah, wait. I am sorry. I do have one more question. So do you still take the position that the sex was without your consent? And remember, you are still under oath," Pontrelli asked as he turned his back on my client and faced the jury with a smile, anticipating June's answer.

"I was scared. I saw fire in his eyes like I never saw before. And I was not strong enough to stop him. He could have hit me in the face and the marks would fade away, or he could have broken my nose and I would have healed. But what is going to take away my scars from when he raped me?"

"Your honor. Instruct the witness."

June continued despite Pontrelli's attempts to stop her.

"But I did not want to end up pregnant."

"Your honor."

June then shouted, "So, yes, I asked him to put a condom on. But that is all I asked him. But I did not ask for sex that night."

"Thank you, Ms. Robbins."

"Or when he raped me again."

Pontrelli abruptly turned to face the witness.

"Raped you again. When did he rape you again?" he asked, surprised.

I looked at June, puzzled.

June took a deep breath and some color came back into her face. "He was angry. He kept texting me but I would not respond. And I kept getting calls from his father's lawyer asking that I drop the case in exchange for some settlement. But I didn't. And I received a check but I never cashed it. It was two weeks later. I had come home from grocery shopping. I put the key in the door but it was open and Steven was sitting on the couch. And he had that same look of fire in his eyes."

"Your honor. Nothing further of this witness."

"Sit down, Mr. Pontrelli," Judge Faust ordered. "As you said earlier, we are in search of the truth. Ms. Robbins. Go on, Ms. Robbins."

"He walked toward me and locked the door," she continued. "And he pulled me by my hair into the bedroom."

"Your honor. I object to any further questioning of this witness," Pontrelli tried.

"Mr. Pontrelli, when you asked the witness the question, *'when did he rape you again?'* you opened the door. The witness may continue. Go on Ms. Robbins, what happened next?"

"He threw me onto the bed and yanked down my pants and flipped me over. And," June paused, "he pushed my legs apart and then he did it like a barn yard animal."

"Your honor. I object," Pontrelli protested.

"So noted," said Judge Faust. "Go on."

"I object," Pontrelli tried again.

"Mr. Pontrelli," the judge said with no patience in his voice. "Take your seat. And if I hear one more word out of you, I will hold you in contempt of court. Do you understand?"

"Your honor."

"Do you understand?"

"Yes." Pontrelli slammed his yellow pad into the counsel table as he took his seat, realizing that he had made the most grievous tactical mistake an attorney can make; that is, asking a question when you are not sure of the answer. And for the briefest of moments, I actually felt sorry for my opponent.

Chapter Thirty Three

Rarely does a defendant ever take the witness stand in his own defense, in order to prevent the district attorney from questioning him on cross examination. Likewise, by remaining silent, the defense attorney has the burden of weaving together all of the evidence that will lead to a conviction without any assistance from the defendant who allegedly committed the crime. As such, the old adage 'it is better to say nothing than something' is most applicable to criminal cases.

But even with June's explosive testimony, and without the defendant's testimony to refute it, that did not mean that Pontrelli was without other means of attack to bolster his client's chances of gaining a dismissal. Instead, he employed a full arsenal of weapons as he paraded several witnesses over the next three days. Each one testified that that June was immoral, often jumping from bed to bed to satisfy her sexual desires. And as each witness recounted lurid stories of June's past, my sole goal was to keep the jury focused on the facts of this case and not let them be clouded or confused by Pontrelli's courtroom dramatics.

Finally, as Pontrelli was about to call his next witness, the judge asked both of us to approach the bench.

"Mr. Pontrelli," he said.

"Yes, your honor," Pontrelli replied.

"Who is your next witness?"

Flipping the page over on his yellow pad, Pontrelli answered "Mr. Andrew Milstein."

"And, let me guess. He is going to testify that he briefly dated Ms. Robbins. And by the third date, there was an amalgamation of desire by both participants and they had sex. Is that right?"

"Not quite, your honor. It was the fourth date."

"Whatever. I think, counsel, that this jury has had its fill of stories about Ms. Robbins. And unless you have another witness that could offer testimony that directly contradicts what Ms. Robbins said happened that night, I am going to ask that you rest."

"But your honor. If I may?"

Pontrelli balked and argued his position. During their back and forth banter, I kept my mouth shut, as it appeared that Judge Faust was about to give me a break.

"Mr. Pontrelli, I will ask you one more time. Do you have such a witness who will unequivocally contradict what Ms. Robbins testified to?"

Pontrelli responded softly.

"No, but…"

"Very well. Counsel, please return to your seats."

"Your honor. I want your decision noted for appeal."

"So noted."

Trying to disguise the smile on my face, I turned to faced June as she was eagerly awaiting my explanation of what had just transpired.

"All right, counsel," Judge Faust announced. "Being that there are no other witnesses, and considering the time of day, this court is adjourned until tomorrow morning at 9 a.m., at which time we will hear from Ms. Landau, who will present her closing argument."

The next day I had butterflies in my stomach as court returned to session.

"Good morning, Ms. Landau, good morning, Mr. Pontrelli. Are you ready to proceed with your close, Ms. Landau?"

"I am, your honor." Slowly rising from my seat, I walked toward the jury box and placed my yellow pad on the small wooden podium that faced the jurors. I had memorized the first six paragraphs of my opening statement as I thought it would be most effective.

"Good morning, ladies and gentlemen," I said assuredly, making sure I made eye contact with every member of the jury. "This is the last time I will have a chance to talk to you. And I want to say right up front that I thank you in advance for the job that you have ahead of you. It is not an easy task to decide one's guilt or innocence. But I am confident that you will make the right decision.

"And this morning as I stand before you, I am here not only as June Robbins' lawyer, and the assistant district attorney who prosecutes persons who commit crimes against others in the county of Los Angeles. But I am also here on behalf of a woman. A woman who has been sexually assaulted against her will. And, despite such a grievous act, incredible allegations have been made against her suggesting that it was consensual."

I approached the rail of the jury box and continued.

"In this country, surely we will always continue to recognize that you are innocent until proven guilty. And if you have been engaged in some conduct people might disapprove of, it doesn't mean you are guilty of a crime. But, if that allegation is of a crime, then the State has to prove all of the elements of the crime beyond a reasonable doubt. And without all the elements, you must find the defendant not guilty.

"Now, at this point you may think that I am doing a wonderful job for Mr. Pontrelli. In fact, perhaps my closing statement sounds like it should be coming from his mouth. But ladies and gentlemen, all of the elements are here. And the defendant was engaged in conduct that was a crime.

"But I guess the first question to ask is whether there has been a crime committed.
Unlike cases of murder, where the presence of a dead body points to the fact that there has been a crime, or in a case of robbery where whatever was stolen and then recovered is marked as Exhibit A, or assault where there are overt signs of physical harm, the perpetration of this act of sexual intercourse against Ms. Robbins did not leave a discoverable trace.

"What then, does a jury start off with? The oath of a woman who says she was raped and the not guilty plea of a man who denies it. As such, in this situation, you must weigh oath against oath. And juries have managed to convict or acquit based on whose oath they decided to trust. But marital rape is the only crime in which, by law, the victim is female and the offender is male. In a court of law, where the victim becomes the complainant, and the offender becomes the defendant, oath against oath at all times means the word of a woman against the word of a man.

"So let's begin to break them down," I said as I returned to the podium and turned to the first page of my notes.

"The defendant would want you to believe that the sexual act between a husband and wife was consensual. After all, my client invited him to her home while they were still married, she shared a bottle of wine with her husband, and they had sex. End of story.

"But it is not that simple. My client and the defendant were separated and not living together as husband and wife when the sexual act occurred. And even if they were together, just because there was at one time a wedding band on her finger, it did not give the defendant the absolute right to have sex with his wife if it was against her will. I repeat," I paused, "if it was against her will."

"Curiously," I continued, "despite the fact that we want to believe that we are a progressive society and have shed our biases, there is still a double standard regarding sexuality. A male who has had many female conquests is still portrayed as virile and a conqueror. While a female who has had many sexual partners is considered promiscuous.

"It is interesting that before 1979, California law did not recognize that a wife could be raped by her husband. But the state legislature in that year wrestled with that notion and decided that a woman does not give up her right of consent to sexual intercourse by virtue of marriage, and that the existing definition of rape treats married women in an unequal and unfair fashion. Further, the legislative intent said that existing law reflects archaic notions that the wife is a man's property to be used or abused as he sees fit.

"I want to read directly from the code, it is Penal Code Section 262 (a), so that there is no doubt or confusion or misinterpretation as to what the code says."

I paused momentarily as I pick up the thick blue code book and opened it to the page that I had paper clipped.

"*'Rape of a person who is the spouse of the perpetrator is an act of sexual intercourse accomplished under any of the following.'*

"And part one reads:

"*'Where it is accomplished against a person's will by means of force, violence, duress, menace, or fear of immediate and unlawful bodily injury on the person or another.'*

"Note, it reads '*of the person who is the spouse.*' And when the alleged act of the defendant, Mr. Robbins, occurred June was still his spouse.

"But Mr. Robbins apparently is a supporter of the notion that June was his property, as he forced himself on his still wife .

"But she is not then, nor ever was, his property," I said, turning to the defendant.

"And whether there is a ring on her finger or not," I paused, looking squarely into the face of each juror, "she always had the right to say no. The defense has also paraded what attorneys refer to as character witnesses. Their sole purpose in testifying is to destroy the character of June, so as to portray her as a woman with a reputation. A reputation to have casual sex. And the defense will argue that she no longer had the right to claim she was raped or had sex against her will because, well, whether it was her husband, or some casual partner, my client wanted it. She asked for it and it was with her consent.

"The truth, however, ladies and gentlemen, and what you must continue to remain focused on, and not let yourself be persuaded by some other version of what happened that night, is that sex was consensual when June agreed to have sex with her husband. But on that night, she did not consent and she was raped," I said, raising my voice, "by that man, the defendant Steven Robbins," I said pointing to him.

I paused briefly to take a sip of water.

"Now Mr. Robbins' attorney is a very fine person." I paused again as I turn to look at Pontrelli. "And he has a job to do. And he is paid to do his job. And paid well. And just like if you were hired to paint a house, or make a delivery, or watch your sister's child, it would be expected that you would do your job well. To the best of your abilities.

"But Mr. Pontrelli, with all due respect, because I do respect him, is providing a disservice to you. He has painted my client as a cold, callous, individual who has had a promiscuous sexual past. And he is asking that you disregard the forced sexual act. And he has tried to confuse you that June Robbins is not a victim but the perpetrator; that she was the reason why Mr. Robbins acted the way he did. And Mr. Pontrelli would like you to forgive his client because he said he is sorry. And we should all go home to our families and friends, forget about what has happened, turn on the television and watch our favorite show, answer our e-mails, and go on with our lives.

"And I know that, after days of testimony and hearing the lawyers argue about technicalities of this and that, and you having to sit through hours and hours of this, that at the end of the day it really does not concern you. That you would like to go home. You would like to relax, turn on the TV and resume your life.

"But for that to happen, it would be awfully selfish on all of our parts. You see, June Robbins cannot go on with her life. Yes, she has filed for divorce to end her marriage. But that is a paper transaction. One day a court issues a license that says you are married and now you are not. But, unlike us, when she leaves this courtroom, she will always carry the memory that she was violated. That she was sexually assaulted, and this act was against her will. It is something that will stay with her for the rest of her life. When she is alone with her thoughts, when she puts her head to her pillow at night, when she thinks about her past, it will always be with her.

"So I respectfully ask that you give her back her life. She can never erase from her mind what happened that night. But by returning a verdict of guilt, you can take that first step to help heal her wounds and send a message that a woman may always say no.

"And there is one more thing I want you to consider. The defendant comes from a powerful family. And he has all the money in the world to fight this charge. However, as you are deliberating, I want you to forget about the size of his family's checkbook. Otherwise, when there is no justice, the rich win and the poor are powerless.

" As you deliberate, remember that someone is lying. So is it my client who has testified that what happened that evening was without her consent? Or was it the defendant who said that his wife wanted to have sex?

"You know, when I hear the phrase 'he said, she said,' it is usually followed by that other phrase that the truth lies somewhere in between.

"The problem is that, if we give in to that statement, that the truth lies somewhere in between, we become victims. And we become weak. And we start to doubt ourselves. And then we doubt our institutions. And then we start to doubt the law. But today, you are the law."

I paused, stepping closer to the jury and repeated my last line. "Today, you are the law. Not some book. Not the lawyers. Not the marble statutes or the trappings in the court. But you. You are the law. And I have faith in you.

"In my religion, we say act as if he had faith. Faith will be given to you if, if we are to have faith and justice, we need only to believe in ourselves and act with justice. I believe there is justice in our hearts."

Looking into the eyes of each juror, I thought about that last time when I saw Jacob. As he asked for my forgiveness, I remembered noticing a blade of grass that had found its way to the surface through a crack in the concrete pavement and was struggling to survive knowing that at any second someone could come along and snuff out its life. If June never called the police, her life would have been snuffed out.

"So ladies and gentlemen. When you walk into that deliberation room, and go over all the testimony that you heard from the last five days, you will get tired. For some, you will think about getting home to see your kids, or having a nice quiet dinner with your spouse, or going to the movies or doing all of that laundry that has piled up.

"But I need your help. And you don't owe me anything but I am asking for your help.

I want you to take a legal pad," I said as I held up my pad. "And as you read the testimony, I want you to consider the full tapestry of June's life with the defendant. To do so, you need to get into her mind. And I want you to make a list of everything you feel.

"If you feel June's fear, write it down.

"It you feel my client was scared, write it down.

"And if you felt she was dominated, write it down.

"And then I ask you to put yourself in the position of my client. Would you fear what my client feared? Would you be scared? Would you feel dominated against your will?

"And I ask that you share these emotions with your fellow jurors. Talk to each other. Engage in conversation. Let it out as June has so that you feel what she feels.

"And when you add up all of these emotions, there can be only one conclusion. And that is that the defendant willfully had sexual intercourse with his spouse without her consent.

"Finally, do not compromise your views. If you believe the defendant is guilty, or if you believe you don't know or if you believe I haven't satisfied you beyond a reasonable doubt, if you believe he may be guilty but you don't know and you're not satisfied beyond a reasonable doubt, don't give in to convenience. Don't give in because you want to get out of here and go back to your families and friends and return to the life you had before all of this. Don't give in for anything. Vote your conscience as you would want it to be voted on your behalf. Thank you."

As I finished, I smiled and panned the jury, making eye contact one last time.

"Thank you, Ms. Landau. Anything further from the People?" asked Judge Faust.

"Nothing, your honor," I said, taking my seat as I prepared myself for the Michael Pontrelli show.

Chapter Thirty Four

"Mr. Pontrelli. Your close."

As Pontrelli rose, the message light started blinking on my Blackberry. Shielding the screen with my hand, I checked the message. It was from Cliff.

"One day to your birthday. And it's a surprise!"

My last surprise was the day I met Jacob. But I knew this one would be much better.

"Thank you, your honor."

Pontrelli walked to the podium. And with all his dramatic flair, he made his case to the jury why his client should be found not guilty, while all I could do was patiently sit as an observer, hoping that the jury would not buy his story.

But after twenty long minutes, I could sense that Pontrelli was reaching the end of argument. And I glanced at the jurors. Were they buying what they heard or had I sold them on June's version?

It was so hard to read their faces and I turned my attention to the clock hanging to the left of the jury box. It looked like the same clock that I use to stare at in high school as I waited for my geometry class to be over. Those last few minutes of every class seemed like eternity. I remembered sitting in fear that I would be called upon by Mrs. Miller to answer a question for which I never had the correct answer. And now, once again, I found myself staring at the minute hand as it clicked its way to 4 pm, knowing that Judge Faust would cut Pontrelli off and have him come back tomorrow morning if he went past Faust's closing time. Finally, Pontrelli flashed once again his expensive veneers at the jurors and spoke his last words.

"And I know, as God is my witness, you will all do the right thing."

I was expecting a more memorable line to end his oration. But I was also relieved this part of the trial was now over.

"Very well. Thank you Mr. Pontrelli." Judge Faust then turned to the jury and began his jury instructions. Moments later, with the sound of his gavel pounding against the bench, court was adjourned.

"Now what?" June asked as we stood and the judge exited the courtroom.

"We wait. This is the difficult part. The jury will go back and go over all of the evidence and hopefully they will decide in our favor," I explained.

"And if they don't?"

"Let's not go there. I will call you as soon as I get word that that the jury is returning."

June and I hugged and I started to call my office when Pontrelli approached.

"Nice work, counselor. I just hoped you didn't ruin your client's life."

"Excuse me?" I asked defiantly.

"I have been doing this a lot longer than you have. And I can read a jury. They will be back with their verdict very shortly. And if I had to bet, it doesn't look good for your client."

Maintaining my professionalism, I smiled politely and walked out.

I decided to take side streets rather than getting onto the freeway and reached my apartment in less than 30 minutes. All I wanted to do was kick off my shoes and lay down.

As I entered the driveway, I was hoping that Beatrice would not be waiting for me as I was just too tired to make conversation. To my relief, she was not. But standing guard and waiting for my arrival was Cabby, who meowed and twined his body through my legs.

"Hi sweetie, you want a treat?" I reached for the purple package of dry snacks that my cat lived for and dropped a few pieces into his bowl.

"I am so tired Cabby. But how was your day?" I asked as I opened the refrigerator door only to be greeted by three containers of days old Chinese food, a plastic container with wilted salad, and a bottle of Diet Coke that had lost its fizz days ago. As Pontrelli's last words resonated in my mind, I stared at the days old food thinking that I should have taken Cliff up on his offer earlier this morning to have dinner. But I also knew he was going to take me to some place special tomorrow night for my birthday and he didn't need to spend more money tonight.

"Cabby, I think you're going to have a better dinner tonight than me." I closed the refrigerator door and walked into my bedroom. But after slipping on my favorite sweats, I returned to the kitchen determined to find something to eat.

"Let's look here, Cabby."

I opened the pantry closet and surveyed my choices.

"I can make myself a tuna sandwich, Cabby. Oh, but wait, there's no bread. How about macaroni and cheese? I don't think so. Wait, what's this?" I said, reaching for a can that had been pushed towards the back of the shelf. "Hmm, Campbell's Vegetarian Vegetable Soup. Ok, Cabby. I think we found dinner."

Also in the back of the pantry was a box of crackers. As I ate my soup and stale crackers and drank my flat soda, I tried to guess what Cliff's surprise tomorrow night would be.

"What do you think, Cabby? Where do you think he is taking me?"

Cabby seemed disinterested and jumped onto his pillow.

"Well, now I have no one to talk to. Ok, let's look at the mail."

For the last couple of nights, I was too tired to go through my mail and I had let it pile up on the kitchen table.

"Target. Ok, let's see what's for sale. Oh. Look. Toilet paper. That's a good price," I mused, thinking how nice it would be to someday push a red shopping cart through the store with my baby in tow and not have to deal with the Pontrellis of the world.

"Did you hear that, Cabby? Toilet paper!"

Cabby lifted his ears when he heard his name.

It was now almost sunset and I reached for the *Yahrzeit* (Memorial candle) that was also in the pantry next to the can of tuna fish. Tonight was the one year anniversary of Nana's death. According to Jewish tradition, Jews commemorate the anniversary by lighting a small candle which burns for 24 hours as a symbol of the flame of life that once burned brightly and illumined the lives of loved ones who now mourn the loss.

Following the lighting, I read from my prayer book:

The light of life is a finite flame.

Like the Sabbath candles, life is kindled.

It burns, it glows, it radiates warmth and beauty,

but then it fades and is no more. Yet we must not despair.

We are more than a memory vanishing in the darkness. With our lives we give life.

Something of us can never die; we move in the eternal cycle of darkness and death, of light and life.

The memorial light we now kindle is a sign of this truth.

As it burns pure and bright, so may the memory of

our dearly beloved brighten and purify our lives.

Amen

Chapter Thirty Five

I was awakened by Cabby's meow.

"Ok. Mommy did not forget you. Let's get you some breakfast," I said to Cabby as his meows grew louder. As he followed me into the kitchen, I paused momentarily at Nana's candle, which was still flickering.

"Here you go, sweetie."

As I poured food into Cabby's bowl, my cell phone rang. It was Cliff.

"Happy Birthday."

"Thank you. You would not believe this. I fell asleep on the couch. I was so exhausted."

"That's ok. Your body was so run down."

"Well now I am going to be late for work."

"If you have any problems, let me talk to Ryan."

"All right big man. I will."

"Anyway, I needed you well rested for your big surprise tonight."

"Cliff. Come on. Give me a hint."

"I can't but I think you will like it."

"You don't have to do anything crazy. Just being with you is the greatest birthday present."

"Well, that is nice. But I am not telling you anything more. Ok. I have to take this call. Love you."

"I love you."

I showered. But rather than taking the time to blow dry my hair, I threw on some slacks and a matching sweater top, and pulled my hair back with a comb, then drove to the office.

"Well, I am sure after your week you would rather be somewhere else than sitting in your office on your birthday. But happy birthday anyway!"

Ellen had been the office manager for the DA for over thirty years and worried about us like her own children.

"Thanks, Ellen." I said, smiling as I flipped through my phone messages. "Yeah, Pontrelli was pretty harsh but one way or the other, I think I held my ground."

"I'm sure you did. Can I take you to lunch for your birthday?"

"That is so nice. But I don't think so, "I said with a grin. "Look at this mess. Can we do it next week?"

"Sure. Do you want to go through everything now or wait a while?"

"I think I'll try wading through my messages first and then we can go over my calendar."

By noon I was famished and Ellen ordered me a tuna sandwich.

"Here you go."

"Thanks, Ellen," I said as I took my first bite. "I'll never get through all of these."

"You will."

Seconds later I heard a tap on my door.

"Ellen, did you forget something?"

"Ms. Landau?"

To my surprise, standing in the door was Pontrelli.

"I am sorry," I said, grabbing a napkin and wiping my hands. "Was I expecting you?"

"No, but we need to talk."

"Ok," I answered, puzzled, as I took one more sip of my Diet Coke and quickly put the smelly tuna fish sandwich back in its wrapper. "Please sit."

As he did, the announcement button on my phone blinked.

"Excuse me. I need to get this."

"Yes, Ellen," I said into the receiver.

"Danielle," Ellen said, "the clerk in 62 just called. The judge dismissed the jury for the day."

"What?" I responded, confused, as I hung up the phone and turned to Pontrelli. "Do you know…?"

"That's what I wanted to talk about," Pontrelli said. "I just came from 62. In light of Ms. Robbins' testimony, and the concerns it raises should my client be subsequently charged, I have told the court that we are willing to entertain a plea with the district attorney. Of course, that is if an offer is still on the table. So Faust asked me to talk to you."

"So that is why he excused the jury?"

"Exactly."

"Well, what do you have in mind? You know what our offer has been."

Pontrelli had lost his arrogant tone and was most conciliatory in his delivery.

"I do. But what I am really asking is that he does not face prosecution for the second act. I don't think you want to put your client through this again."

"Well, I have to talk to my boss."

"I know you do."

"I'll try to have an answer for you by tomorrow."

Pontrelli got up from his seat and left my office like a field mouse running for cover. A week later, without the jury, without the media, and without Pontrelli's pomp and circumstance, Robbins pleaded guilty to marital rape in return for probation and no jail time. We also agreed not to file charges for the second rape. And just like that, the biggest case of my nascent career started with thunder and ended with a thump.

Chapter Thirty Six

Cliff took me to the same Mexican restaurant where we had our first date. And two margaritas later, I asked, "So what is the surprise?"

"Not yet. But I think we need to walk off this dinner."

Moments later, as the Ferris wheel operator was securing us in our seats, I thought I saw Cliff nod to him in a weird way.

"Do you know him?" I asked.

"Who?" Cliff responded.

"The ride operator."

"How would I know him?"

"Well it seemed like he knew you."

"I don't think so. The last time I was here was with you and I doubt he remembers everyone who rides the Ferris wheel."

"Whatever," I said, casually borrowing a line from my father.

It took several minutes to load the wheel before it climbed to the top. But as we slowly inched our way higher, I felt a pulse in my throat and I feared that my Mexican dinner was going to reappear but not in the way it was presented in the restaurant. To my relief, my body relaxed into a brief state of normalcy which was quickly erased as the wheel continued its rotation and we descended quickly back to Earth and then stopping again at the top.

"Oh come on," I lamented in frustration. "We didn't even have one full turn!"

Oddly, Cliff was smiling.

"What's so funny?"

"It's pretty up here, isn't it?"

"Sure."

"And look at the moon. It is so low in the sky."

The moon was full and its light reflected onto the shore below.

"Yeah, but it is supposed to be a ride," I said, puzzled at Cliff's apparent indifference. "And I can look at the moon from the ground as well."

"Well, here is something you may want to take your time to look at."

Cliff reached inside his pocket.

"What?"

Inside his hand was a small black lacquered box.

"I love you, Danielle," he said in the most adoring voice as he placed the box in my hands.

Like a little kid, I turned the box upside down and shook it to see if it made any sound.

"Is this my surprise? What is it?"

"Well, you won't find out unless you open it."

I shut my eyes as I slowly pried open the box. And when it would not open any wider, I opened my eyes and screamed.

"Oh my God. Oh my God. This is amazing," I screamed, staring at its contents.

"I can't get down on my knees. But will you marry me?" Cliff asked.

"I don't know what to say," I answered crying.

"Well I hope you say yes."

My eyes were now alternating between looking at his beautiful brown eyes and the most beautiful shining stone.

"Yes. Yes. Of course yes."

With my enthusiastic response, Cliff placed the ring on my finger.

"The lighting is perfect," he announced.

Cliff was right as the brilliance of the moon lit up every facet of the perfectly round diamond.

"I love you. You have made me so happy," I said as I kissed my fiancé.

And as Cliff rose up his right hand and waved it several times, a loud cheer and applause erupted from below.

"He knew," I said, smiling.

"Of course."

The Ferris wheel quickly descended to its starting point where we were met with more cheers and applause from the operator and the other passengers who were told in advance of the proposal.

"One more time around for our bride and groom," shouted the operator as he snapped a picture of us with Cliff's cell phone.

And as the Ferris wheel ascended to the stars, the only star I chose to stare at was Cliff.

Chapter Thirty Seven

Cliff said that it was only a ten minute ride from the Newark train station to Parsippany. But it seemed a lot longer as my cab driver made one turn and then another and another as if we were in a maze. I started to wonder whether he was trying to run up the fare.

Finally, after passing street after street of very small, boxy structures that all looked so familiar except for their color, we turned into a neighborhood of very large, expensive homes. Even the streets were wide and lined with old elm trees. Each home was set back from the street on very large lots. It looked almost as though the neighborhood was from a different time.

We stopped in front of a wrought iron gate with a sign draped over it that read "Sunrise Manor."

"This is it, lady. 756 Richmond Knolls," the driver announced as he stopped the meter. "That's $12.80. Do you want a receipt?" he asked, turning up the volume on the radio station.

"No thanks." I handed him three five dollar bills.

I nudged open the gate and began my walk up the long expanse of brick path as I gazed at the most beautiful Victorian style home. The house was a pale yellow with green shutters and a steeply pitched roof over dormer windows. A large wraparound porch complete with spindled railings offset the double wooden entry doors.

As I reached the entrance, two elderly women sitting in wheel chairs on the porch greeted me.

"Are you visiting?" I was asked by one of the ladies.

"I am."

As I spoke, a sense of nervousness came over me. Only days ago, I successfully held my own against one of the most artful courtroom litigators. But now, I felt unprepared.

Both women smiled and nodded their heads as I pushed the entry door which opened into a very wide foyer with a long planked hardwood floor partially covered by an oval rug.

Irene's daughter told me that Irene had been living in this assisted living residence for the past five years after she had become very frail, as it was too difficult for her daughter to care for her in her home.

"Hello, I am here to see Irene Walczak," I said to the pretty young girl seated at the information desk. Behind her and on the wall was a collection of photos that appeared to be of residents and I wondered if Irene was in one of the photos.

"Sure, you must be Rose's granddaughter. Welcome."

I was surprised she knew that.

"Would you like one?" The receptionist gestured to the plate of chocolate chip cookies on the counter. "We bake them fresh every afternoon."

"No thanks. But maybe later."

"Irene has been so excited since she heard that you were coming. Everyone here knows. If you would just please sign our guest book," she said, pointing to the blank line on the middle of the page. "Irene is on the third floor and the elevator is just down the hall to the right. I'm going to call and tell the aide that you are on your way."

"Thanks."

There was a mirror on the back wall of the elevator and I quickly checked my makeup before pressing the button. As the elevator slowly rose, my nervous feeling was replaced by that of excitement.

The doors opened, revealing a very attractive middle aged woman. She had wavy gray hair pulled back and clipped and wore a large smile.

"You must be Danielle. So nice to meet you. I am Frances, Irene's daughter." The smiling woman came towards me with open arms. We embraced as if she had known me her whole life.

"It is so wonderful to meet you. I hope this is a good time?" I said.

"This is a wonderful time. Mom has not been able to sleep since she heard you were coming."

"Neither have I."

"You know, my Mom is going to be 100 soon and her voice is weak.

But when she got the news that you were coming, it's like she was a new person."

"Well, I am so excited."

"Come this way, sweetheart."

Frances placed her arm tightly around my waist as she led me past the recreation room where three women and a man were playing what appeared to be a very heated game of cards.

"Hi, Mrs. Dubin." Frances waved to one of the older ladies playing cards who returned the gesture as we continued to walk.

"This place is lovely," I commented.

"It is," Frances agreed. "And they keep the residents very busy."

We entered the long hallway, which was painted in very bright colors and filled with more pictures of the residents involved in various activities.

"My mom's room is down this way."

Each room door bore a small gold plaque on which was etched the name of the resident who lived there on. Hanging on the wall to the right of the door was a shadow box with a collage of photos of the resident. Finally, we stopped at the last door on the floor and my eyes were immediately attracted to the photos. In the center was a black and white photo of a young woman with her hair pulled back in a bun wearing the sweetest smile.

"Is this?"

"Yes, my mom was probably 21 when that picture was taken. About the time when she met your grandmother."

"Your mother is beautiful."

"Thank you. Mom was resting a few minutes ago so let's see if she is up."

The opened door revealed a very frail woman sitting in a wheelchair by the window. She had a white sweater draped over her shoulders and a peach colored afghan blanket on her lap.

"Mom. I have a surprise for you. This is Danielle, Rose's granddaughter."

Irene slowly raised her two hands and opened her eyes, motioning me to approach her. As she did, her unmistakable smile broadened her face, reflecting her golden heart. And her tired eyes could still outshine any star.

"It is such an honor to meet you," I said. Tears immediately began to flow from my eyes.

I bent down to hug her and she kissed my forehead as I held her hands that were soft as silk and full of love.

"Mom is hard of hearing. You need to look directly at her and talk slowly."

I got down on both knees and stared into this sweet, kind face that saved my grandmother from the worst atrocity known to mankind. Irene did not speak but instead kept looking into my eyes.

"She's a beautiful girl, isn't she, Mom?" Frances said.

Irene smiled and we continued to exchange glances. And then she gently touched my hair with her weak hand.

"My mother told me that your grandmother had the most beautiful silky, thick blonde hair," Frances said.

"As did your mom's. And my Nana and your mom would take turns brushing each other's hair," I said as I opened my purse, removing the brush and putting it into Irene's hands.

A huge smile came over Irene as she examined the brush finding the initials I. O. etched on the handle. And in a very weak voice, Irene spoke.

"I gave this to Rose," she said clutching the brush.

I held her hands in mine. "I know. And now, it has made its journey back to you."

Irene alternated between looking at me and admiring the brush.

"Mom, can I get you something? Are you thirsty?"

Irene slowly raised one hand shaking no.

"She hasn't been eating," Frances explained to me. "Mom, are you hungry? Did you have lunch today?"

Irene did not answer but continued looking at the brush.

"What else can you tell me about my grandmother?"

Rose mumbled something.

"Here Ma. Drink this. It's 7-Up." Francis held a can with a straw and brought it to Irene's mouth.

"Take a sip."

Irene complied.

"That's better, Mom. The doctor said you have to drink."

Taking another, longer sip, Irene looked up at me and miraculously found the strength to speak.

"It was a terrible time. And Rose had trouble sleeping. It was a terrible time. She slept all alone in this dark basement with no light. And it was so cold. And she was scared."

Irene took another sip.

"And I feared that one day they would take her back to the camp. So I taught her a song to sing to herself when she was frightened. And to think of herself as a ballerina dancing on a big stage. And she would be safe.

Tumbala, Tumbala, Tumbalalaika
Tumbala, Tumbala, Tumbalalaika"

"Oh my God," I cried as Irene sung the song my Nana taught me.
"Tumbalalaika, shpil balalaika
Tumbalalaika freylekh zol zany"

Irene repeated the song and we sang together:
"Tumbala, Tumbala, Tumbalalaika
Tumbala, Tumbala, Tumbalalaika
Tumbalalaika, shpil balalaika
Tumbalalaika freylekh zol zayn"

I started to cry.

"Here, sweetheart." Francis handed me a box of tissues that were on the small table next to Irene's bed. "My mother use to sing that song to me, too."

"Thank you."

"Your ring is beautiful," Frances said, admiring my engagement ring. "Look at this ring, Mom. When are you getting married?"

"In a few weeks."

"You must be so excited."

"I am."

"Here." Irene handed me the brush and I look startled.

"I think my mom wants you to keep it. Right, Mom?"

Irene nodded her head in agreement. "For your wedding. Something old."

"I can't."

"Please," she said, and with the sweetest smile Irene pushed the brush back into my hand.

"Thank you. My grandmother loved you," I said as I clutched her small body and kissed her again on her forehead as Irene stroked my cheek.

"And I so loved her," she replied.

We talked for a few more minutes but it soon became apparent that Irene was very tired and wanted to rest.

"I am going to go now," I said, holding Irene's hands in mind and feeling my grandmother who had held the same hands. "But I want to again thank you so much." As I spoke, tears continued to pour down my face. "And I will be thinking of you on my wedding day. And you will always be in my heart."

"Send us a picture," Francis said as she started to walk me to the door.

"I will. Goodbye, Irene."

As I began to walk to the door, I stopped as I heard Irene's voice.

"My mom wants to say something," Frances said. "What is it, Mom?"

Irene took another sip of the soda and spoke.

Irene repeated the same last words that Nana said to me.

"Save one life, seed a generation."

And hearing those words, it was as if Nana was also in the room with us.

Chapter Thirty Eight

The morning dawned sunny and bright, and I knew that it was one of those days that were going to be a beautiful one. Upon waking up and looking at Cliff who was still sleeping so peacefully beside me, I thought about how today was going to change my life. I had no regrets, cold feet or qualms about this day. This time felt right and I so loved Cliff. For the first time in my life, I knew love for all the right reasons.

"So have you finally decided how you are going to wear your hair?" Cliff asked as he rolled over and stared at me with his beautiful eyes.

Unlike the first time around, I had read every bridal magazine and had experimented with every imaginable hair style in anticipation of this day.

"Not yet," I responded.

"Ok. I guess I will be surprised," he said, walking into the bathroom.

Taking Nana's brush from the nightstand, I began brushing my hair and shouted, "Either down or up?"

"Thanks for all the information," Cliff shouted back. "And did you finish that book?"

"Which one?" I asked.

"The one Ellen gave you. I think it is called *BEFORE YOU SAY I DO AGAIN!*"

"Funny. Anyway, I think it is too late."

"Ok, just asking."

"Look at the sky." I pulled back the drapes and moved open the plantation shutters. The sky was a peaceful shade of blue and the pure white clouds looked like cotton candy floating by.

Cliff and I had stayed at the hotel and had planned to spend the morning going over any last minute details. But instead, we decided to enjoy the morning by walking along the surf. As we strolled hand in hand, the sun stroked the shore where two young boys were trying unsuccessfully to fly a kite. Each time they tried, the kite bobbed for a moment before crashing into the sand.

We moved closer to the rushing water and the waves gently crested and then crashed over one another, forming little prisms of rainbows from the ocean spray. As the first waved rolled over my feet, it left foam and bubbles. I could taste the salt in the air.

It was now almost noon and I did not want this moment to end. But we had to get ready.

"When will I see you again?" I kiddingly asked my groom.

"Well, I don't know," he joked back. "I have to be somewhere around 5. After that I am free. How about you?"

"I also have something I need to do. But maybe we will run into each other later."

"Ok. See you then."

As we kissed goodbye, I knew that the next time we kissed would be under the Chuppah as husband and wife.

I spent the afternoon with Marcia, who helped me with my makeup. And after much discussion, I decided to wear my hair up.

"You look beautiful," Marcia said as she placed the tiara on my forehead and we both gazed into the floor length mirror.

Marcia said that I looked like a princess in my white strapless gown. It was far less ornate than my mom's gown but not ordinary.

"Do you feel different? You know, this time."

"I do," I said, looking at my reflection in the mirror. "I feel alive!"

The sun was about to disappear over the horizon as another day was about to give way to night. It was one of the most enchanted sunsets; the sky was a cocktail of red, purple, pink and orange, and the water shimmered and shone with the yellow highlights glowing upon the waves. The slight breeze perfected the atmosphere.

"You're so beautiful. My precious little angel," my dad said as he clutched my hand.

"I somehow remember you saying that line once before."

"I did. But this is your wedding."

I was so thrilled that my dad was here.

"I love you, Dad."

The string quartet played my Nana's favorite wedding song Erev Shel Shoshanim and I clutched my small bouquet of white roses.

"It's time," my dad whispered as we took our first steps walking slowly in sync on the wooden planks that had been placed over the sand, while my flowers bobbed up and down with each fluid step.

Looking at the end of the aisle, the night suddenly paled in comparison to the love I saw in Cliff's eyes. I felt like I was walking on this morning's cotton candy clouds and my heart felt as if it were going to burst with the love I felt as I looked at him. Our gaze never wavered from one another. I could see every thought in his eyes, which were welcoming and seemed to playfully dance in the light of the candles. But it was his smile that told the whole story; I knew everything good would happen just by his smile. And never once did my mind flit back to my past.

As we finally reached the end of aisle, a slight breeze picked up as the gentle surf greeted the white sand and quickly retreated, leaving foam. I curled my toes and dug my heels into the chalky white sand as Cliff and I stood before the Rabbi.

"Do you take this man to be to be your lawful wedded husband?"

I looked up into the changing sky and closed my eyes. As if on cue, a quickly passing cloud sprayed a gentle rain. Not long enough to cause anyone to take cover. But long enough for me to lift my head to the clouds and see my Nana's sweet smile blessing us.

"I do," I whispered.

"*Mazel Tov*," the crowd erupted as Cliff smashed the glass. And, with the Ferris wheel in the background, Cliff arched me backwards, giving me the most amazing kiss a girl could ever imagine.

Save one life, seed a generation. Two years later, our daughter Rose Irene Warner came into this world. She had her dad's brown eyes and her Nana's sweet smile. And oh yes--she was always hungry!